★ PLANET ★
★ ★ ★ STORIES ★ ★ ★

T. T. SCOTT, President and General Manager   MALCOLM REISS, Editor

D1569752

Volume 1.
No. 1

Winter Issue
20c per copy

PLANET STORIES: Published by Love Romances, Inc., 461 Eighth Ave., New York City. Printed in U. S. A. The entire contents of this magazine are copyrighted, 1939, by Fiction House, Inc. All rights reserved. This issue dated November 1, 1939. While due care is always exercised, the publishers will not be responsible for the return of unsolicited manuscripts. For advertising rates address THE NEWSSTAND FICTION UNIT, 9 Rockefeller Plaza, New York City.

THE GOLDEN AMAZONS OF VENUS

By JOHN MURRAY REYNOLDS

Dakta death, horrible beyond the weirdest fever-dreams of Earthmen, faced Space Ship Commander Gerry Norton. The laconic interplanetary explorer knew too much. He stood in the dynamic path of Lansa, Lord of the Sealy Ones, the crafty monster bent on conquering the fair City of Larr and all the rich, shadowless lands of the glorious Amazons of Venus.

THE space-ship *Viking*—two hundred feet of gleaming metal and polished duralite—lay on the launching platform of New York City's municipal air-port. Her many portholes gleamed with light. She was still taking on rocket fuel from a tender, but otherwise all the final stores were aboard. Her helicopters were turning over slowly, one at a time, as they were tested.

In the *Viking's* upper control room Gerry Norton and Steve Brent made a final check of the instrument panels. Both men wore the blue and gold uniform of the Interplanetary Fleet. Fatigue showed on both their faces, on Steve's freckled pan and on Gerry Norton's lean face. Gerry in particular had not slept for thirty-six hours. His responsibility was a heavy one, as commander of this second attempt to reach the planet Venus from Earth. Well—he would have a chance to catch up on sleep during the long days of travel that lay ahead.

The two officers finished their inspection, and strolled out onto the open deck atop the vessel. For a while they leaned on the rail, staring down at the dense crowds that had thronged the airport to see the departure of the *Viking.* In this warm weather the men wore only light shorts and gayly colored shirts. The women wore the long dresses and metal caps and thin gauze veils that were so popular that year. Around the fringes of the airport stood the ramparts of New York's many tall buildings, with the four hundred story bulk of the Federal Building a giant metal finger against the midnight sky.

"When are we going to pull out, Chief?" Steve Brent asked.

"As soon as the ship from Mars gets in and Olga Stark can come aboard."

"Funny thing—I've never been able to like that gal!" Steve said. Gerry smiled faintly.

"That puts you in the minority, from all reports. However—that's aside from the point. She's the most capable Space-pilot in the whole fleet, and we need her. What's she like personally?"

"Tall, dark, and beautiful—with a nasty tongue and the temper of a fiend," Steve said. He yawned, and changed the subject. "Y'know—I've just been wondering what really did happen to the *Stardust!*"

Gerry shrugged without replying. That was a question that was bound to be in the minds of all members of this expedition, whether or not they put it in words. Travel between Earth and Mars had been commonplace for more than a generation now, but there had not yet been any com-munication with Venus—that cloud-veiled planet whose orbit lay nearer the sun than that of earth. Two years ago the exploring ship *Stardust* had started for Venus. She had simply vanished into the cold of outer space—and never been heard from again.

GERRY NORTON thought the *Viking* would get through. Science had made some advances in these past two years. His ship would carry better rocket fuel than had the *Stardust,* and more efficient gravity plates. The new duralite hull had the strength to withstand a terrific impact. They would probably get through. If not —well—he had been taking chances all his life. You didn't go into the Interplanetary Service at all if you were afraid of danger.

"There comes the ship from Mars now!" Steve Brent said, suddenly pointing upward.

A streak of fire like a shooting star had appeared in the sky far above. It was the rocket blast of the incoming space liner. Yellow flames played about her bow as she turned on the reverse rockets to reduce the terrific speed. The roar of the discharge came down through the air like a faint rumble of distant surf. Then the rockets ceased, and the ship began to drop down as the helicopters were unfolded to take the weight and lower her easily through the atmosphere.

"It won't be long now!" Steve said in his low, deep, quiet voice.

"Aye, not long!" boomed a deep voice behind them, "but I'm thinking it will be a long day before we return to this braw planet of ours!"

Angus McTavish, chief engineer of the *Viking,* was a giant of a man with a voice that could be heard above the roar of rocket motors when he chose to raise it. He had a pair of very bright blue eyes —and a luxuriant red beard. There were probably no more than a dozen full sets of whiskers worn in the earth in this day and age, and McTavish laid claim to the most imposing.

"Fuel all aboard, Chief," he said, "The tender's cast off and we're ready to ride whenever you give the word."

"Just as soon as these people come aboard."

"Tell me, Mac," Steve Brent interposed, "Now that we're all about to jump off into the unknown—just why do you sport that crop of whiskers?"

"So I won't have to button my collar, ye feckless loon!" the big engineer replied instantly.

"The Scots are a queer race."

"Aye, lad—the salt o' the earth. We remain constant in a changing world. All the rest of you have forgotten race and breed and tradition, till ye've become as alike as peas in the same pod all over the Earth. We of Scotland take pride in being the exception."

"And in talking like some wild and kilted highlander of the twentieth century! You're out of date, Angus!"

"If you two are going to argue about that all the way to Venus," Gerry said grimly, "I'll toss you both out and let you drift around in space forever."

"Speaking of the Twentieth Century," Steve said, "one of the ancient folk who lived in that long ago and primitive time would be surprised if they could see the New York of today. Why, they made more fuss about one of their funny old winged air-ships flying the Atlantic than we do about a voyage to Mars or the Moon."

· The ship from Mars settled gently down on the concrete landing platform, and her helicopters ceased to turn. From a hundred nozzles along the edge of the platform came hissing streams of water, playing upon the hull that had been heated by its swift passage through the outer layers of the Earth's atmosphere. Then, as the hull cooled, the streams of water died away and the doors opened. The passengers began to emerge.

A platoon of police, their steel helmets gleaming in the glow of the lights, cleared a path through the crowd for a small group that hurried across to the waiting *Viking*. A few minutes later three newcomers came aboard. All wore the blue and gold uniform of the Interplanetary Fleet. The two men were Martians, thin and sharp featured, with the reddish skin of their race. The other was an Earth woman. Olga Stark stood nearly as tall as Gerry Norton's own six feet. She had a pale skin, and a mass of dark hair that was coiled low on her neck.

"Pilot-Lieutenant Stark and Flight-Ensigns Tanda and Portok reporting aboard, sir," she said quietly.

"You'll find the officers' quarters aft on B-deck. I'm calling a conference in the chart room as soon as we get clear of the stratosphere."

GERRY NORTON stood on the little platform at the top of the control room, under a curved dome of transparent duralite that gave him a clear view along the whole length of the *Viking's* superstructure. The last member of the expedition was aboard, the airport attendants had all stepped back. The time of departure had come at last!

"Close all ports!" he snapped.

"Close ports it is, sir," droned Chester Sand, the Safety Officer. Warning bells rang throughout the ship. Tiny green lights came winking into view on one of the many indicator panels.

"All ports closed, sir!" the Safety Officer sang out a minute later. For a moment Gerry bent over the rail of the platform and himself glanced down at the solid bank of green lights on the board.

"Start helicopters!" he ordered.

There was a low humming. The ship began to vibrate gently. From his place in the dome, Gerry could see the *Viking's* dozen big helicopters begin to spin. Faster and faster they moved as Angus McTavish gave his engines full power. Then the ship rose straight up into the air.

"Here we go, boys—Venus or bust!" Steve Brent muttered under his breath, and a low chuckle swept across the control room.

The lighted surface of the airport fell swiftly away beneath them. The myriad lights of New York were spread out like a jeweled carpet in the night, dwindling and seeming to slide together as the drive of the *Viking's* powerful motors carried her steadily upward. At the three thousand-foot level they passed a traffic balloon with its circle of blue lights, and the signal blinker spelled out a hasty "Good Luck!"

AT the thirty thousand-foot level they passed an inbound Oriental & Western liner, bringing the night mail from

China. She hung motionless on her helicopters to let the *Viking* pass, her siren giving a salute of three long blasts while her passengers crowded the decks to cheer the space-ship. After another ten thousand feet they were above ordinary traffic lanes. The glass windows of the control room were beginning to show a film of condensing moisture, and Steve Brent brought the heavy duralite panes up into place.

"Stand by rocket motors!" Gerry commanded. "Stand by to fold helicopters. Ready? *Contact!*"

There was a muffled roar. The *Viking's* nose tilted sharply upward. Momentarily the space-ship trembled like a living thing. Then she shot ahead, while the helicopters dropped down into recesses within the hull and duralite covers slid into place over them. Gerry climbed down from the dome into the main control room. Momentarily he glanced at the huge brass and steel speed indicators.

"Twelve hundred miles an hour," he said. "Fast enough for this density of atmosphere. Hold her there. Summon heads of departments and all deck officers to the chart room."

The call was quickly answered.

The assembled officers stood leaning against the walls, or perched on the chartlockers. Now that the trip had actually begun, uniform coats were unbuttoned and caps laid aside. Angus McTavish had a battered brier pipe clenched in his teeth. The stem was so short that the swirling smoke seemed to filter upward through his whiskers.

"Better be careful, Mac," said Portok the Martian. "Maybe the air filters won't be able to handle that smoke of yours."

"Never mind the air filters, sonny!" grunted the big Scot with imperturbable good humor. "They'll handle the smoke of good 'baccy better than the fumes of that filthy *grricqua* weed you smoke on Mars."

A radio loud-speaker had been left on, and they heard the voice of an announcer on some European station:

"We now bring you a brief sports résumé. In Canton, China, the Shantung Dragons played a double header with the Budapest Magyars. The score of the first game was . . ."

"Wonder if they ever heard of baseball on Venus!" Steve Brent chuckled.

"Maybe they'll learn as fast as we of Mars," said Portok. "I seem to remember that in the last Interplanetary Championship Series we . . ."

"Skip it!" Steve growled. "I lost a week's salary on that series."

McTavish and Portok grinned.

Gerry Norton watched them with a smile on his lean, dark face. They were a good crowd! The *Viking* was going on the most dangerous journey mankind had ever attempted, a journey from which no one had ever before returned alive, but he could not have asked for a better group of subordinates. They were people of his own choosing, and all but two were old shipmates. Though he had never sailed with Chester Sand, the Safety Officer had been highly recommended. Neither had he ever sailed with Olga Stark before, but he knew her by reputation as an excellent navigator and when she applied to go he felt he should accept her.

FOR half an hour Gerry held them together, while he set the watches and checked assignments and outlined other routine details. Then the meeting ended, and only Steve Brent remained with him. They walked forward into the darkened control room, where the only light was the dim glow from the indicator boards. The Quartermaster on watch stood motionless beside the steering levers.

Gerry noticed that he had a tendency to rise a couple of inches off the floor with each step. The pull of Earth was already lessening! He threw the switch that controlled the attraction-gear, and heard a faint hiss of shifting gravity plates beneath their feet. The feeling and impression of normal weight returned.

For a moment Gerry and Steve stood looking out one of the big duralite windows of the control room. At this level the legions of stars gleamed with an unreal brilliance in the dead black of the heavens. The Earth was a vast globe behind them, glowing for a quarter of its surface with the familiar outlines of the continents still visible. With the lessening pull, the *Viking* had increased speed to five thousand, but she seemed to be standing still in comparison with the vastness of space.

"Funny thing, Chief," Steve Brent said meditatively, "Olga Stark and Chester Sand are not supposed to have met before they came aboard this ship—but I saw them whispering together in that dark corner off Corridor 6 as I came forward."

"Maybe she's just a fast worker," Gerry said. For a moment the incident irritated him, but then he shrugged and forgot it. On a purely scientific and exploratory expedition of this kind, there was no possible motive for any underhand work.

THE days passed in slow progression. The *Viking* had attained her maximum speed of fifty thousand miles an hour as the ceaseless drive of her great rocket motors forced her ahead, a speed possible in the void of outer space where there was no air to create friction. For all her great speed by Earthly standards, she was but crawling slowly across the vastness of Interplanetary space.

Life on board had settled down to a smooth routine. Now and then alarm bells would suddenly ring a warning of the approach of a small planetesimal or some other vagrant wanderer of outer space, and the ship would change course to avoid a collision. Otherwise there was little excitement. Astern, the familiar Earth had dwindled to a shining disc—like the button on an airman's uniform. Ahead, the cloud-veiled planet of Venus drew steadily nearer.

Passing along one of B-deck corridors one day, Gerry met Olga Stark coming out of the recreation rooms. She was off duty at the moment, and instead of her uniform she wore a long gown of green silk. Her dark hair was surmounted by a polished metal cap, and a thin gauze veil hung to her chin. Gerry stopped her with a gesture.

"Very decorative, Lieutenant," he said with a twitch of his lips, "but this is supposed to be a scientific expedition. I must ask that you wear your uniform outside of your cabin."

"I am off duty!" she retorted, her dark eyes suddenly angry and sullen.

"It's true that you're not on watch at this moment, but everybody is on duty

twenty-four hours a day till this expedition is over. Resume your uniform."

"And if I refuse?" she asked.

"You'll go into double irons. When I'm commanding a ship, I do just that!"

For a moment their glances met, the woman's hot and angry, the man's cold and unyielding. Then, without another word, she swept away to her cabin. Gerry Norton sighed, and went on his way. He had never become entirely reconciled to the presence of women in the Interplanetary Fleet. They made good officers most of the time, but occasionally they had fits of feminine temperament.

AT last there came the day when the yellowish, cloud-veiled mass of Venus filled half the sky ahead. Watches were doubled up. Rocket motors were cut down as the attraction of the planet pulled them onward. Then the forward rocket-tubes began to let go for the braking effect, and the flame of the discharges filled the control room with a flickering yellow light.

As they entered the outer atmosphere layers of Venus, the effect of air on the sun's rays gave them natural sunlight and blue skies again for the first time in over six weeks. Something about the effect of yellow sunlight slanting in the port-holes raised the spirits of all of them, and men were whistling as they went about their work. Gerry brought the ship to a halt a few thousand feet above the endless, tumbled mass of clouds that eternally covered all of Venus. They were now near enough to be fully caught in the rotation of the planet's stratosphere, so that they had normal night and day instead of the eternal midnight that had gripped them for weeks.

Early the next morning, with all hands on duty, the *Viking's* helicopters began to drop her down into the cloud-mass. The cottony billows swept up to meet them— and then they were submerged in a dense and yellowish fog. Moisture gathered thickly on the windows of the control room.

"This reminds me of a good London fog!" said Angus McTavish, who had come up from his engine rooms for a few minutes. "I wonder if they have any good pubs down there!"

The soupy, saffron-colored fog enshrouded the *Viking* as she dropped lower and lower. Gerry Norton checked the altitude personally, watching the slowly moving hand of the indicator. Twice he held her motionless while he sent echo-soundings down to make sure they were not too close to land. Then they went a little lower —and suddenly came clear of the cloud mass. They were sinking slowly downward through a peculiarly murky, golden light that was the normal day-time condition on the planet of Venus. They had arrived!

Below them stretched the rippling waters of a vast and greenish sea. It was broken by scattered islands, bare bits of rock that were dotted with a blue moss and were utterly bare of life except for a few swooping sea-birds. On a distant shore were lofty mountains whose peaks were capped with snow. In one or two places a narrow shaft of sunlight struck down through a brief gap in the canopy of eternal clouds, but otherwise there was only that subdued and peculiarly golden light. Nothing moved but those few oddly shaped birds.

"Lord—but it's lonely!" Gerry muttered.

There was no sign of human existence, no trace of the towers and buildings of mankind. Not even any sign of life at all, except for those sea-birds. It was like a scene from the long-ago youth of the world, when the only life was that of the teeming shallows or the muddy shores of warm seas. The place was desolate, and forlorn, and inexpressibly lonely.

They had opened some of the ports for a breath of fresh air after long weeks of the flat and second-hand product of the air filters, with its faint odor of oil and disinfectant. The breeze that came in the open ports was warm and moist and faintly salty.

"Rocket motors — minimum power!" Gerry commanded quietly. "There's no use landing on one of those bare islets. We'll see what lies beyond the mountains."

The subdued blast of only two rocket tubes began to drive the *Viking* forward at a slow speed of about 300 M.P.H., while long fins were thrust out at the sides to carry the weight and free the helicopters. All hands were crowded at the windows and ports. After a moment Olga Stark turned to Gerry.

"Our magnetic compasses are working again, Captain," she said quietly. "I suggest going across the mountains and then turning southwest."

"Why there—rather than in any other direction?" Gerry asked quietly. The girl shrugged.

"Just a hunch. Of course, it's all guess-work."

The *Viking* had to go up to a level of 18,000 feet above this lonely Venusian sea before she was above the peaks of the mountains. Then Gerry turned her inland. Just before they left the shore-line they passed some sort of a flying *thing* that swooped down to prey on the sea-birds. It had a reptilian body, and a spread of leathery wings about twelve feet across.

"Will you look at that!" Steve Brent muttered.

"I'd hate to meet that on a dark night!" Gerry said grimly. Along the shore-line as they flashed inland he could see monstrous, crawling things that moved sluggishly along the beaches or in the shallows. It began to seem that life on Venus was on a different level than that of the Outer Planets.

The *Viking* drove steadily westward across the mountains. From the lower control room windows Gerry could see only drifted snow and naked boulders, and the gauntly lonely peaks. The air was thin and cold. The canopy of yellow clouds was only a little way above them. Then, across the mountains at last, they dropped down toward a broad table-land covered with patches of forest and alternate stretches of open grass-land.

"Cut rockets!" Gerry snapped. "Prepare to land!"

A few minutes later the *Viking* settled gently down in a broad clearing, where the coarse grass was knee high. For the first time in over six weeks the sound and vibration of the motors ceased. The expedition had landed on Venus!

THE landing party filed out a door that opened in the lower part of the hull. The moist air was a little warmer than that of Earth, and it had an unfamiliar smell of growing things, but its density seemed about the same. Since the size of Venus was similar to that of their own planets, neither Earth-man nor Martian had much trouble in walking as soon as they became accustomed to a slightly lesser gravity. Gerry found he could leap eight feet in the air without any trouble.

Gerry split the landing party into four groups, sending them spreading out like the spokes of a fan.

"Don't go more than three miles from the ship without further orders. Study the countryside thoroughly, and then report back on board."

All the landing party wore light armour of steel coated with duralite, and carried ray-tubes at their belts. Every third man had a heavier ray-gun with its cylindrical magazine, not unlike the old-fashioned machine gun. Their polished armor took on a golden tinge as they tramped away across the grass-land, while behind them the *Viking* lay motionless in the grass like a great torpedo of steel and blue.

Gerry took personal command of the southernmost exploring party, leading them into a broad belt of forest. It was very still beneath the giant trees, where strange yellow flowers hung from the branches and their path wound between clusters of ten-foot ferns. Huge toad-stools of purple and green rose higher than their heads, and once they saw a giant ant some three feet long who scuttled off through the underbrush with the speed of a galloping horse.

Gradually Gerry became separated from the rest of his party, bearing more to the southward as he caught a glimpse of more open country through the trees. Then, on the edge of a small clearing, he abruptly halted as half a dozen men appeared on the far side.

That is, Gerry thought of them as men for lack of a better term. They were like nothing he had ever seen on either Earth or Mars or any of the planetoids between. Lean bodies were covered with glistening gray scales. Though the hands seemed human, the feet were clawed and webbed. Short, flat tails hung behind them. The faces were scaleless, low-browed and green-eyed, with a jutting mouth and nose that came together in a sort of snout. They had pointed ears that stood sharply erect. Their general appearance was a little more on the animal side than the human, but they had swords slung at their belts and carried short-barreled rifles.

In the center of the group was a woman. She was naked except for a scarlet loin-cloth and golden breast-plates. This was no semi-reptilian creature, but a woman straight and clean-limbed and beautiful, with long blonde hair that hung nearly to her waist. She had blue eyes, and her skin was about as white as Gerry's own, though it had a faintly tawny tinge so that she appeared all golden. At the moment her hands were tightly tied behind her back and a cloth gag distended her lips, while one of the Scaly Men led her along by a rope about her neck.

Gerry stepped out into the clearing with his ray-tubes swinging free in his hand. His wide shoulders were thrown slightly forward, his whole muscular body was tensed and ready beneath his armor. As always when he went into a fight, his lean and normally somber face was smiling.

THE captive girl saw him first, and her eyes widened in utter surprise. Then the half dozen reptilian men caught sight of the lone Earth-man standing there in his gleaming armor, and their snout-like mouths sagged open. Gerry walked quietly forward.

He was half across the clearing before the Venusians recovered from their surprise. Then one of the patrol flung his short rifle to his shoulder. There was a hiss of escaping gas, and a split-second later an explosive bullet struck him in the chest with a flash and a loud report. It would have instantly killed an unprotected man, but it did no more than slightly dent Gerry's armor.

The Earth-man half crouched, his eyes narrowing and his jaw jutting suddenly forward. He had meant to try and parley, but diplomacy had no place with creatures who shot first and challenged afterward. His ray-tube swung up to the level. There was a sharp crackling sound, and for a second a murky red light played around the open end. The nearest Venusian crumpled and went down. He twitched for a second, and then lay still. The gray scales had turned dead black in the area where the death-ray had struck him.

At least the Scaly Men had courage! The remaining five came forward with a shrill and almost canine yelping, advancing at a bent-legged run. Their rifles hissed as the compressed gases were released, the explosive bullets crackled all around Gerry. Twice more his ray-tube let go its deadly blast—and then his weapon was empty. He cursed himself through clenched teeth for having strayed away from the patrol while armed only with a light tube with simply three charges. Two more of the reptile men lay twitching in the tall grass, but the other three were almost up to him. After that one volley they had drawn their swords, which probably meant that their compressed-gas rifles were cumbersome things to reload.

And then Gerry Norton suddenly remembered the greater strength of his Earthly muscles. As the foremost Venusian lunged for him with long blade swinging, Gerry bounded high into the air. He went clean over the head of his antagonist, coming down squarely on top of the next behind. They both went sprawling, but Gerry recovered first. Gripping the fallen Venusian by the ankles, the Earth-man swung him around his head like a flail and hurled him squarely at the other two. The three of them went down in a tangled heap.

By the time the reptile men again scrambled to their feet, Gerry had snatched up the sword of one of the men he had killed with the ray-tube. Now he had something to fight with! The long sword whistled as he jerked it free from its scabbard. For an instant he tested the blade in both hands. It was forged of some bluish metal that seemed as strong and flexible as well-tempered steel. Then, still smiling his thin-lipped smile though his eyes were as cold as the wintry seas, Gerry Norton waited the onrush of the three Venusians.

There were a few seconds of clashing steel. The reptile men were good swordsmen, but they were no match for the speed and strength of the Man from Earth. Two of them were stretched on the ground with cloven skulls, and then the last survivor turned and ran. Gerry could have caught him easily, for the webbed feet of the Venusian did not make for great speed, but he was content to let him go.

When the scaly tail of the fleeing creature had vanished in the underbrush, Gerry thrust his sword upright in the ground—where it would be handy if he needed it again in a hurry—and freed the golden-haired girl from her bonds.

"I wonder where *you* fit into this picture, Bright Eyes!" he muttered, knowing she would not understand.

There was certainly nothing of the shrinking violet about this girl! When her hands were free she faced Gerry without any sign of either fear or even much gratitude, standing erect with her hands on her hips and her eyes nearly on a level with his own.

"*Jaro quimtar*—who are you?" she asked in Martian.

GERRY stared at her in startled surprise. The girl had unquestionably spoken in Martian. It was a very old and antique form of the language that she used, a dialect that had not been heard on Mars itself for countless generations, but it was possible for Gerry to understand it. The last thing he had expected to find on this planet of Venus was anyone who spoke one of the tongues common on the Outer Planets!

"I'm Gerry Norton," he said.

"Geree!" the girl repeated. "You talk funny."

"Same to you, sister," Gerry grinned. "And just who are you, anyway?"

"I am Closana, of course, the daughter of Rupin-Sang!" the girl said haughtily. "Don't you see the Golden Arrow?"

She touched a small golden arrow that hung from a light chain about her neck. It seemed to be some kind of an insignia of rank. Her deep blue eyes were looking at him thoughtfully.

"You wear queer clothes, Geree," she said at last. "Where do you come from?"

"From Earth."

She frowned.

"Where is that? Is it one of the lands beyond the Great Sea?"

"Much farther away than that. It's another planet, far off in outer space."

"You lie," she said. "Such a thing is not possible."

"Okay, sister," Gerry snapped, "we won't argue about that right now. Who were your unpleasant friends here? What do we do next?"

Closana walked across to take the sword of one of the slain Reptilians. She tested its balance, seemed satisfied, and then belted the scabbard about her own waist. She handled the long blade with the experienced ease of a warrior, and for the first time Gerry noticed the play of corded muscles beneath the smooth and tawny skin of her arms and shoulders. Closana, daughter of Rupin-Sang, was feminine enough but there was nothing of the clinging vine about her! She threw her long hair back over her shoulders and faced Gerry with the sword in her hand.

"You should have killed the last of the Scaly Ones," she said, "instead of letting him get away. Now he will bring the whole raiding party down on us."

"Who are they, those things you call the Scaly Ones?"

"Their region lies beyond the frontier of our land of Savissa," the girl explained. "We are near the boundaries now. There is constant warfare between ourselves and the Scaly Ones. Now and then their raiding parties break through our ring of barrier forts, and it was a group of five hundred such raiders that captured me this morning. That one who escaped will bring the rest back with him."

"Then I guess we'll need help!" Gerry said grimly.

THERE was a two-way, short-wave radio set built into his helmet. He reached up to adjust the switch, then flashed the alarm signal. A few seconds later he heard the answering voice of Portok the Martian, who was in command of the nearest of the *Viking's* exploring parties.

"Jumping ray-blasts, Chief, we were wondering what had happened to you!"

"Guide on my transmitter and get here as soon as you can!" Gerry snapped. "Hurry!"

A few minutes later they saw a glint of armor through the trees, and then the half dozen members of the exploring party emerged into the clearing. Their eyes were wide with surprise as they saw Closana standing beside Gerry.

"Who's your yellow-haired friend, Chief?" Portok asked with a broad grin. He had spoken in Martian, the two tongues being practically interchangeable with the men of the Interplanetary Fleet. Closana's eyes flashed fire.

"Speak of me with more respect, little Red-face!" she snapped. Portok's jaw sagged open, but before he could say anything further the underbrush on the far side of the clearing suddenly vomited a yelling horde of the Scaly Ones.

They came in close-packed masses, yelping shrilly. Their scaly skins and the blades of their swords gleamed in the subdued yellow light. Evidently bent on capture of the small group of strangers, they were not using their gas-guns.

"Keep together! Fall back toward the ship!" Gerry roared, drawing the sword he had captured earlier in the day.

There was a sharp crackle of ray-blasts as the Earth-men fell back before the charging horde of the Scaly Ones. The short hand-tubes were soon exhausted, but the heavy ray-guns carried by two of the men fired steadily. Murky light continually played about their stubby muzzles. Dozens of the Scaly Ones dropped, twitching, in the tall grass before the deadly blast of the rays, but the shouting hordes came on unchecked. And then a bugle sounded somewhere off on the flank!

"Now, you scaly devils!" Closana screamed, facing about and waving the sword high above her head, "The frontier guards have arrived!"

Long lines of warriors charged out through the bushes to take the reptile men on the flank. The front line of skirmishers carried heavy bows and had quivers of arrows slung on their backs, the ranks behind were armed with shields and spears. Rank by rank and company by company they came, nearly a thousand strong, the ringing clamor of brazen trumpets urging them onward. Gerry Norton stared at them blankly, scarcely able to believe what he saw. All the warriors were women!

They were tall and clean-limbed, with long golden hair that streamed behind them as they ran. Like Closana, they wore bright-colored loin cloths and had round gold plates fastened across their breasts. The might of the Golden Amazons of Venus swept forward like a giant wave, with a spray of tossing spear points above it. Then the trumpets sounded again, and the arrow storm began.

The front ranks loosed their long shafts swiftly, and the air became full of the twang of bow-strings and hiss of speeding arrows. A shouting officer of the Scaly Ones went down with a pair of shafts feathered in his chest. His men were dropping all about him as the gold-tipped arrows struck home.

THE reptile men were using their gas-guns now. The sharp hiss of the discharges rose above the twang of the bow-strings, the snap of the exploding bullets was like a crackle of old-fashioned musketry. The projectiles ripped holes in the front ranks of the Amazons, but they still came bounding forward. Then the sharp reports of the exploding bullets died away, for the gas-guns were cumbersome things to re-charge and there was no time. The two lines met with a clash of steel.

Gerry Norton had thrown his armoured Earth-men and Martians as a guard around Closana when she ran toward the center of the Amazon line. On two occasions small parties of the Scaly Ones cut their way through the guarding spears to reach them, and each time the blast of the heavy ray-guns mowed them down. The clatter of meeting blades was like the noise of a thousand smithies, the shrill yelping of the reptile men was drowned out by the triumphant blast of the Amazon trumpets. The Scaly Ones were giving back all along the line, under pressure of superior numbers and the greater agility of the lithe Amazons.

Gerry fought with the long, blue-bladed sword in his hand and the shield of a fallen Amazon on his left arm. With the greater strength of his earthly muscles, he raged through the fighting while his heavy blade wrought deadly execution. And then it was over! The Scaly Ones broke up into scores of fleeing groups and fresh companies of Amazons bounded in pursuit with their long bows twanging. Closana leaned on her dripping blade and held out her hand.

"It was a good fight, Geree. I think I will take you for my husband."

"I think," Gerry said, "We'll just leave

that idea for discussion some other time."

THE fleeing survivors of the Scaly Ones had gone, with companies of light armed Amazons in hot pursuit. The others were tending the wounded and gathering up the dead, picking up fallen weapons, doing all the routine tasks that are the aftermath of battle. Closana was now surrounded by a body-guard of tall, blonde Amazons whose lion-cloths bore the same design of a golden arrow-head as her own.

"I think," she said to Gerry, "that you should come to see my father Rupin-Sang, who is ruler of this land."

Quite a thinker, decided Gerry.

"We can take you there in the ship if you show us the way," he said shortly.

A horde of Amazons thronged around the big blue-and-silver hull of the *Viking* where she lay in the knee-high grass. As the members of the landing party filed on board and turned their ray-tubes in to the Ordnance Officer to be recharged, the other members of the crew came out to stare at the visitors. Angus McTavish stood on the steps of the ladder with his big fists on his hips.

"Will ye look at all the bonny lassies!' he said, "This may not be such a bad planet after all."

The feminine warriors of Venus saw McTavish then, and a sudden murmur swept over the throng. An instant later a hundred blades flashed in the air in salute, and then all the Amazons dropped down on one knee.

"Now what the devil . . .?" muttered Steve Brent who had come out of the ship just behind McTavish.

"Just a proper tribute to my outstanding personality, lad!" the big Scot muttered aside. Closana read the surprise in Gerry Norton's eyes.

"There are few men in this land of Savissa," she explained, "And the wearing of a beard is the sign of a noble of the highest rank."

"Wonder how long it will take me to grow a good crop of whiskers!" Steve said.

Closana and a dozen of her body-guard came aboard, looking curiously about them. As the Venusian princess walked into the control room she came face to face with Olga Stark. For a long moment the two women stood looking at each other, their clashing glances hard and intent. The golden Venusian and the dark haired Earthling. Then Closana shrugged and turned away.

"I do not like her," she said calmly. A slow flush spread over Olga Stark's face, and her eyes smoldered, but she did not answer.

With helicopters spinning, the *Viking* rose a thousand feet in the air. Then she moved ahead at minimum cruising speed. Closana stood at one of the control room windows to point the way.

IT was a strange land that they saw moving past below them, though a pleasant one. There were rolling uplands, and patches of forest, and occasional villages surrounded by broad tilled fields. Except for the yellowish tinge to the vegetation, and the odd shapes of the trees, it might have been an Earthly countryside. Then Gerry noticed another thing! Though it was broad daylight, as bright as it could become on this planet, there were no shadows at all. The diffusing effect of the eternal cloud barrier kept the light equal on all sides.

"The Land of No Shadow!" he said aloud. For the first time in this busy day he thought of the fact that they were forty million miles from home. If anything happened to the *Viking*, they would spend the rest of their lives here.

They passed some of the barrier forts, square and stone walled buildings reminiscent of medieval castles on Earth. In the misty hills beyond, Closana told Gerry, lay the country of the Scaly Ones.

"What is it like?" he asked. She shrugged, but her eyes were shadowed.

"All I know about it is legend, the sort of tales that old women tell in the evenings. Many of our people have been taken there as prisoners in raids, but none has ever returned alive."

Leaving Steve Brent in command in the control room for the moment, Gerry went aft to his quarters where he had a compact Tri-dimensional-cinema outfit. He was passing along one of the corridors on B-deck when he abruptly halted. A faint humming was coming from behind the closed door of the radio room!

The *Viking's* sending outfit was not strong enough to bridge the vastness of interplanetary space. Such outfits existed, of course, but only a small set had been installed on the space-ship because of the extra weight involved. The radio room had been closed and locked weeks ago. No one was supposed to have access to it except Steve Brent and Gerry himself. And yet —the unmistakable hum of a generator was coming from behind the closed door!

Gerry cautiously tested the knob of the door. It gave under his hand. As he opened the portal a crack, he clearly heard the sharp murmur of the sending apparatus. Then he swung the door wide on its noiseless and well oiled hinges. A dim light gleamed across the room! A dark figure was crouched tensely over the table that held the sending set. At the moment Gerry could not see who it was.

Two steps Gerry took into the room. Three steps. The rubberoid soles of his shoes made no sound. Then a crushing weight descended on top of his head! In the half second before he lost consciousness, he realized that there had been a second interloper in the radio room. Someone who had been crouching against the wall by the door, and who had slugged him as he passed.

WHEN consciousness returned to Gerry Norton, he was lying alone on the floor of the darkened radio room. He sat up, and rubbed his aching head, and swore softly. There was no sign of the interlopers, nor any clue to their identity.

The whole incident puzzled him. His assailants must have been from among the *Viking's* crew. That was surprising enough in itself, but there was also the problem of motive. Why would anybody be sending a secret message when there was no receiving set within millions of miles? The thing just didn't make sense.

Closing the radio room behind him Gerry went back to the control-room and drew Steve Brent aside.

"Look here, Steve! I just found someone sending a secret message out over the radio, and got knocked on the head before I could see who it was."

"You must have been reading some of those funny old Twentieth Century gangster yarns of evil deeds!" Steve grinned.

"I'm serious. That really happened." Gerry snapped. The grin faded from Brent's freckled face.

"Then it must have been Chester Sand," he said promptly.

"Why do you say that?"

Brent shrugged.

"Because he's the only man aboard that I don't know too well to suspect."

"Interesting logic," Gerry grunted, "But we can't lock a man up on such negative grounds. Keep your eyes open. I'm going to try to sweat some information out of someone as soon as we get through this ceremony of visiting the king of this place."

WOMEN working in the fields looked up as the *Viking* passed, lifting a hand to shade their eyes as they stared aloft at the soaring space-ship. Other women drove small carts along the white roads that wound through the fields. There did not seem to be any men in this land at all. Then, along the far horizon ahead, there began to lift the domes and towers and minarets of a mighty city. Closana proudly lifted her arm.

"The Golden City of Larr!" she said, "Capitol of our land of Savissa. None but our own people have ever penetrated those walls except as prisoners of war."

The walled city of Larr dominated the plain in all its towered splendor. Its walls of polished yellow stone were more than a hundred feet high. The serrated battlements at the top were faced with plates of thin gold. Domes of blue and scarlet gleamed within the walls. Slender minarets lifted their lattices high in the air. In the center was a massive round tower whose top was shaped like the point of a golden arrow.

"But surely your people never built this place!" he gasped. Closana shook her head.

"The city was not built by my people as they are now. Larr, the Golden City, is very ancient. It was built by the Old Ones—they who lived here long ago, in the dim dawn of time. I have forgotten most of the tale but my father can tell you."

As they passed over the outer walls, Gerry saw some long steel tubes mounted on swivels above the battlements. They were protected by gleaming metal shields. He touched Closana's arm.

"What are those things that look like giant ray-guns?"

"Those are the defences of the walls," the girl answered, "We also have them at the barrier forts. In some way they send out rays of heat that burn and shrivel all things within reach. I do not know much about them, but my father can tell you."

"Looks like he's going to tell me a lot of things," Gerry said. Closana shook back her long hair and looked at him thoughtfully for a moment.

"Yes, Geree. He will also tell you why you had better marry me as I suggested."

"I told you we'd have to let that subject wait till later!" he said grimly. Steve Brent prodded him gently in the ribs.

"Persistent souls, these Golden Amazons!" he said in English.

THE appearance of the *Viking* in the air over Larr created a mounting excitement among the citizens of the city. Through the open windows of the control room Gerry could hear the brazen clamor of many trumpets, sounding the alarm. Crowds appeared on the roofs. Arrows streaked up at the space-ship, futile shafts that fell short of the mark. As they neared the central tower, gun crews swarmed about two of the ray-tubes. Knowing the resisting power of the *Viking's* duralite hull, Gerry was not greatly worried, but Closana seemed to feel that things had gone far enough.

Hitherto the girl had been quite evidently enjoying the consternation that the *Viking's* arrival had caused among the defenders of the city. Now she leaned far out from the open window and waved reassuringly. As she was recognized, defense preparations ceased and the gun crews began to cover their weapons up again.

The *Viking* settled gently down on the worn stone pavement of a square plaza directly before the central tower. A ring of amazon spearmen instantly formed to keep back the curious crowds, and other companies were drawn up as a guard of honor. They saluted Closana with a shout and a surge of uplifted spears when she and Gerry stepped out the opened starboard door. Then, when Angus McTavish came out with a group of senior officers a few seconds later, all the Amazon warriors dropped instantly down on one knee while their spear-points rattled on the stones. The big engineer beamed through his beard, and tilted his uniform cap to a more rakish angle.

"I have already stated that these folk are a verra discriminating people!" he said with deep satisfaction. Closana turned to Gerry.

"It would be better to take only a few of your people along when we go into see my father."

Gerry faced about, his glance running quickly over those of his crew who had emerged from the hull and were standing nearby.

"Steve Brent stays here in command," he said quietly, "You come with me, Angus. And Portok. And one other. . . ." He hesitated, then named Olga Stark. Later he was to wonder what evil genius had led him to select her as one of the party. He could not quite remember. Probably it was just a desire to take as varied and representative a group along with him as possible. Closana looked annoyed at his choice, but did not comment.

THEY passed through the ranks of the spear-guard, and up to the octagonal main door of the tower where carved golden leaves slid back into the wall on each side. A blue light glowed around the inner frame of the door, and Closana held up her arm.

"Wait till the blue light fades, for it is Death," she said quietly. Then, as the light died out, they all stepped inside while the golden leaves of the door closed clashing behind them.

They were in a winding corridor whose stone walls were faced with polished stone and hung with ancient tapestries. The place was lighted by metal discs set flush in the ceiling, discs of a substance that gave forth a soft and golden glow. Even this light, Gerry noticed, was so diffused as to be shadowless. "The Land of No-Shadow!" he muttered under his breath, remembering the phrase that had come to him earlier. Somehow the friendly old Earth seemed very far away at that moment!

In an ante-chamber they met the first man they had seen since they reached Venus, aside from the half-animal raiders of the Scaly Ones. This man was short and slight, with a very high forehead and unusually large eyes. His skin had the same tawny tinge as that of the feminine warriors of his race, but he was more lightly built than they. He wore a loose yellow tunic, and his hair and thin beard were heavily shot with gray. Somehow he looked tired, and old even beyond his years, as though the sands of his race were running very low.

"Rupin-Sang awaits your coming," he said to Gerry. As Portok and the others from the *Viking* came into sight, the Venusian stared at them with strangely startled eyes. He said nothing more, but his glance seemed to hold a strange, terrible haunting fear.

At the end of the corridor they stepped into a small golden car. A door closed behind them. The floor shot rapidly upward. A few seconds later the door of the lift-car swung open again and they stepped out into a round chamber near the top of the great tower.

"Enter to His Highness Rupin-Sang, Lord of Savissa and the Mountain Lands, ruler of field and forest and castle, hereditary Warden of the Great Sea!" the Venusian courtier said sonorously.

The room was circular, with glassless windows set in the walls every few feet. A warm breeze blew in to stir the tiny metal discs that hung around near the tops of the walls in a sort of frieze, setting them swinging till they clashed together with a continuous jingling. A small fountain murmured in the center of the room. A peculiarly shaped telescope stood by one wall, and there were other scientific instruments of a type unfamiliar to the Earth-men.

IN a big carved chair in the center sat a very old man, a rolled parchment lying across his knees. What remained of his hair and beard were pure white. His face was lined and sunken. He half raised his arm in a ceremonial gesture of welcome, but then a sudden expression of alarm came over his face. He pointed with one shaking hand.

"*Aie*—woe to the City of Larr! The

hour of the fulfilment of the prophecy is at hand! Woe to Larr, with its walls and towers!"

Closana hurried to her father's side. A moment later the old man had regained his calm. He greeted them with formalized speech of welcome full of old phrases, then added:

"Forgive my agitation when you first entered, *hiziren,* but it brought to mind the doom-filled phrases of what we of Savissa call the Prophecy of Jeddah-Khana."

"What is that?"

"It is a very old prophecy, carved in an ancient runic script on the stone walls of one of the vaults under this tower. Tradition says it was put there by the Old Ones who built this city, and of whose science we are the unworthy heirs." Rupin-Sang bowed and touched his forehead as he mentioned the Old Ones. "The Prophecy states that the day will come when a red-skinned man and a dark-haired woman and a ruddy, bearded giant will come together to the city from afar, and that within a month thereafter the Golden City of Larr will crumble and return to the dust."

"But surely you don't take such old legends seriously!" Gerry said. The old man smiled.

"My head tells me not to, but supersition is strong in we of Savissa. However —I can take comfort from the fact that the old legend also prophecies a rebirth for Savissa after the great catastrophe. But enough of this talk of portents and legends! I give you welcome to Savissa, and to the city of Larr. Also, I thank you for rescuing my youngest daughter from the Scaly Raiders. Whence come ye?"

Gerry sketched in hasty phrases the outline of present conditions on Earth and Mars, and told of their trip through space to Venus in the *Viking.* Rupin-Sang nodded without showing any particular surprise.

"And so that's the story," Gerry concluded. "We're curious about some of your conditions here. The women warriors, for instance. . . ."

"It was not always so in the land of Savissa," Rupin-Sang said with a faint smile. "In the days of the Old Ones there was a natural balance of the sexes. But, as the slow centuries passed, the birth rate gradually changed. Now one child in five thousand born in Savissa is a male. The few men we do have are needed for certain administrative and scientific work, particularly the supervision of the alta-radium mines in the mountains from which we get the raw material for the alta-ray tubes that are our greatest protection against invasion."

"I saw the tubes on the walls," Gerry said, "but why is it that your mobile forces are armed only with primitive weapons like bows and arrows?"

"Because we cannot possibly mine and produce enough of the alta-radium to do more than supply the defences of the city and of the barrier forts. The possession of the secret of that ray has kept our borders free from the Scaly Ones except for isolated raids like the one you encountered today, but we cannot arm our troops with the ray."

"And the gas-guns of the Scaly Ones?"

"They are a good weapon—but we have not the materials to manufacture them on this side of the border."

"Sounds like what we used to call a 'balance of power' in the days when Earth was torn by wars," Gerry said with a smile. "But tell me one thing more. I notice that in this land you speak an archaic form of Martian."

"The Tempora-scope can tell you the story better than my words."

Rupin-Sang nodded to his attendant, and a cloth cover was removed from a broad metal disc that was attached to some kind of a machine. He touched a control lever, and the mechanism began to hum. Blinds were dropped down over the windows, so that the room was filled with a murky twilight. The humming sound grew steadily louder. Now the metal disc glowed with a brilliant light. Momentarily its polished surface clouded over, as though obscured by a thin fog, and then the mists drifted aside.

BEFORE them they saw the Universe as it was in the youth of the world, when roaring volcanoes were still active on the Moon and the rings of Saturn were just drifting out from the girth of that spinning sphere. It was as though they were looking out through a circular window somewhere in the sky. The machine gave a perfect illusion of reality, not merely tri-dimensional but touching all the senses as well. They could hear the roar of new-made satellites spinning off into the void, and the rush of burning gases. They could smell the scent of molten rock.

Then time passed! The planets began to cool. The mud-flats steamed under a cloudy sun, the mountains shouldered their way upward through the tilted and riven fields. On the edges of inland seas, the hot shallows were filled with slimy things that crawled with their bellies dragging. They could hear the ripple of the waters, and the rustle of warm winds blowing through the flowerless and fern-like forests. Gerry could smell the rank odors of the steaming and primitive jungles. There was a pungent taste on his lips. Once he stretched his hand out toward a trilobite that seemed to be crawling up to his feet—and he felt the coarse surface of the shell before he pulled his hand back again.

The picture changed once more, centering on a ruddy planet that swept toward them while Portok exclaimed at the sight of Mars in the ancient days before the planets were built. Men and women walked its smooth fields, among the flaming scarlet flowers. Music and laughter and the voices of women drifted on the scented winds. But Mars was changing. It was drying up. Life could no longer be the same. Some of the people were beginning to draft the plans for the great canals that were to conserve the planet's failing supply of water, but others took to space-ships and sailed off into the void.

Then, for the first time, they saw the planet Venus as the Martian space-ships dropped down through the veiling clouds. They saw those first pioneers of space land on Venus, and subjugate the natives, and build mighty cities in the plains. But something happened to the birth-rate, and most of the science of the Old Ones was lost when a series of great quakes swept the planet. The holdings of the descendants of those interplanetary travelers of long ago dwindled to only the city of Larr and the land of Savissa itself.

The humming of the Temporascope died away. The big metal disc again became

2—Planet Stories—Winter

blank. The machine had ceased to function, and the illusion of the reality of the past was gone. They were simply in a shaded tower room with a tired old man who sat on a carved throne.

"And that is the tale of the rise and decline of our people, *hiziren*," he said sadly. "Now the sands of our nation run low. I am half inclined to believe that the old prophecy will come true, and that this is the twilight of Savissa and its people. But— enough of that. Raise the blinds again, Rotosa, so that we may have light while we can. And I ask you visitors from afar to dine with me tonight before you go back to your space-ship."

THE banquet table was set on the ground floor of the Arrow-Tower, in a room where an open colonnade looked out on a walled garden behind the palace of the rulers of Savissa. A carved wooden table was set with golden plates. Faint music came from some hidden source. In the garden outside, night birds sang softly and there was a constant sound of running water from many fountains.

In addition to Rupin-Sang, there were three of his male attendants and about twenty women. On this ceremonial occasion they supplemented their usual scanty garb with long and graceful robes that gleamed like silk. Thin veils were attached to jeweled circlets. Catching a glimpse of the sullen discontent on Olga Stark's face, Gerry suddenly realized that the Earth woman was jealous of her own appearance.

"Probably hating my guts right now for making her wear her uniform!" he thought. "Women are queer!"

To Gerry Norton, that meal was a peaceful interlude between the monotonous strain of the long interplanetary voyage and the uncertainty of what lay ahead. Though some of the native dishes tasted strange to his Earthly palate, the food was generally good. Fragrant, heady wines from the hill country bordering Savissa were served in colored glass goblets. A sound of distant singing drifted across the garden.

Gerry was wondering what disaster had overtaken the first expedition that had set out to reach this planet, the space-ship *Stardust* that had left Earth over two years ago under command of Major Walter Lansing. Perhaps it had landed in some less friendly part of the planet and been overwhelmed by the natives before it could get away again. Perhaps it had met some swift disaster in outer space and was now spinning endlessly in the void—a lifeless and man-made planetoid. In any case, he would make a thorough search for some trace of the *Stardust* before he started back to Earth again.

WHEN the meal was over and they all arose from the table, Gerry noticed that Angus and Olga Stark walked out into the garden together. It struck him as an odd combination, for Olga was the one person on board with whom the genial Scot was not friendly. Then he forgot about it.

A few minutes later Closana took Gerry's arm and led him out into the garden. Colored lanterns hung here and there along the paths, but most of the light came from globes of glowing metal that were concealed near the tops of the trees. The effect was much like Earthly moonlight, except that the moon was golden instead of silver. Angus and Olga should have been a few yards ahead of them, but both had disappeared. Gerry wondered about it—and then a dim figure rose up in the shadows immediately before him. A cloud of choking gas, hurled squarely in his face from some sort of flask, filled his lungs with the pain of many fiery needles.

Gerry crumpled soundlessly to the ground. He could see and hear what went on, but otherwise he was paralyzed and incapable of sound or movement. For a moment he thought that Closana was behind some form of treachery. Then dark figures swarmed around him, lifting him from the ground, and he saw the dim light gleaming on gray scales. The Scaly Ones had penetrated to the innermost sanctuary of the City of Larr!

Gerry's head fell back as they lifted him, and he could see that Closana was equally helpless in the grip of more of the raiders. A section of grass and bushes was swung back on a hidden trap door, revealing a flight of moss-covered stone steps leading downward. The two prisoners were carried down, and the door dropped hollowly into place above them.

THEY were in a narrow and very ancient stone passage. Moss and lichens covered the walls, moisture dripped from the ceiling. On the floor in the midst of another group of the Scaly Ones lay Angus McTavish, evidently also a victim of the paralyzing gas. Olga Stark stood nearby, her long dark hair loose about her shoulders and an expression of savage triumph in her eyes.

"Tie them securely!" she snapped to the officer in command of the Scaly Men. His long-nosed, brutish face creased in a grim smile.

"It shall be done, Mistress!"

Closana was stripped to her loin-cloth. A cloth gag was twisted into her mouth, her arms were tied behind her back. Gerry and Angus were treated in the same way. Control of his muscles was returning swiftly to Gerry Norton now, as the effects of the gas wore off, but he was already secured and helpless.

Grim rage filled Gerry then, but even greater than that emotion was his utter amazement. The thing was completely beyond his understanding. This was no routine raid of the Scaly Ones against the people of Larr, but a definite attempt to capture *him!* Strangest of all was the part played by Olga Stark, who acted as though she was in command of the Scaly Men. It just wasn't possible—but it was happening.

The three prisoners were pulled to their feet. Guards gripped their elbows. At the first bend in the passage a small waterfall came down from above and formed a gurgling stream that ran in a deep gutter at one side. The air was hot, and moist, and heavy with the scent of running water and fungus growths. Other jets of water came down from above to add to the trickle of water until, as the passage widened, a gurgling torrent ran along beside them. Suddenly Gerry realized where they were. This was the sewerage system that carried away the waste of the city's many flowing fountains!

At last they came to the main drain, a vaulted stone passage where a twenty-foot stream of black water flowed along beside the narrow foot-path. Tied up there, looking like a sea-monster in the dim light of the lanterns carried by the Scaly Men, was a metal boat that had only a narrow deck and a round dome above the water. A crude submarine!

The three prisoners were forced aboard. Their gags were removed, now that silence no longer mattered, but their arms remained bound and they were chained by the necks to a steel bar as they sat in a row at one side of the narrow hull. The raiders cast off, came aboard, and closed the dome behind them. Motors hummed softly, and then the submarine moved sluggishly down the stream.

At the moment the three of them were alone. They could see the scaly skins of some of their captors busied at various tasks in adjoining compartments, but there was no one within hearing. After twisting futilely at his bonds for a moment, Gerry leaned back against the steel bulkhead behind him and looked over at Angus.

"Well—here we are!" he said.

"Aye—so it seems!" The Scot's broad face was grim. "I should have known that black-haired witch had some deviltry in mind when she asked me to walk in the garden with her!"

"But where does she fit into the picture? How does she get her control over these scaly devils?"

"How do I know?" snorted McTavish angrily. "Ask me some more riddles! What's more to the point is where they're taking us in this queer craft."

"I can guess that," Closana said quietly. The girl was very pale, but she smiled faintly as she met Gerry's eyes. "This drain empties into the Giri river, and a few miles farther along that river forms the boundary between Savissa and the lands of the Scaly Ones. We have never known they could travel beneath the water this way."

"What will happen after they get us there?"

"Torture and death. Once any of our people are taken across into the land of Giri-Vaaka, they never return alive."

"Nice little trip we're taking, Gerry lad!" McTavish growled. "Too bad you didn't bring your cinema camera along!"

THE submarine moved sluggishly ahead, silent except for the hum of its motors. As Gerry looked around he could see that it was a crudely constructed and makeshift craft. Even so, it was more than he would have expected from men of the apparent mentality of the Scaly Ones.

"This is a funny sort of submarine!" he said to Angus. The big engineer, who had twisted around to peer at the bulkhead directly behind them, growled deep in his throat.

"It's funnier than ye think, lad! Look at this!" McTavish nodded toward one of the sheets of thin steel from which the bulkhead had been built. On the edge there were stamped a few words. The letters were small, and in the dim light Gerry had to narrow his eyes for a moment before he could read them.

U. S. Gov't Steel Works
Atlanta, Ga.

"How in Heaven's name did they get that . . . ?" Gerry's voice trailed off without finishing the sentence. McTavish shrugged.

"Ye don't need more than one guess. The *Stardust* must have been wrecked somewhere near here, and these devils took some of her parts to build this outlandish craft."

At last, long hours later, the submarine came to a stop. As his captors led him up on deck, Gerry saw that the ungainly craft had grounded in the shallows on the shore of a broad river. It was just daylight. A pale yellow light filtered down through the canopy of clouds, and a flight of marsh-fowl was winging by just overhead.

"Where are we?" asked Gerry.

"This is the Giri River," Closana said. "Savissa lies on the far shore. This is the land of the Scaly Ones."

Some of the reptile men hauled the submarine into a cove and began to cover it over with piles of reeds. Some twenty others formed up in a column with the three prisoners in the center. Then the officer in command barked an order and they all moved out along a dirt road that led away from the river. Olga Stark was walking beside the first rank of scaly warriors. She had not looked at the prisoners at all.

They tramped steadily onward through the dust in silence except for the dull slap of the webbed feet of the reptile men and the jingle of their equipment. After a while the officer in command came back to look at the prisoners. He was a grizzled veteran with shaggy ridges above his eyes and the long-healed scars of half a dozen old wounds on his scaly body. McTavish glared at him for a moment.

"Take a good look, sonny boy!" the big Scot growled. "What's your name—if you have one?"

"I should tear out your tongue for speaking in that tone to an officer of Giri-Vaaka," the officer said. His voice had the high pitched and metallic quality typical of his race, and he bared his pointed teeth in a not unfriendly grin, "but the torturers of the Lord Lansa will take care of you soon enough. I am Toll, commander of a *strikka* in the border guards."

"Where are you taking us?"

Toll grinned wickedly.

"To the palace of Lansa, overlord of all Venus."

GERRY noticed that this countryside of Giri-Vaaka was very different from the pleasant and cultivated fields of Savissa over which he had passed the day before. The roads were dirt and half overgrown. Not much of the country was under cultivation. Strange purple bushes with thorns a foot long covered much of the land, crowding close on the patches of forest where ten-foot ferns towered high overhead. Sometimes they came upon a grazing herd of the yard-long giant ants, who would go galloping away with their antennæ waving in the air and their hard-shelled leg-joints clicking loudly.

Depression hung on Gerry Norton's chest like a physical weight. It was not alone the fact that every stride carried them deeper into a grim and hostile land—prisoners whose doom was probably already sealed—that set him biting his lower lip till he tasted the salt blood on his tongue. Nor even the fact that Closana shared the same fate because she happened to have been with him at the time of the raid. It was also the utter strangeness of everything. Yesterday, in Savissa, the people and the mode of life had been nearly enough to normal so that he was not deeply conscious of the strange vegetation and the

other things in which Venus differed from Earth and Mars.

Now everything seemed different, and alien. The lowering yellow skies of Venus were ominous. The hot winds brought strange smells and seemed to carry a hint of doom. The one thought that gave him any real hope was the fact that Portok the Martian had not been captured with the rest of them. He must have missed them soon after the abduction. There might be a chance that he and Steve Brent would bring the *Viking* to look for them.

THEY had begun to pass occasional small farms. These were scanty fields carved out of the creeping masses of purple thorns, usually with a roughly thatched hut in the center. On one such occasion the farmer and his family stood apathetically at the roadside to watch the patrol of Reptile Men go by.

"But they're not scaly!" Gerry exclaimed. Closana shook her head.

"No. They are of the Green Men of Giri. Once they held this land while the Scaly Ones dwelt in the marshes of Vaaka farther west, but the Scaly Ones have now been masters of this place for many generations."

The Green Men, Gerry noticed, looked like ordinary Earthlings except for a slight greenish cast to their skin. Probably, like the Golden Amazons, they were also descended from the Old Ones who had come from Mars so long ago. The ragged and mud-stained farmer gave Toll a perfunctory salute, and then leaned on his hoe to watch the column pass by.

The warriors of Toll swaggered along the road with the insolent assurance of men who know themselves masters of all around them. The farmer's green face was carefully expressionless, but there was a gleam in his eyes that spoke of no great liking for his scaly masters. When his glance lingered on Gerry's for an instant, the Earth-man read a definite sympathy in it.

They camped that night in a clearing beside a small stream. One of the guards shot a giant ant with his gas-gun, then cracked open the horny shell with his sword. They cut long strips of the meat and roasted it over a fire. Though the taste was peculiar the stuff was edible, and the three prisoners managed to swallow it.

"The condemned man ate a hearty meal!" Angus McTavish said with grim humor, wiping his fingers on the coarse yellow grass beside him.

Olga had gone on with a faster-moving detachment, and only a dozen Scaly Ones remained with Toll to guard the three prisoners. Gerry and Closana sat side by side before the fire, their bare shoulders touching. The ruddy and flickering glow of the firelight touched Angus' giant frame a little farther around the circle, and then the scaly skins and long snouts of the reptile men watching them. Gerry clasped his arms around his knees.

"Y'know Angus, at the moment we're living as our ancestors must have lived long generations ago. No ray-tubes or dura-steel armor. No portable electrophones. Not even a low-speed rocket car to carry us along. It must have been this way back in the days when they built that little old building that's now used for a museum in New York. The Empire State Building."

"You've got your dates mixed, laddie," McTavish yawned. "The Empire State was built in the twentieth century, and even the people of those queer old days were more advanced than most of what we've seen of life on this planet of Venus."

"I don't suppose those Ancients knew what they were missing."

"Maybe they were better off! At least they only got into trouble on their own Earth instead of wandering off to other planets like a pack of fools as we have!"

Toll and two of his men came toward them, carrying the ropes with which they had earlier been bound.

"Sorry, but I must tie you up for the night," he said. For an instant Gerry thought of making a break. If he could get away he might find some way of rescuing the others. Then he decided against it. One of the reptile men would be almost sure to bring him down with a gas-gun before he got out of the circle of firelight, in spite of the greater strength of his Earthly muscles. So he shrugged, and allowed the guards to tie him up again. For quite a while he lay awake, hoping to hear the hum of the *Viking's* motors, but at last he fell asleep.

ON the third day of their journey, the trail led upward, into a range of bleak and rocky hills. A few mean huts were the only signs of human habitation. Then, as they rounded a bend in the trail which at this point clung to the face of a cliff, they saw the answer to a mystery that had puzzled the civilized world for two years.

It was the wreck of the space-ship *Stardust*. She lay at the foot of a cliff across the valley, her steel and duralite hull still gleaming brightly through the thick green creepers that had grown up around it. Even from this distance Gerry could see the hopelessly crumpled rocket-tubes at the stern, and the gaping holes where plates had been ripped away to make the submarine that had brought them out of the city of Larr.

"So that was the end of the *Stardust!*" Gerry muttered. "I wonder what happened to her crew!"

"We'll probably find out soon enough!" McTavish replied grimly. "I'll bet all the gold in Savissa against an empty rocket-oil tin that we're headed for the same fate right now."

"Poor devils—I suppose the Scaly Ones did get them. I never liked Walter Lansing, as you know, but I could have wished him better luck than this!"

At last they crossed the hills and saw a broad valley before them. Dim and snow-capped mountains notched the yellow sky on the far side of the valley. A river wound through the plain, and on the shore of the saffron waters of a mighty lake they saw the gray walls of a city. Toll, the reptilian captain, pointed across the valley.

"Yonder lies the city of Vaaka-hausen. Soon you will stand before the Lord Lansa, and then," he added with a grim and ghoulish humor, "neither I nor anybody else will be bothered with you any more."

The countryside immediately around the city of the Scaly Ones was better kept and more cultivated than what they had seen of the rest of Giri-Vaaka. There were a number of small villages. Then they passed in through the walls, gray stone ramparts that seemed to be very old and were in poor repair. The muzzles of heavy caliber gas-guns peered over the battlements here and there.

The crowds in the streets stared curiously as Toll led his prisoners toward the center of the city. Tall reptile men swaggered through the crowds with their swords slung on their hips, but the shorter Green Men were in the great majority. Most of them, men and women alike, stared at the captives without any particular sign of emotion. This gray and crowded city of Vaaka-hausen had none of the atmosphere of pleasant friendliness that Gerry had noticed in Larr. It seemed a place of fear and oppression.

THE palace of the ruler of the Scaly Ones was a squat gray building in the center of the city. An arm of the river swept along beneath one wall, with the muddy waters lapping at the aged gray stones. An iron gate swung aside to let the newcomers into the courtyard. Men who wore black metal breast-plates over their scales took over the prisoners from Toll, leading them down a long flight of stairs into the dungeons beneath the palace. They waited in a vaulted chamber where the only light was a shaft of yellow radiance that came from a narrow slit high up near the ceiling.

"It won't be long now!" Gerry muttered.

Then a gong sounded somewhere nearby. It was a very resonant and deep-throated gong, and instantly the rock-walled chamber became filled with a green light. It had no visible source, seeming to come from the walls or from the very air itself. Again the gong rolled.

"The Lord Lansa comes!" barked the captain of the guards, "the overlord of Venus is at hand. Down on your knees, captives and slaves."

Closana went to her knees, though otherwise holding herself proudly erect with her hands tied behind her back. In the greenish light her long blonde hair looked like molten gold. Angus McTavish muttered savagely in his beard and stayed on his feet. Instantly one of the reptile guards drew his sword and held the blade horizontally behind the Scot's knees.

"Kneel—or I cut the tendons!" he snapped.

"Come down, you stiff-necked idiot!" Gerry growled. With a muttered oath

Angus dropped to his knees, and the guard stepped back into line.

Then the door opened, and three men came slowly into the room. Two were gray-scaled guards who carried their gas-guns cocked and ready. The third was a tall man in a loose green robe. His head was hooded, so that nothing of his face could be seen at all, his hands were tucked in the sleeves of his robe. There was something deadly and almost grotesque about that silent figure. Gerry knew that at last he was in the presence of Lansa, Lord of the Scaly Ones and ruler of Giri-Vaaka, self-styled Overlord of all Venus!

THE seconds passed in silence. The guards were frozen motionless at attention. At last Lansa spoke, his voice coming hollowly from the shadows of his hood.

"Take them to the cells. Their doom shall be decided when the Serpent Gods have spoken. I have ordered it!"

The tyrant of Venus gestured sharply, and the guards closed in about the prisoners. For a fleeting instant Gerry had a glimpse of a thin green hand, a hand where the finger was missing at the second joint. Then Lansa went out and the door closed behind him. The deeply resonant gong sounded again, and the pulsating green light instantly vanished so that there was again no light except for the thin trickle of yellow radiance that came in the single high window. The prisoners were pulled to their feet.

There was no chance to speak to Angus or Closana again. Gerry's guards led him down a narrow corridor, past the steel doors of cells. It was very dim and silent. From some of the cells he heard a faint rattle of chains, from others a low groaning. Otherwise there was no sound but their own footfalls. At last the guards opened the door of a cell, pushed Gerry inside, and cut the ropes that bound his arms. As they slammed the heavy steel door behind them he heard the rasp of bolts. Then the slapping tread of the guards' webbed feet died away and he was left alone.

Dim as the light in the corridor had been, that in the cell was so much less that Gerry had to wait half a minute before he could see at all. Then he made out the outlines of a small, bare cell with a bunk made of a light and flexible metal at one side. There was nothing else in the place. Gerry rubbed his wrists a moment to restore circulation, then sat down on the edge of the bunk and dropped his head in his hands.

He seemed to be about at the end of his trail. Well—that was fate. He did not mind so much for himself and Angus. You knew you were taking risks when you signed up for interplanetary travel in the first place! But he was sorry that Closana had been dragged into it.

Gerry had now lost all hope of rescue by the *Viking*. He did not doubt that her duralite hull could withstand the explosive bullets of even the heaviest caliber gas-guns, nor that her three-inch ray-tubes could blast a way into these underground dungeons in a few minutes. If only Steve Brent knew where to come! That was the rub. There was now no way for Brent to learn where the prisoners were being held, and he could not search all the land of Giri-Vaaka.

Something small and furtive was moving about on the floor a few feet away. Gerry scuffed his feet on the stones, and the creature scampered quickly away. Probably a rat! It seemed that he was going to have pleasant company during his stay in this place.

Restless and gloomy, Gerry stood up again. He started to walk up and down the few feet that the length of his cell allowed him. Then he froze motionless! A faint tapping was sounding from somewhere to his left. Someone was knocking lightly on the wall of the adjoining cell. Then a voice spoke softly in Martian.

"You there! You in the next cell! Can you here me?"

GERRY knelt down on the damp floor and put his head close to the base of the wall. Now he could hear the man more clearly, could even hear his heavy breathing. Gerry's groping fingers found a place between two of the stones where the mortar had been picked away to leave a small air space.

"Yes, I hear you!" he called softly. He heard a dry chuckle.

"Good! I have been waiting a long time for them to put someone in the next cell. Some of the stones are loose. I will come in."

There was a soft rattle of falling mortar, and a scrape of sliding stones. Gerry saw the head and shoulders of a man thrust through the opening, and then the man crawled laboriously into the cell.

"Who are you?" he whispered. "Your accent is not like that of the Green Men of Giri. Wait, I have a light here."

A small flashlight clicked on. Its beam pointed up into Gerry's face. Then the man gasped.

"Good Lord!" he whispered. "It . . . it's Gerry Norton!"

Then the man swung the light so that it swung on himself. Gerry saw a tall, gaunt man in the tattered remains of a blue and silver uniform. It was Major Walter Lansing, once of the Interplanetary Fleet, who had commanded the ill-fated *Stardust* when she set out on her voyage into space!

"Norton!" he gasped in a hoarse whisper. "Man, I never expected to see anyone from Earth again!"

"We thought you were dead."

"I might as well be!" Lansing said grimly. "But tell me how you come to be here."

As they squatted there in the darkened cell, Gerry whispered the story of the *Viking's* expedition and of his own capture. Lansing told him how the *Stardust* had been wrecked on the rim of the mountains when landing, and how the Scaly Ones had captured all the crew.

"They have kept me alive because the signs pointed that way when they cast the omens before the Serpent Gods," Lansing said, "but all the rest of the crew were used as bait for hunting the giant Dakta. They died. You and your companions will probably meet the same fate."

"Pleasant prospect!" Gerry said grimly. Lansing gripped his arm.

"There's a chance, Norton! Listen! I've been able to get these scaly devils to bring me a good many things from the wreck. I couldn't get a ray-tube, they were too wise for that, but I did get a portable radio by telling them it was my tribal god. I have it in my cell. We'll go over and you can phone your ship to come after us." He eyed Gerry eagerly. "Let's go!"

They both crawled through the gap in the wall. It was like Gerry's own, but it was piled with an assortment of junk from the wrecked space-ship. In one corner stood a compact two-way radio telephone set with its tubes still intact.

"Think you can tell them how to come?" Lansing whispered.

"I'm not sure. They marched us along the roads, and the route was winding, and . . ."

"I'll draw you a map!" Lansing interrupted. "You hold the light."

While Gerry held the flash, the other man spread out a piece of crumpled paper on the floor and began to draw on it with the stub of a graphite stylus. He talked as he wrote, in a shrilly, excited whisper. Gerry had never liked the man in the old days, considering him excitable and undependable, and it was evident that the long captivity had not improved Walter Lansing's self-control. That did not matter. The main thing was to get out of this place. And then Gerry saw something that stiffened every muscle and made the short hair prickle all down the back of his neck. The ring finger of Lansing's left hand was missing at the second joint!

THE suspicion that had come to Gerry Norton seemed impossible. Walter Lansing . . . the Lord Lansa. It couldn't be. And yet—he was sure he had seen that same mutilated hand thrust out from the sleeve of a green robe an hour before! Lansing was still talking as he bent over the improvised map.

"Here's the line of the Giri River. Tell them to cross by the bald gray hill, then bear west-six-north, using Venusian magnetic bearings. After that . . ."

He suddenly stopped and looked up, catching Gerry's grim glance fixed on his left hand. Hastily he jerked it aside into the shadows. He must have read in Gerry's eyes that his move had been too late, for his own gaunt face hardened.

"*You rat!*" Gerry hissed between his teeth. His right hand shot out, clutching for the other man's throat, but Lansing twisted aside and jerked a dark object from his pocket. An instant later a sting-ing cloud of the paralysis gas took Gerry in the face, and he fell limply to the floor.

Lansing straightened up and tossed aside the flask that had held the gas. There was a savage gleam in his narrow eyes.

"All right, Norton," he said, "we'll do it the other way. Ho—guards!"

A gong sounded in the corridor, the pulsating green light immediately flooded the cell. Scaly-skinned guards swarmed in and saluted. Lansing ripped off the torn uniform, revealing a tight-fitting green garment beneath it, and one of the guards helped him on with the cowled robe he had worn before. He glanced down at Gerry for a moment.

"Bring him and the others up to me when he recovers the use of his muscles," he said.

BY the time Gerry Norton recovered from the effects of the gas he had been securely bound again. Two guards led him to the end of a corridor and up a flight of stairs to the level above. This was also part of the prison zone of the castle, but built in an entirely different manner. Walls and floor were of a polished green metal. Super-charged electronic locks fastened each door, holding death for anyone who attempted to tamper with them. Metal globes gave a steady light. Mirrors above each cell door gave the guards who lounged in the corridors a complete view of the inside of every cell.

This, Gerry realized, was actually the prison used by the lords of Giri-Vaaka. He had been placed in the old and abandoned dungeons beneath as part of the scheme to lure him into calling the *Viking* to her doom. Glancing in the door-mirrors of the cells as he went by, Gerry saw that most of the occupants were men and women of the Green Race of Giri, with a fair number of Golden Amazons and a few reptile men who had been guilty of some crime or infraction of discipline.

Then he saw Closana! The girl was tightly spread-eagled against one of the polished metal walls of her cell, her outstretched wrists and ankles held by steel cuffs. Gerry's jaw jutted stubbornly forward, and for a moment he twisted helplessly against the cords that held his arms behind him.

The guards halted before a door deep in the interior of the palace, where a pair of scaly warriors stood on guard with gas-guns cocked and ready. The opening itself was not closed by any door, but by what looked like a tightly stretched curtain of some transparent green material. On closer inspection he saw that it glowed with a steady pulsation, while occasional specks of green fire ran through it. When one of the guards moved incautiously back so that the tip of his scabbard touched the green glow filling the door, there was a crackling hiss. The tip of the scabbard simply vanished. It was as though it had been cleanly cut off by a very sharp knife.

A challenge came from within, and one of Gerry's guards shouted a reply. The green glow suddenly vanished from the doorway. Whatever elemental force it was that blocked the passage had been withdrawn, and they walked freely in through the opening.

THE wide room before them was walled with slabs of polished black marble. The figures of writhing snakes and rearing reptiles were inlaid into the black walls with some iridescent green stone. Their eyes were inlaid jewels. Thin trails of pungent smoke drifted upward from their nostrils. A low and throbbing music, full of the thunder of muted drums, came from unseen source. At regular intervals around the walls stood tall golden standards with glowing globes atop them.

This was the throne room of Lansa, Lord of Giri-Vaaka, who had once been an officer in the flying forces of Earth. The man himself sat on a black marble throne with a dozen of the higher officers of his scaly warriors grouped around him. These Inner Guards wore breast-plates and helmets of a bright green metal, and their pointed ears protruded upward through twin openings in the sides of the helmets.

Lansa's swarthy face was gloatingly triumphant. It had always been Gerry Norton's private opinion that Walter Lansing was slightly mad. Brilliant in many ways, but definitely unstable. At last he appeared to have slipped over that shadowy border that divides the rational from the insane.

"It is unfortunate that my little scheme to have you summon your space-ship here did not work," Lansa said in English. "But we will find some other way of persuading you to do it."

"You think you're quite the little tin god, don't you?" Gerry sneered.

"I *am* a god—to these people," Lansa replied quietly. "Though the *Stardust* was damaged too badly to return to earth, little of her equipment was harmed except for the rocket tubes themselves. Within six months after landing I had made myself master of these primitive but obedient people. The submarine that brought you from the city of Larr shows what can be done with them. In the meantime I had communicated with friends on Earth by means of a secret radio frequency, and waited for the sending of the next space-ship. . . ."

He broke off as a door behind the throne opened and a woman came into the room. It was Olga Stark, now wearing a long gown of shimmering green. Metal strands of the same color were braided into her dark hair, which was crowned by a circlet bearing the design of a rearing serpent. All the officers and courtiers lifted their arms in salute. The woman walked over and stood beside Lansa's throne, looking down at Gerry with a cold and impersonal scorn. It had not taken Olga Stark very long to fit herself into the role of the queen of Giri-Vaaka!

A NUMBER of things were clear to Gerry Norton now! It had been Olga Stark with whom Lansing had secretly communicated after he made himself master of the Scaly Ones, and that explained her insistent requests to join the expedition. Again, it had been Olga who had been surreptitiously using the radio to talk to Lansing that day when Gerry had stepped into the radio room on hearing the hum of the generator. They had been arranging the details of his abduction. Only —who was Olga's confederate who had knocked him over the head when he had walked in on them that time? There was still some traitor on board the *Viking*.

"I have now developed the resources of this country to the point where the final campaign is ready," Lansa boasted, "all these reptile men needed was a man of sufficient brains and initiative to lead them. We are making ray-tubes, modeled on those aboard the *Stardust,* and will soon be able to blast down the guardian forts of Savissa and to conquer those few other portions of this planet that still stand against me. Then I will return to the Earth in your *Viking,* taking with me enough gold to buy a vast fleet of ships. There is more gold available here on Venus than all your banks on Earth have ever imagined! I could make myself ruler of Earth with all that gold, but I will choose another method. I will bring back the space-ships, and load them up with my scaly warriors —and then sail to conquer the Outer Planets and whatever else may lie beyond the Solar System!"

Gerry Norton stared at Lansa in a grim silence. The man was undoubtedly mad. Stark, raving mad! No one but a maniac would cherish such a wild dream of Universal conquest. He had that dangerous combination of natural cleverness and distorted values that has often distinguished leaders who have taken nations into the shadowy valleys of ruin. For a moment Lansa hesitated, his narrow eyes blazing and one arm flung up in a dramatic gesture. Then some of the fire went out of him, and he returned to more prosaic and immediate things.

"But all that lies in the future. At the moment I must ask you to radio-phone the *Viking* to come to this city and land in the plain just below the walls."

"I'll see you in hell first!" Gerry snapped. Lansa shrugged.

"I expected you to indulge in some such heroics! Your type always does. I have not forgotten your attacks on my reputation back on Earth some years ago, Norton, nor your charges that I was unfit to command the *Stardust.* It will give me considerable pleasure to watch what is about to happen to you. Ho—guards! Bring him down to the torture chamber."

THE place of torture was a circular and low vaulted chamber. Gerry was led across to one of the walls, and his bound hands fastened behind him to a metal ring. The place was lit by a dim green light that had no visible source, though in one spot there was a ruddy glow where

irons were heating in a brazier of burning charcoal. A bench was placed for Lansa and Olga to sit on, and four of their guards stood beside them.

The torturers themselves had been selected from among the Green Men of Giri, instead of the scaly skinned warrior race of Vaaka. They were squat and heavy men, those torturers, evidently of the most brutal and debased type that Lansa had been able to find. One in particular, whose wide green face was made hideous by an old scar that had put out one of his eyes, licked his thick lips in ghoulish anticipation as his fingers prodded the flesh about Gerry's ribs and felt the Earth-man's muscles.

"Bring in the other two," Lansa commanded.

All about the room were the tools of the torturers art. Some were familiar things that have been used since men first began to mistreat his fellow creatures—leaded whips and stretching-racks and cradles lined with pointed spikes. Others were strange looking and probably even more horrible mechanisms of coils and wires and electrodes. Gerry licked his lips. The place had the hushed stillness of a chamber that has been thoroughly sound-proofed. Probably no screams of agonized victims ever penetrated beyond those smooth walls of polished green metal.

They brought Angus McTavish in first. He looked like some shaggy red giant, wearing only a loin-cloth with his hair and beard all awry. Then came Closana. Her crossed wrists were tied together before her by a cord that was held by one of the guards, and she was very pale.

Lansa nodded quickly.

"Let them begin," said Lansa tonelessly.

"A suggestion, sir!" Olga leaned forward on the bench. The glance of her brooding eyes was fixed on the young Amazon princess. "Let them work on the girl first. It will probably succeed more quickly. I think the man Norton has fallen in love with that empty headed young savage, and you know how men are."

"You are right. Let it be done that way."

Closana was spread-eagled in mid-air, her upstretched arms fastened to ropes that led to the ceiling and her ankles lashed to metal rings in the floor below. She could move nothing but her head as Olga Stark walked up to stand before her.

"This will repay for the condescension with which I was treated in Savissa!" the Earth-woman said venomously. Closana looked at her in silence for a moment, and then suddenly spat squarely in the other woman's face.

"*Atta girl!*" roared Angus with all the power of his big lungs. Olga struck the helpless girl twice in the mouth with her clenched fist, then returned to her seat.

"Begin!" she commanded.

One of the torturers tossed Closana's long hair forward on either side of her neck, to leave her back entirely bare for the lash. The girl's eyes were closed again, and there was a thin trickle of blood at one corner of her mouth. The torturer shook out the lash, whirled it once through the air, and then brought it smashing across the middle of Closana's back.

THE girl's whole body writhed convulsively for a moment. There was an instant red welt where the whip had struck. A low moan escaped between her clenched teeth. Then Gerry Norton leaned forward where he stood bound against the wall.

"You win, Lansing!" he said hoarsely, "stop it! Make them leave her alone and I'll do as you say."

"I thought you would," the renegade officer said softly. There seemed to be a definite disappointment in his cruel eyes. "I will have the radio set brought here and you can call the ship right now."

"Have them lower the girl down."

"She stays where she is until you have finished."

The portable radio-phone from the wrecked *Stardust* was brought in and set up on a stand immediately in front of Gerry. Olga set up the sigmoid antenna on its duralite frame, and twisted the dials to the space-ship's wave length. Then she took the transmitter.

"Calling Steve Brent on the *Viking!* Calling Steve Brent on the *Viking!* Please come in!" she repeated over and over.

At last the answering signal lit up, and Steve's familiar voice came from the receiver.

"This is Steve Brent. Who is calling?" Olga held the transmitter before Gerry's

mouth. Lansa nodded to one of the torturers, who drew a white hot iron from one of the braziers and held it a little way from Closana's face.

"One false word and that iron goes into the girl's eyes," the Lord of Giri-Vaaka warned in a low hiss. "After that, all of you will live in agony for weeks before we have finished. Tell him to land near the city and bring all but a single watchman to the east gate where they will be well received."

"Hello Steve. This is Gerry Norton!" Gerry said. Brent's voice shook with excitement.

"Jumping ray-blasts, chief, we all thought you were done for! Where did you go? What happened? Where are you now?"

"I'm being well entertained in the city of Vaaka-Havson. These Scaly Men are very pleasant and friendly when you get to know them. Cross the Giri River by a bald hill. . . ."

Gerry finished the directions for the coming of the *Viking* and the landing of its crew as ordered by Lansa. As the radio was turned off, the Lord of the Scaly Ones stood up with his thin lipped smile.

"Good! Our plans progress. Now you three will go back to a cell. And, since you are no longer of any value to us, you will be used when we hunt the giant Dakta on the shore tomorrow."

THE three prisoners were placed in the same cell, all spread-eagled against the wall with their outstretched arms held by metal cuffs. Angus McTavish's face was sour and glowering as he turned to Gerry.

"That was an ill thing that ye did, Gerry Norton," he growled.

"I could not see them whip her any more."

"The three of us will probably meet as bad a fate soon anyway, from what that thin faced devil said at the end, and, meanwhile, ye've lured our comrades to detruction."

"It couldn't be helped," Gerry said, and closed his eyes. He had taken what was probably the longest chance of his career, and he was not in a mood to talk about it. Particularly when every faintest syllable uttered in one of these metal cells could be heard by the guards in the corridor outside!

There was little rest for any of them, chained in that awkward position and with the cell always filled with that pitiless green light. Gerry dozed fitfully from time to time. Closana seemed to have fallen asleep, drooping forward in her bonds with her head hanging low, but her long hair covered her face and it was hard to tell. Angus made no attempt to sleep at all, and for most of the intervening time he was muttering many tongued curses into his beard.

At last they were freed from their chains. They were given water in metal cups, and a bowl of some kind of stew to eat. For perhaps an hour they rested and eased their stiffened muscles. Then more guards came and bound their hands behind them and took them away.

It was again broad daylight when they were taken out into the streets of the city, the peculiarly yellow daylight that filtered through the cloudy canopy overhead. The three prisoners were surrounded by a heavy guard of reptile men who marched them across the city and out through a gate in the far wall. Here a broad plain swept down to the waters of a saffron colored lake, a sheet of water so vast that its far shore was no more than a dun line along the horizon. A sort of grandstand had been erected along one side of the plain.

"I think I begin to understand the point of this little game!" McTavish muttered, squinting as he peered ahead, "and I don't fancy the idea at all."

"I don't get what you mean?"

McTavish snorted.

"Did ye never see a piece of cheese in a mouse-trap?"

Then Gerry himself began to understand. On a broad platform before the grandstand stood a line of men armed with gas-guns. Some were gray scaled officers of the fighting forces, and others were dandified Green Men of the decadent minority that had fawned upon and mingled with their conquerers. In the flat and marshy expanse of the plain before them there had been driven a number of short but heavy stakes like tent pegs, each with a metal ring set in the top. There were long rows of them. Gray scaled guards were busy fettering prisoners to the pegs, making them fast by tying to the metal ring the other end of the long cord with which their hands were tied behind them. The hunters and the audience were ready, the bait was being prepared.

Closana was a few feet away from Gerry, fastened to the next stake. She stood erect, her shoulders drawn back by the strain of her bonds and her long hair blowing in the wind.

"This is the end, Geree," she said, "if not today, then tomorrow or the next day. This was the tale told in Larr of what happens to the prisoners of the Scaly Ones, but I never believed it till now."

THERE were sixty or eighty prisoners fastened in the field to serve as bait for the giant dakta. About half were Golden Amazons captured in various raids. The remainder were men and women of the Green People of Giri, prisoners condemned to death by the grim and ruthless tribunals of the Scaly Ones. Now a dozen attendants carrying leather buckets ran up and down the lines of the captives, splashing each victim with a dipper full of a purple colored and very pungent oil.

"Now what's the game?" Gerry muttered. Angus bent his head to sniff at the heavy liquid trickling down his hairy chest.

"It smells like a harlot's dream!" he muttered sourly, "probably intended to make us more attractive to whatever kind of creature it is that's coming after us!"

The attendants had hurried away with their buckets of oil, and now the crowds in the grandstand and on the plain settled down to wait. They were in holiday mood, laughing and talking in their shrill voices.

Then a black dot appeared high up in the sky. A murmur of anticipation ran over the crowd. The dakta came plummeting earthward as its super-keen senses saw and smelled the attractive bait waiting below. The thing, as it came near, was like some figment from a night-mare. It had a reptilian body between a twenty-foot spread of leathery wings, and a long beak with a double row of pointed teeth. One of the things that Gerry had seen flying over that lonely sea when he first brought the *Viking* down through the canopy of clouds that covered the planet of Venus!

"So *that* is a dakta!" Angus muttered, "bonny little creature!"

The winged lizard checked its flight momentarily some ten feet off the ground, directly above one of the captive Amazons. Then he dove down. The girl screamed and twisted away to the length of her tether, and the toothed beak just missed her. The first of the hunters fired as the dakta whirled and lashed out again, but the bullet exploded off to one side.

Gripping the writhing Amazon with his beak and his clawed feet, the dakta flapped his great wings and soared upward again. Two more of the hunters fired together. One of the explosive bullets missed entirely, the other blew one of the girl's legs to pieces but did not harm the monster that held her.

Then Lansa tossed aside his green robe and stood up. Gerry saw that he held a ray-tube, either one from the *Stardust* or one of the new ones he now claimed to be able to make in Giri-Vaaka. The tube slanted upward. Murky light played around its muzzle. The dakta gave a shrill and almost human scream. Then it dropped its mangled victim and fell twitching to the ground. Its leathery skin was turned black where the ray-blast had struck it. Along the edge of the field, the close packed crowds broke into wild cheering and Lansa acknowledged it with a condescending gesture of one upraised arm.

The hunt went on. Sometimes the dakta came singly, sometimes in pairs. The hunters had the range better now, and dropped them consistently. On several occasions the flying lizards were brought down before they had time to seize a victim at all, but most of the time one of the prisoners was killed or mortally wounded before the dakta was slain. A Green Man tethered to the stake next beyond Closana had been ripped about the throat by the raking teeth of a dakta's bill, and was breathing with a sort of gurgling moan as he bled to death. So far, that was the nearest that one of the flying lizards had come to Gerry or his two companions.

And then Gerry saw the thing for which he had been watching. There was a streak of fire along the eastern horizon. The blast of speeding rocket tubes! A cigar shaped hull of gleaming blue and silver came streaking across the saffron sky with a trail of smoke behind it. The *Viking* had come!

A SWELLING uproar came from the crowds which began to mill about in confusion. Lansa had risen to his feet and was peering upward with one hand raised to shade his eyes. Yellow flames played about the *Viking's* bow as the reverse rockets checked her momentum. A pair of swooping dakta veered away from her, then dropped down toward the bait tethered below. One of them was headed straight for Angus McTavish.

Instantly one of the forward ray-guns on the space-ship glowed into life, and the winged lizard crumpled in mid-flight. Gerry knew then that someone on board had been looking down through the powerful viewing glasses, and had recognized him and Angus. He shouted hoarsely, knowing he would not be heard but unable to keep silent.

Drums were throbbing a swift alarm, and the milling crowds were in wild confusion. Companies of the scaly warriors were firing by volley, but the explosive bullets only flashed harmlessly against the *Viking's* duralite hull. Some of the heavier gas-guns set on the battlements above hissed into life then, but even the larger caliber explosives could make no impression on tempered duralite. With her ray-guns flashing and ripping black swathes in the scaly ranks below, with her helicopters spinning to take the strain as the blast of the rockets died away, the *Viking* settled rapidly groundward.

"By Lord, Steve came a-fightin'!" McTavish roared.

"Of course, you old goat!" Gerry shouted back, "did you really think I'd call the ship into a trap? You're as bad as that maniac who calls himself Lansa. I knew that if I spoke *too* strongly of what nice fellows these scaly devils are, Steve would have the sense to know that I was under pressure and in a trap."

And then came swift disaster! Over the edge of the nearest black and battlemented wall of Lansa's palace thrust the muzzle of a large caliber ray-gun. Steve Brent saw it, too, and tried to lift the nose of his ship to bring his own guns to bear on this new menace, but he was too late. The muzzle of the ray-gun on the battlements glowed dully, the blast of the supoderays struck the row of spinning helicopters on top of the *Viking's* hull. The blades of the big propellors went spinning into space, their shafts bent and crumpled like straws in a gale. Robbed of their support, essential when lacking rocket power of at least 300 miles per hour, the spaceship plunged downward like a falling star. She struck the waters of the lake with a mighty splash. Spray dashed as high as the walls of Lansa's castle, and when it was gone the space-ship had vanished.

GERRY NORTON stood motionless. He was staring at the muddy and foam flecked waters of the lake, and at the spreading ripples that still beat on the shore as the effect of that mighty splash subsided. At the moment he felt old and tired and defeated, his brain numbed. The *Viking* was gone! Freckled Steve Brent, and the cheerful Portok, and all the rest of them were gone. Buried deep in the muddy bottom of a Venusian lake.

The second expedition from Earth to this cloud-veiled and ill-fated planet had also ended in disaster. In the future the *Viking* would be classed with the *Stardust* —simply another luckless space-ship that sailed away into the void and vanished. The men of her crew and what they tried to accomplish would be forgotten, their names would only remain on some yellowing record buried in the maze of government files. So deep was Gerry Norton's bitter brooding that he scarcely heard the words Angus McTavish was shouting in his ear.

"Come on, Gerry lad! Let's get away while there's all this confusion."

EVER since they had been brought to this field beside the lake, Angus had been working at his bonds. He was a very strong man anyway, and the swell of his earthly muscles was far greater than the strength of any of the races that the Scaly Ones were accustomed to making prisoners. While the attention of all the guards was absorbed in the appearance and subsequent wreck of the *Viking*, Angus had managed to snap his own bonds and was now unhurriedly freeing Gerry's wrists.

Gerry ran to Closana and untied her hands, while Angus freed the nearest other prisoner who was a stocky and broad shouldered Green Man with a heavily lined face. As soon as his hands were free, the latter wheeled to face them.

"My thanks, *hiziren!*" he panted, "now go while you can. You are more easily spotted in a crowd than I. Hurry! I will free as many of these others as possible. Get into the city, and try to reach the place men call 'The Square of the Dragon.' Say that Sarnak sent you. Hurry!"

Even though he was carrying Closana in his arms, Gerry's Earthly muscles allowed him to run in mighty six-foot bounds. Angus went leaping along before him. So great was the confusion that they were half way across the plain to the city before anyone noticed them at all. Then a shouting officer of the Scaly Ones threw himself in front of them with his drawn sword in his hand.

The big engineer roared like an angry bull, and leaped clean over the man. Before the scaly warrior could turn the Scot had him from behind. An instant later Angus had the sword and was racing ahead, while the Venusian lay sprawled in the mud with his neck broken and his long head twisted grotesquely awry.

The half dozen guards posted in the arch of the gate stared indecisively at the white skinned trio racing toward them. Angus had a sword in each hand by this time, and he leaped at the guards with a shout. The fugitive broke through the line of swordsmen by sheer momentum and dashed into the city. There was no pursuit. The first of the panic stricken throng rushing back for the shelter of the city reached the gate a moment later, and the guards were swamped by a jostling mob of mingled Scaly Ones and Green Men.

Gerry and his two companions darted into the nearest of the many narrow alleys that twisted about this part of the city. They dodged from one dingy thoroughfare to the next. When they met a woman of the Green People, Gerry unceremoniously tore off her robe and shielding veil and flung them to Closana to hide her own tawny skin and golden hair. Later, when he and Angus had also disguised themselves in the rough garments worn by the poorer folk of this city of Vaaka-hausen, they were able to walk quietly down the streets without fear of detection unless they met a patrol at close range.

At last they came to a dingy plaza that was surrounded by ramshackle buildings of great age. It had probably once been a prosperous and fashionable part of the city, centuries ago, before the Scaly Ones overran the land of Giri. Now grass grew up between the paving stones, and the roofs of the dingy buildings sagged close to the breaking point, and piles of festering rubbish lay along the gutters. The place was a slum of the sort that had not existed on the more enlightened planets of Earth and Mars for many generations. A canal flowed along one side of the square, and in the center of the plaza stood the eroded and ancient black marble statue of a rearing dragon.

"This must be the place!" Angus muttered from the shadows of the hood that he had drawn up over his head.

A S they hesitated, a few people peered furtively out at them from the broken windows and sagging doors of the houses around the square. Then a man came toward them. He was bent and crippled, a beggar wearing filthy rags. His matted hair hung down over his eyes, and his whole body seemed covered with the caked filth of one who had never thought of washing. As the man came forward with a sort of limping shuffle, Gerry instinctively laid his hand on the hilt of the sword he carried concealed under his cloak, while Closana drew the concealing veil more closely over her face.

"Alms, *hiziren!* A little charity of your generosity!" the beggar whined as he came closer.

"What place is this?" Gerry asked, trying to give his voice the soft tone and lisping accent characteristic of the Green Men.

The beggar limped a little closer and peered up into the shadows of Gerry's hood. What he saw seemed to satisfy him.

"Take your hand from your sword hilt, friend!" he said in a low voice quite unlike his previous whine, "what place do you seek?"

"The Place of the Dragon."

"This is it. Who sent you?"

"Sarnak sent us."

"It is good." The beggar pointed down a flight of worn stone steps that led to the canal whose surface was some eight or ten feet below the level of the plaza. "Go down there, below the bridge, and tap on the stone that bears a rusted iron ring. You will find friends. Go quickly, while there are no strangers to observe you."

"Do you trust that man?" Angus whispered in English as they turned away. Gerry shrugged.

"We've got to. It's our only chance, We're too easy to recognize, in spite of these clothes, to stay free in this city for long."

The black waters of the canal flowed sluggishly along between slimy stone walls. Refuse drifted on the surface. The water itself had a foul and penetrating odor. Gerry walked down the steps, and then along the walk that stretched beside the water at one edge of the canal until he was under an arch that served as a bridge to support the street above. The arch was wide enough so that they were now completely hidden from the view of anyone in the plaza above.

On one of the stones of the arch, at about the height of his shoulder, Gerry saw a rusted iron ring. He tapped on that stone with the hilt of his sword. He heard a faint click, and though there was no visible change in the surface of the pitted stone wall before him he heard a whispered question:

"Who knocks?"

"Friends," Gerry replied.

"Who sent you?"

"Sarnak sent us."

There was a low, metallic jingle. A section of the wall about the height of a man and some three feet wide swung quietly inward. As soon as the three of them had stepped through the opening into a small room that was built in the interior of the arch, the door swung shut behind them.

T HERE were half a dozen men in this low roofed and stone walled chamber. All were of the Green People, dressed as ragged beggars but with the bearing and appearance of warriors. Drawn steel gleamed in their hands. Their faces were heavy with suspicion. One of the men had gone to stand with his back against the closed door behind them.

"Who are you, that come using the name of Sarnak?" snapped the leader.

Suspicion became blended with puzzled surprise as Gerry and Angus threw back their hoods and the outlaws saw their white skins. Hastily Gerry told the tale of the dakta hunt and of their subsequent escape.

"So Sarnak got away!" the leader of the Green Men exulted. "Ho! That is the best news that we of the Dragon's Teeth have heard in many weeks! All right, Slag, take these strangers through to the inner places."

One of the Green Men beckoned to Gerry to follow him down a narrow flight of steps at the back of the room. It ended in a circular pool of water like a large well, the steps going on down below the surface. Their guide opened a cupboard built into the wall and took out four glass helmets. The helmets were attached to leather pads that fitted tightly about the shoulders and chest, with straps to hold them in place. A cylindrical metal tank was attached to the back of each helmet, with a tube that led to a valve at the side. The guide also took out some heavily leaded sandals.

"Put on these helmets and then open the valves," he explained, "then follow me down the steps. Be careful not to fall in the darkness. After we get around the first bend in the corridor below there will be light."

Gerry put the globular glass helmet over his head, opening the valve as soon as he had adjusted the straps. The air in the helmet immediately took on a faintly chemical odor, but it was pleasant and in no way oppressive. As soon as all of them were ready, the man called Slag beckoned and then started down the steps.

Warm black water rose to Gerry's knees, then to his waist. As it came up to his shoulders he saw the top of Slag's helmet disappear below the surface ahead of him. For a moment the smooth surface of the water was level with Gerry's eyes as it rose around his own helmet. Then he stepped down into a darkness as black and impenetrable as though he were immersed in ink.

Gerry guided himself with his left hand on the slime covered stones of the wall beside him. He reached back with his other hand to steady Closana who was just behind. All together he counted thirty steps, feeling carefully with his feet each time, before the floor leveled off. The wall curved around to the right. Gerry followed it, rounded a bend, and was no longer in darkness.

They stood in a straight passage that was lined with blocks of polished stone. Metal plates, set in the ceiling at regular intervals, glowed with a greenish-yellow light that was nearly as bright as the cloudy Venusian daylight. The place was completely filled with water.

It was an eerie sensation! Slag was standing a few feet ahead, grinning at them through the glass of his helmet, but now he turned and walked slowly down the corridor. Gerry followed him, bent well forward as he walked, forcing himself ahead against the resistance of the water. All their movements were sluggish and slow, but the heavily leaded sandals held them down and gave their feet purchase.

SMALL fishes swam past them along the passage, their round eyes peering in through the helmet glasses as they passed. Clumps of colored seaweed grew out from the walls and ceiling, their long streamers waving gently in the slow currents set up by the passage of the men. In spite of the brightness of the light from the ceiling plates, the effect of the water made it difficult to see far down the passage ahead. The outlines of Slag were clear enough as he plodded along directly ahead of Gerry, but everything beyond him was a little blurred and uncertain. It was like living in a mirage.

At last they came to a point where the passage branched. Here they passed a sentry who wore a glass helmet and a tight fitting green rubber uniform. On his chest was the insignia of a rampant black dragon. He was armed with a very thin, almost needle-like sword whose point was razor keen. Gerry realized the reason for that peculiarly designed weapon when the sentry swung his sword upward to salute their guide. The blade was so thin that it offered little resistance to the water, and its power of being quickly wielded made it a far more effective weapon under water than a heavier sword would have been.

They passed more branching passages, and more rubber-clad sentries who stared at them curiously as they went by. There was a whole network of corridors in this underwater world! At last Slag opened a metal door at the end of the particular passage he had followed, and they all crowded into a small room. Slag closed the door and dogged it, then tapped on a glass panel across the room.

A silvery flood of air bubbles came pouring out the end of a pipe that protruded through the wall. At the same time Gerry heard the thud of heavy pumps starting to suck water through gratings at the base of the wall. The water level dropped rapidly. When it was down to their waists, Slag took off his helmet and slipped the leaded sandals from his feet. He motioned to the others to do the same.

"We are about to enter the hidden realm of Luralla, the home of the Dragon's Teeth!" he said. "If you can prove your right to be here you will be welcome. Otherwise you will go back into one of these waterlocks—without any helmets on."

He grinned cheerfully.

THE water dropped below the level of the door sills. The pumps sucked noisly on the last few foaming inches for a moment, and then they ceased. The inner door was opened by a sentry whose tight fitting green uniform with its black dragon was made of dry cloth instead of dripping rubber. He wore a plumed metal helmet, and carried a heavy sword instead of one of the thin water blades.

"Come in, Slag," he said, "who are these strangers?"

They were in a sort of guardroom, a square chamber where glass water helmets stood in long rows on metal shelves and many weapons hung in racks on the walls. The control levers of the pumps were just to the left of the door. There were half a dozen uniformed men standing about the room, one of them bearing the silver insignia of an officer on his chest. When

Slag had given a hasty account of the coming of Gerry and the others, the officer nodded toward an inner door.

"Prince Sarnak has just returned. You will find him in the great hall. Take these strangers there."

The sound of music and laughter, and the confused babel of many voices, came to Gerry's ears as soon as the far door was opened. They entered a vast hall. It was low ceiled, as were all the water-locked chambers of this strange place, but it was broad and spacious. Heavy stone columns carved like giant sea-horses supported the roof. Patterns of seaweed and star fish and other denizens of the deep were intermingled wth rearing dragons in the painted designs along the walls. The room was filled with wide tables flanked by long benches.

The men and women who sat at the tables, or stood gossiping in noisy groups in corners of the hall, were nearly all of the Green People of Giri, but there were a few escaped Golden Amazons who came flocking eagerly around Closana. In outward appearance these green skinned men and women were similar to the folk who lived in the city overhead with their scaly masters, but there was a subtle difference. These people had none of the cowed and subjugated air of the citizens who lived above ground. There was a different look in their eyes, a more confident note in their voices, a firmer set to their shoulders. These folk had the air of free men and warriors, not slaves.

A stocky and merry eyed man caught sight of them and came striding across the hall. It was Sarnak, the man who had been tethered next to them in the field of the dakta hunt.

"Welcome to the halls of Luralla!" he boomed, "we are glad to have you come to the hidden realm of the Dragon's Teeth. *Hiziren* and comrades, these are the outlanders from afar who freed me this afternoon so that I and a dozen more of our people escaped death at the hands of the Scaly Ones!"

"Thrice hail!" roared the crowd, while a hundred blades flashed in the golden light. Angus McTavish rung the water out of his dripping beard.

"These look like men of spirit," he rumbled cheerfully, "I think I'm going to enjoy myself again."

A LITTLE later, wearing dry clothes, the three of them sat down with Sarnak and his officers at a table in the corner of the hall. Young girls brought them dishes of fried sea-urchins, and broiled steaks of the grappa fish, and other savory dishes.

"We who call ourselves the Dragon's Teeth are outlaws descended from outlaws," Sarnak explained. "Our ancestors were men and women who never acknowledged the rule of the Scaly Ones when they overran this once pleasant land of Giri. I was born in this hidden place, as was my father before me and his father before him. We live here in the waterlocked Halls of Luralla, and harass the tyrants in what ways we can, and try to keep alive the traditions and glory of the old days when the Dragon Kings ruled in this city and the Scaly Ones were still lurking in their Vaaka marshes to the westward."

"Does Lansa know of this place?"

"He knows that the Dragon's Teeth exist, as all rulers of the Scaly Ones have known it, but the location of our hiding place has never been betrayed."

"Then," roared Angus, pounding his big fist on the table till the dishes rattled, "why don't you revolt? I'll go with you myself to strike a blow against those reptile skinned devils up above!"

"Count me in, too!" Gerry said quietly.

Angus' voice had boomed out through the big hall. It was answered by a lilting shout as men sprang to their feet. Hundreds of sword blades flashed clear of their scabbards. Only Sarnak himself remained seated, slowly shaking his head. There was a twisted smile on his broad and heavily lined face. His eyes held bitterness.

"It would only be pointless suicide, *hiziren!*" he said grimly. "We number only about a thousand all together, we hunted men of the Dragon's Teeth, against the countless thousands of Lansa's scaly hordes. It would be different if our countrymen up above could be inspired to a mass uprising, but the time is not yet. Too long have they lived under the rule of the tyrants. They are cowed. They have lost their spirit, and some of the younger ones

have even become fawning satellites of the conquerors! If there comes a day when the forces of the Scaly Ones are engaged in some major war along the frontier, as in this suggested assault upon the barrier forts of Savissa that Lansa is said to be planning, then we may be able to do something. For the present we must continue to lie hidden and bide our time."

Gerry Norton was uncertain about his own course. Now that the *Viking* and her crew had been lost, with all hope of a return to Earth cut off, he felt hopelessly adrift. Sarnak urged his visitors to stay in Luralla. The place was a remarkable engineering feat, completely under water and with its air constantly re-conditioned and preserved, but Gerry felt restless and cramped there. Though the outlaws carried on a constant guerilla warfare with the Scaly Ones, it was all on a small scale. Gerry felt that he would rather return to Savissa, where at least the people were free and the Amazon warriors kept ceaseless watch on their frontiers. Closana, of course, was very anxious to return home.

"Suits me, too," Angus rumbled, "in that country they at least show a proper respect for a man of my attainments."

"Meaning your whiskers?" Gerry asked.

"Look out, Angus," Closana warned with a smile, idly running her slender fingers along the keen edge of her dagger. "Some Savissan princess will choose you for her husband as I have chosen Geree here."

"I told you we wouldn't talk about that for the present. . . ." Gerry began. Closana's hand moved swiftly as a striking dakta. The keen blade bit through the cloth of Gerry's sleeve and pinned it to the table top.

"You'll never get away from me, Geree," the girl said quietly. Angus McTavish burst out in a great roar of laughter.

"Might as well admit you're licked now, lad! These Venusian women seem to be verra strong minded lassies!"

THEY started two days later. There was, of course, neither night nor day in the sub-aqueous halls of Luralla but the outlaws ran their lives on a normal schedule. Sarnak supplied Gerry and the others with rubber uniforms and complete equipment including the thin bladed water-swords in the long feathery scabbards.

"I will have you guided out to one of our exits that is a quarter mile off shore from the place where the dakta hunt was held," Sarnak offered.

"I thought that water was a lake," Gerry said. Sarnak shook his head.

"No. It is an estuary, an arm of the Great Sea. The chemical tanks on your water helmets will keep the air pure for several days travel, and the sentries at the last outpost will give you trained saddle-dolphins so that you will make better time toward the coastal regions of Savissa."

Sarnak went with them to the guard-room at the edge of the water filled passages, and personally checked over their equipment.

"These are our new type of helmet with the audiphones that let the wearers talk to each other under water," he said, touching the tiny microphones set into the curved glass. "Well—you had better start. May the Dragon Gods be with you!"

They strapped on their helmets and adjusted the valves. A uniformed guide stepped into the water-lock with them. Sarnak shook hands, saluted, and then stepped back through the door which closed behind him. The guide lifted his hand in a signal, and a second later a torrent of water rushed out of the gratings to foam about their feet. They were ready to leave Luralla!

Again they went through the maze of water-filled passages, passing occasional sentries. After a while the character of the corridor changed. It was wider, and was arched instead of square, and there was a carpet of soft natural sand beneath their feet instead of a stone floor.

"We come to the last outpost of Luralla, *hiziren!*" the guide said.

They stepped out of the end of the passage and found themselves in the open sea, many fathoms down. A broad and slightly sloping floor of smooth sand studded with lumps of coral and clusters of sea-weed stretched before them. Some were giant ferns stretching twelve and fifteen feet high, others were low and sponge-like growths. A school of tiny red fishes shot swiftly past them. Larger fish sailed majestically by overhead. The top of the water was a gleaming golden ceiling far above them, the greenish yellow light lessening in intensity as it came down to the depths.

The end of the passage was surrounded by a barrier of piled coral. Outlaw swordsmen stood on guard, also armed with a sort of compressed air cross-bow that shot a heavy metal needle with great force. From a corral at one side an orderly brought three saddle-dolphins.

The big fish were equipped with rubber saddles strapped around the body, and short stirrups. They were guided by a bridle similar to that used on Earthly horses. As Gerry swung up to the saddle his dolphin bucked once or twice with quick flips of his tail, then steadied down as he felt the tight pressure of his master's knees. When the other two were mounted, the officer commanding the outpost lifted his arm in salute.

"The Dragon Gods be with you!" he said. At a distance of fifteen or twenty feet the sound of his voice was slightly muted, but the words were perfectly clear in the ear-pieces of Gerry's helmet. He lifted his own rubber gloved hand to his globular helmet and returned the salute.

THEY rode off at an easy pace, the dolphins rising above the tops of the tallest vegetation. Gerry found that it was easy to sit the saddle as long as he bent a little forward to overcome the resistance of the water against his chest. They were about thirty or forty feet down. On Earth such a depth would have been uncomfortable, but the lighter gravity of Venus made it easily bearable.

Gerry glanced back. Closana was riding a few feet behind him, slender and erect, controlling her restless dolphin as easily as though she had been accustomed to such steeds all her life. Angus was grinning broadly through his globular glass helmet as he sat astride a particularly big dolphin and swung his light bladed water-sword from side to side.

"If any of our friends back on Earth could see us now in some sort of an astral spectroscope," the big Scot cried, "they'd think themselves crazy. Maybe this is only a nightmare at that! Do you think we'll wake up soon and find ourselves safe back on board the *Viking?*"

"I'm afraid not," Gerry answered. He wondered in what part of this vast sea the twisted hulk of the *Viking* was now lying.

All day they rode, roughly following the shoreline to the northward. Whenever it got so deep that nothing was visible below but a vast green shadow Gerry headed inland until the tops of the sea gardens again came into view. Sarnak had told them that by the middle of the next day it should be safe for them to come above water and check their maps and put fresh chemical cartridges in the cylinders of their helmets. The Scaly Ones patrolled their coast line in shallow open boats, but they did not go beyond their own borders.

Once Gerry checked his dolphin and then headed downward as he caught sight of something big and dark lying on the sand. The others followed him. It was the broken and rusting hulk of a spaceship, a vessel of a strange type with a name in an unknown tongue still visible on the shattered stern. The wreck must have been there for a very long time, for the sand was heaped high about it and sea-weeds grew up through the open hatches.

"Leaping ray-blasts!" McTavish said softly. "Yon craft never came from either Earth or Mars."

"Probably from some far distant planet in outer space that we've never heard of," Gerry said. "Some adventurous wanderer of the interstellar regions who came to grief in this lonely spot."

IT was desolate and forlorn, the sight of that wrecked vessel from so long ago. It made Gerry think of his own lost command. There were clean picked white bones of strange shape lying about on the sand. Gerry saluted, a tribute to those strange and forgotten wanderers of space, and then urged his dolphin to a higher level again.

When the dimming light showed that it was dusk above the water they rode in to the four-fathom shallows and halted in a smooth patch of yellow sand. Gerry unsaddled the dolphins and tethered them to lumps of coral where they browsed contentedly on the short vegetation. Then the three exiles sat down in a circle on the sand. McTavish stretched his long legs, bouncing a few feet off the ground as he did so and then floating slowly down again.

"I'll never forget this journey if I live to be older than the whole Solar System itself!" he said. "Also—I'm hungry."

"There's nothing we can do about that until noon tomorrow," Gerry grunted. "Maybe the fasting will make you lose some of that surplus bulk of yours. But I'll admit I could do with some of that special coffee Portok used to brew in the ward room on the *Viking* in the evenings."

"I'd give a lot for a drink of plain water," Closana said wistfully. "Acres of water around us and nothing to drink!"

When the last of the light was gone they lit a small lamp that Sarnak had given them. It illumined a circle some twenty feet across, a little patch of light in the midst of the utter blackness of the depths of the sea. They sat there talking for a while, then Gerry stretched out on the sand with one arm hooked around a lump of coral to hold himself in place. He was thankful that the waters of Venus were always warm. It would scarcely have been possible to sleep at the bottom of one of Earth's oceans in this manner, even with the equipment with which Sarnak had supplied them.

For a while Gerry drowsed. The audiphones of his helmet picked up all the faint sounds of this watery world. A muffled splash as Angus McTavish stirred restlessly . . . the steady movement as their drowsing but apparently sleepless dolphins fed on the fields of sea-weed . . . an occasional steady churning as some larger denizen of the deep swam past above them. Then he slept.

IT was well past midnight by the illuminated dial of the waterproof chronometer that Sarnak had given Gerry when he awoke. Angus was shaking his shoulder. The light had been put out hours before, and there was no illumination at all except for an occasional flash of green phosphorescence where some fish sped by.

"Either I'm an overgrown sponge," the big engineer muttered, "or there's a light shining through the water off to the west."

Gerry yawned and sat up, instinctively starting to rub is eyes before his hands bumped against the hard glass surface of his curving helmet. Some of the bits of coral around them glowed with an eerie green radiance, and a tall frond of sea-weed had tiny specks of light on the tips of its constantly waving leaves. Then, far off to the left, Gerry caught a faint glow.

It was hard to tell what kind of a light it was, so great was the refraction of the water, but there was something there. It was little more than a lessening of the deep gloom that otherwise surrounded them on all sides. Gerry got to his feet and picked up his rubber saddle which he had been using as a pillow under his helmet.

"We'd better investigate," he said. "Wake Closana."

They saddled their dolphins and rode out at an easy pace, holding the big fish down with a tight rein. As they rode the glow ahead of them became more definite. It seemed to come from a long row of twenty or more lights. Then they were near enough to see each other in the reflected glow.

"It's some kind of a ship," Gerry said. "Those lights are her port holes!"

"It's more than that!" snapped Angus. "It's the *Viking!* I know the lines of her stern anywhere, even in this sunken and God forsaken spot!"

The space-ship lay quietly in the soft mud of this part of the ocean bottom. All her port holes of transparent duralite were glowing with the reflected light from inside. The twisted wrecks of her helicopters were still visible on top of the hull, but otherwise she did not appear to be damaged.

Gerry was in the middle as the three of them rode their dolphins up close to one of the big windows of the control room. The ship had evidently survived the fall into the water, for they could see dim figures moving about inside.

"I told you that duralite hull could stand a little thing like a fall into the ocean!" McTavish exulted.

As they crowded their finny steeds close to the glass of the control room window, Portok the Martian came to peer out. His red skinned face went pale as he saw them, and even through the ship's hull their audiphones picked up his agonized cry.

"Steve! Tanda! I just saw the ghosts of Norton and McTavish looking in the window!"

Steve Brent came into the control room. He looked haggard and unshaven, and he was stained with oily grease.

"What are you raving about, Portok?" he snapped.

"It's no raving, Steve!" the little Martian chattered, "I tell you I saw the three of them. The Chief, and Angus, and the Amazon girl—all riding on some kind of big fish and peering in that window!"

"You're going crazy!" Steve Brent snapped, but he walked to the window. His own eyes widened as he saw the strangely clad trio sitting their mounts outside. Gerry waved violently to him.

"Let us in, you idiot!" he shouted, forgetting that the *Viking* did not carry any audiphones that could pick up his words. He heard Steve's unsteady voice.

"Maybe we're both crazy, Portok, but I think they're really out there. Open the outer door to the starboard space-lock."

A SMALL door swung open on the starboard side of the *Viking's* blue and silver hull. That small compartment had really been designed for dropping objects into the void of outer space, or for testing the quality of the atmosphere on any stray planetoids the *Viking* might have visited on her journey across the vastness of interplanetary space, but it would do for a water-lock in this instance.

Gerry and the others dismounted from their dolphins and let the reins hang. Angus gave his mount a slap on the flank. With a flip of its tail the big fish wheeled and swam off, and after a second the others followed it. Gerry led the way into the space-lock and closed the door behind him. It only took a few seconds for the blast of the *Viking's* powerful compressed air tanks to blow out the water. Then, as Gerry unstrapped his helmet and lifted the big glass globe off his head, Steve Brent opened the inner door and stepped into the space-lock.

"I don't know if I'm crazy or dreaming or what, Chief," he said, "but I'm damn glad to see you back."

"You're sane enough," Gerry snapped, "it's a long story, so skip it for the moment. I thought *you* were done for!"

"Not the *Viking!*" Larry affectionately slapped the laminated duralite shell of the space-ship. "She can stand more than being dropped in the drink from a few hundred feet up. Our problem is how to get going again. We've been able to crawl along the bottom by using minimum power of one rocket tube and scaring hell out of all the fish, but that's the best we've been able to do. Now that Angus is back he can take over. What do you think about the helicopters?"

"I could forge new ones in a week out of that blue metal they have in Giri-Vaaka," McTavish muttered. "But God knows how we'll ever get hold of a supply. Anyway, I think I can reverse enough of the gravity plates to give this craft reserve buoyancy so she'll navigate on the surface instead of hugging the bottom."

"I never thought of that!" Steve said admiringly. Angus grunted, and began to strip off his green rubber uniform.

"It takes a Scotsman to show the rest of the Universe how to get out of a tough spot!"

IT was afternoon on the following day when the *Viking's* long hull finally broke the surface. She lay in the water like a half submerged cigar, the yellowish ripples lapping on the curved blue duralite of her superstructure. The twisted remains of the shattered helicopters were ugly stumps along the space-ship's sleek back. A single rocket tube flamed and smoked astern, its blast driving the vessel through the water at a good pace while her wake smoked and bubbled.

Gerry Norton opened the duralite dome of the upper control room and stepped out on the wet deck with a few of the others. They were well out on the great sea, with the green hills of the Giri-Savissa border a low smear along the horizon to starboard. This was the same lonely sea they had seen when they first dropped down through the clouds to Venus.

The vast and greenish-yellow waters were broken by scattered islands, bare bits of rock that were dotted with blue moss. Sea birds swooped about them. Lofty mountains on a distant shore were capped with snow. In one or two places a narrow shaft of sunlight struck down through a brief gap in the canopy of eternal clouds, but otherwise there was only that subdued and peculiarly golden light in which there moved only a few oddly shaped birds.

So much had happened since they first saw that lonely sea! It seemed as though much more than a week had elapsed. Savissa and its Golden Amazons . . . the arrow tipped tower of Rupin-Sang . . . the Scaly hordes of Vaaka and the dread palace of the insane Lansa who had once been an Earthly officer . . . the secret and water-locked halls of Luralla where the outlaws of Giri dwelt—many scenes went through Gerry Norton's mind. He seemed to have aged ten years since the day he brought the *Viking* down through the cloud screen. Well—the immediate problem was to get some suitable metal to repair the smashed helicopters. The *Viking* might possibly get up into the air with the power of her rockets alone if they beached her on a sloping shore with her nose upward, but she could never come down safely without helicopters.

"I'll hold her on this course a while," Gerry said. "In the morning we can strike over and try to pick up the frontiers of Savissa."

It was just at dusk that they saw white towers against the sky. They rose out of the sea as Gerry turned the *Viking's* blunt nose toward them—the mighty battlements of a vast city. Closana, who was standing on deck beside him at the time, rested her hands on the rail and stared in utter amazement.

"But it isn't possible, Geree!" she gasped, "there isn't any civilization out there on the islands of the Great Sea!"

"Could it be a mirage?" he suggested. "A reflection of some Savissan city on the mainland?"

"No." The girl shook her head. "There are no cities of that sort in any of these lands. Geree—there is something strange here. I do not like it. There *cannot* be any city ahead of us there!"

"But there it is!" Gerry said grimly. "We can't all be seeing things. We'll go closer and get a better look."

It was sunset, the unspectacular Venusian sunset which was simply a swift lessening of the golden glow from the cloud veiled sky above. Lights were gleaming from most of the tall buildings of the towering city as the *Viking* drove toward it through a quiet sea. Sea birds swooped low about the ship's wake. The watchers on deck could see the low shore line of the island on which the city was built. Then they heard distant bells, pleasant bells that seemed to be chiming a farewell to the day and a welcome to the night. And then a red light flashed on top of the tallest building and in an instant the entire city vanished.

ONE minute the strange city had been clearly visible before them, its graceful towers agleam with lights as they notched the sky. The next instant the whole place was gone. There was nothing in sight at all but a low shoreline. It was as though a thick veil of concealing mist had been suddenly drawn across between the ship and the city. Only—the air was clear and without a trace of mist. Gerry walked across to the open dome of the upper control room.

"Cut rockets!" he snapped. "Get some kind of an anchor overboard. We'll just stay right here off shore until morning. There's something queer going on."

Gerry and Steve Brent leaned on the rail together, peering through the darkness toward the island. Nothing was visible in the faint phorphor-glow that marked the Venusian night, but they could just hear a distant singing as of many voices lifted in chorus.

"What do you think happened to the city so suddenly?" Steve asked. Gerry shrugged.

"I suppose some mist hid it."

"There wasn't any mist," Steve said flatly, "anyway—we could see the low hills on shore just as clearly after the city disappeared as before. Anyway. . . . ."

"Listen!" Gerry interrupted.

Now they could again hear the sound of bells coming across the water. Half the time the sound was swept away by the night breeze, half the time they could just hear it. The bells were of many blended tones and notes, an immense carillon. They were singing some outland melody that was full of the surge of ocean breezes and the cries of the sea birds. It rose, and swelled, and died away again.

"The city's there, all right," Gerry said slowly. "Though I can't imagine why we

don't see any lights with the sound of the bells that close. But we'll see in the morning."

"I tell you there is no city," Closana said, her voice troubled. "We have often sailed ships into these waters from the Savissan coast, and we know that none of these Outer Isles are inhabited. What you have heard must be the ghosts of the Old Ones, ancient phantoms speeding through the skies. There is a legend that the bells of their phantom ships can sometimes be heard off the coast at night."

"Ghosts or no ghosts, we're going ashore there in the morning!" Gerry said stubbornly.

ALL night the *Viking* rode to a crude anchor that Angus had improvised from some spare parts on board. The space-ship's designers had never expected her to lie in water. Most of the crew were on deck as soon as it grew light enough to see. Ahead of them, less than half a mile away, stretched a sandy shore backed by a line of low hills. The island had a wealth of the yellow vegetation typical of the mainland of Venus, so that it had a more friendly appearance than the other specks of land which dotted the Great Sea and were only bare rock, but there was no sign of life. Certainly there was no trace of any city! There was not even an indication of human habitation at all. As the dawn-mists cleared away they could see that another range of hills stretched along the horizon some miles behind. Their greenish-yellow slopes were clear and sharp against the cloudy sky beyond, and they were located well in the rear of where the city had appeared to be in that hasty glimpse the night before.

"Ready the landing party!" Gerry commanded. "Full armor and equipment!"

They gently beached the space-ship on the sloping expanse of sand, running her nose a little way up above the water level while the light surf lapped her dripping sides. Some giant crabs scurried away across the beach in startled surprise.

"Want to go ashore, Angus?" Gerry asked as McTavish's red bearded face came up through an escape hatch. The big engineer shook his head.

"I'll just stay aboard here and brood

over my broken helicopters, thanks. My last trip ashore took care of all my wanderlust for the present."

Gerry took half the vessel's crew with him, leaving the other half on guard. Closana went with the landing party. With their armor gleaming in the golden light, ray-guns and other weapons ready, they tramped up across the loose sand of the beach. Beyond the shore line was firmer ground, a field of some low plants that grew in orderly yellow rows.

"I'll swallow my ray-tube if this isn't a field cultivated by man! Nature was never that orderly." Steve Brent muttered. Gerry shrugged.

"Lord knows! If we ever get those helicopters fixed, I'm all for a quick return to Earth. This planet is certainly no peaceful garden of Eden, and I've had pretty near all I want of it. Savissa was the only place I really liked. I wonder what's happening there now!"

"We'll know if anything very exciting turns up," Steve said. "When we started out on our search after you disappeared that night, I left Tanda behind with a portable radio to keep us posted. Sort of figured it was our base on Venus, and anyway there was always the chance you might wander back there."

"Great planetoids—I just thought of something! As soon as we get back to the ship, remind me to radio Tanda to tell Rupin-Sang that the Scaly Ones had learned to use the old sewers, and that he must either block them off or place a heavy guard there."

For a mile they walked inland, across those odd fields. The orderly rows of plants stretched off to the horizon on both sides. And then they came to a kind of level plain. The ground before them was strange looking, so strange that Gerry called a halt while he stared down the slight slope at it.

MOST of the plain was of bare rock, rock that was absolutely smooth and level without any sign of weathering at all. Along the outer edge it was pitted at regular intervals by what looked like shallow wells a foot in diameter. Beyond that zone were many excavations of many sizes and shapes, all cut down into the solid

rock with the sides perfectly straight and smooth. Gerry took off his helmet and scratched his head.

"Now what do you make of that?"

"I know what it looks like to me," Steve said. "It looks just like the foundations of a city—without the city. Those round pits are the anchorages of the outer wall. Those square holes are the basements of tall buildings. Only—somebody has lifted the whole city away."

"You're crazy!" Gerry growled. Steve shrugged.

"Maybe we all are! Anyway, I'm going to take a look into one of those holes."

Steve walked quickly forward toward the nearest of the round pits. Suddenly, just as he reached the very edge of the zone of bare rock, there was a dull clash of steel. Something had seemed to pick Steve up bodily and hurl him backward. He landed flat on his back on the ground, his helmet bouncing off and rolling a few feet away.

"It hit me," he shouted.

"What did?"

"I don't know." Steve sat up and rubbed his head. "Y' know, Chief, it really felt more as though I'd just walked squarely into a solid stone wall."

"It has just occurred to me," Gerry said slowly, "that maybe that's exactly what you *did* do!"

Gerry walked forward cautiously, a foot at a time, one hand stretched out before him. When he reached a spot on line with the place where Steve had been stopped, his hand encountered something cool and firm and smooth. It was like the surface of a highly polished stone wall. Or a sheet of heavy and invisible glass. He ran both his hands over it. The thing was continuous and solid. There was nothing visible to the eye, and he could see far ahead of him across the strangely surfaced rocky plain, but there was an impenetrable barrier blocking the path.

Stepping back a few feet, Gerry picked up a pebble and tossed it upward. The stone bounced sharply back as soon as it came in line with the invisible barrier. He threw the pebble higher and the same thing happened. There was something mysterious and disquieting about the way the stone would soar up into the clear air—and then sharply bounce back from a point in space where nothing at all was visible.

"Magic!" Closana said nervously. Even the Earth-men of the landing party had drawn together in a compact group, ray-tubes ready and eyes alert.

Gerry moved back a few feet farther, then hurled the stone forward and upward as high as he could. This time the pebble did not bounce back. It simply vanished in thin air. And then, from somewhere off in the emptiness of space above them, there came the sound of a deep and mocking laughter!

AS though that first laugh had somehow eased the necessity for a carefully enforced silence, there came a whole burst of unseen and eerie merriment. There was a murmur of many voics. Then it died away again. There was still nothing visible, and the silence was once more unbroken.

"For Lord's sake, let's get out of here!" Portok gasped. "This place is ghost ridden!"

"There are no ghosts here, little red-faced man!" boomed a voice.

The sound had seemed to come from somewhere overhead. From the empty void above, where there was nothing at all until the cloud canopy was reached many thousands of feet up. One of the *Viking's* crew bared his teeth in a sudden panic and lifted his ray-gun to fire blindly upward. Before he could pull the trigger there was a blinding blue flash and a crash like summer thunder. Captive lightning! The ray-gun flew from the man's hands and landed a few feet away, its wooden stock badly charred and its barrel a glowing mass of fused metal.

"Let your weapons rest, for they are useless here!" commanded that same booming voice from above. "Whence came ye, strangers in odd clothing who have traveled in a ship like a blue whale? What do ye seek here in the Outer Isles?"

Gerry stepped forward, a few feet ahead of the group. He shouted that they were a scientific exploring party who had come from Earth in a space-ship. There was a brief period of silence, as though men consulted in whispers. Then the voice called him again.

"You there—the leader! The Council of Elders will talk with you. Go fifty paces to your right, to where there are two white stones, and then come forward between them. Do not be afraid. You will not be harmed."

"Are you going to take the chance, Chief?" Steve whispered. Gerry nodded.

"I'll have to."

About fifty yards to his right Gerry saw two white stones. They were set some twelve or fifteen feet apart, on the very edge of the invisible barrier. Gerry walked over, turned left, and then walked squarely in between the stones. He held one arm protectingly in front of him, but this time his hand did not encounter any barrier. Instead—he found himself standing under the arch-way of a gate with a mighty city spread before him!

THE city had simply appeared in a flash, with its mighty towers soaring up to the sky, as soon as he stepped over the outer line of the arch. Whatever it was that held the place invisible from outside, it had ceased to function for him as soon as he came within the limits of the outer surface of the walls. Glancing back, he saw that his companions were still staring blankly at the spot he had just quitted. They were evidently unable to see either him or any part of the city.

"It's all right, Steve!" he shouted. "Just hold everybody there till I come back."

Doors of heavily carved glass slid noiselessly out of recesses within the wall to close the gate through which Gerry had just entered. The arch in which he stood was inside the thickness of the wall, faced with white marble, inlaid with designs in gold. Ahead, he could see a broad avenue that ran from the gateway down through the center of the city. It was tree lined and pleasant, thronged with people. Flowers grew in little plots in front of the gold and white houses. Small furry animals, dogs, were evidently kept as pets. They drowsed on the doorsteps or scampered about the neat gardens.

Half a dozen men were standing around Gerry, within the arch of the gate. They were slight in stature though wiry, with heads a little larger than normal and exceptionally high foreheads. Their skin bore a tawny tinge, similar to that of the Amazons of Savissa. Two of them, who immediately took up posts just inside the glass portals of the gate, wore a semi-military uniform that included a gilded helmet. The others wore white cotton tunics and high leather shoes. It suddenly struck Gerry that this was the first place on Venus that he had visited where the majority of the citizens did not go heavily armed at all times. Perhaps it was a good omen.

One of the men stepped forward, a bearded and gray-haired man who bore a gold-tipped staff.

"I am Gool, chairman of the Council of Elders of Moorn," he said in the deep voice that Gerry had heard outside. "The Council has decided to see you at once. You are the first outsider who has been permitted to enter the city of Moorn—White Queen of the Outer Isles—in countless generations. It would not have been permitted even now if you had been a man of this planet. Come with me."

THEY went up a flight of steps and climbed into a metal car that hung from an overhead rail supported by columns along the street. Gool touched a button, and the car shot ahead at high speed along the overhead mono-rail. The old man, who had settled comfortably back on one of the upholstered seats, was faintly smiling as he watched Gerry's face.

"You are puzzled, stranger?" he asked at last.

"Yes. There seemed to be nothing on the plain but a lot of holes bored in the rock, and now . . ."

"And now you find yourself in the city of Moorn," Gool said. "A knowledge of dimensional control is one of the reasons why we of this city have lived in peace and safety for so many centuries while the rest of the planet is torn by constant wars."

"Dimensional control?" Gerry said slowly. Gool nodded.

"Yes. It is hard to put it into language that will be clear to one who has no knowledge of our science. Perhaps I can explain it by saying that the human eye is a three-dimensional organism, and therefore capable of perceiving only things that fall into that same category. There are a great many things in the universe, some of the greatest importance, that the ordinary man's senses are incapable of perceiving. We have learned how to cast a protective screen of fourth-dimension rays about our city, and the effect is that it becomes completely invisible to the human eye. Do I make myself clear?"

"Not entirely," Gerry grinned. "But I do know that your screen works! But, since your science is so far ahead of the other people of Venus, why don't you rule the entire planet?"

"The other races are all barbarians," Gool said with a sort of disdainful gravity. "We prefer to live here in our peaceful isolation and not bother with them. That is an essential part of our philosophy."

The speeding mono-rail car mounted higher as it neared the center of the city. The track seemed to end on the blank wall halfway up the tallest of the buildings, but as the car came near a circular doorway suddenly opened just in time to let it through. They halted in a circular chamber where heavy springs caught and allayed the last of the car's momentum, and a pair of gold-helmeted guards saluted Gool as they helped him to alight.

"The Council is ready and waiting, my Lord," said one. Gool nodded over his shoulder to Gerry.

"Follow me," he commanded.

The Council of Elders of Moorn sat at a U-shaped table in a high-ceilinged room whose walls were hung with heavy and very ancient tapestries. The dozen members of the council were all old men, graybeards who seemed dwarfed by the high-backed chairs in which they sat. They listened with grave attention to Gerry's account of what he had seen of conditions on Venus, but their austere faces showed no sign of animation when he again suggested that they should intervene in the planet's affairs.

"We are not interested," Gool said listlessly.

Suddenly the short-wave alarm in Gerry's helmet buzzed loudly. He pressed the receiving switch.

"Listen, Chief!" Steve Brent's voice was tense and excited as it came from the earphones, "I just got a message from Tanda back in Larr. There's hell to pay back there! The Scaly Ones have in some way managed to storm one of the barrier forts, and now they're pouring over the borders of Savissa in great hordes. They're armed with supode rays, too!"

Gerry switched off the radio, and leaned forward with his hands on the carved table.

"Now is the time for you to act!" he snapped. "Lansa is a mad-man. He plans to overrun all Venus. If you come to the aid of the Amazons at this time, it will . . ."

"Our isolation of centuries is not to be broken," Gool interrupted. Watching the emotionless faces of the Council of Elders, he felt as though he were wading through mud. He was getting nowhere! The inertia of these gray-beards was a leaden and tangible thing.

"But if Lansa wins he may come after you!" he urged. "Your walls are invisible, but they're there. I could feel them with my hands. Now that Lansa has the equipment to project the supode ray, he may bring them down and . . ."

"We take no part in what goes on outside our walls," Gool repeated firmly. "We will give you the metal to repair your own ship. If you and some of your men wish to return quickly to the mainland in the meantime, we will send you across in our flying cars. That is the most that we can do."

HALF a dozen flying cars rested on a broad platform on top of one of the walls of the city of Moorn. Many bells were tolling the noonday chimes as Gerry Norton led his armored men from the *Viking* aboard the compact little flying machines. There was room for six men in each car, the pilot and five passengers. Only Angus and the necessary assistants had remained behind to repair the spaceship with the materials supplied by the men of Moorn. Gerry leaned from his car to shake hands with Gool, who was leaning on his gold-tipped staff.

"Thanks for this much help," Gerry said. "Next time we meet I'll tell you . . ."

"We shall not meet again, my friend," Gool said with a half smile. The words seemed definitely ominous to Gerry, but before he could say anything more the old man had bowed ceremonially and then stepped back off the landing platform.

The flying cars of Moorn were shallow bowls of some gleaming blue metal, oval in shape and with three comfortably upholstered seats. They had no visible means of propulsion. Curved windshields of heavy glass protected the passengers from the air-blast of swift motion. Gerry got in beside the pilot of the leading car, who was a slight and taciturn Moornian with the big head and high forehead of his race. A complicated control board was fixed in place before him. Closana and Portok were in the seat next behind, while two more members of the *Viking's* crew occupied the rear seat.

"Ready?" the pilot asked. Gerry nodded.

The pilot touched a switch on the control board before him, and three globular dials glowed with an iridescent light. The space-car rose easily from the landing platform, moving upward and outward at a steep angle. There was neither noise nor vibration. The city vanished as soon as they passed outside the zone of dimensional-control on its outer walls. Looking back and down, Gerry saw only the pitted rock of the foundations far below. A cart was moving toward the beach with some bars of metal for the *Viking*.

Then the next flying car came into sight as it sped out beyond the walls. Its nose came into sight first, then the middle section, finally the whole car. One after another, the rest of the flotilla took off till they were flying in a V-shaped formation like a flock of wild geese.

"What kind of power makes these cars go?" Gerry asked.

"Iso-electronic rays," the pilot replied shortly, not taking his eyes from the indicator board.

"And can they be made invisible like the city?"

"Yes. The dimensional-control lever is here." The pilot pointed at many of the controls, then again lapsed into silence.

It was evident that Gerry was not going to be able to have any extended conversation with the driver of the car. That might be due to instructions the man had received from his superiors, or simply to his own nature. Probably a combination of both! These men of Moorn were a cold and self-centered race. Probably they were an isolated off-shoot of the original Old Ones who had first settled this planet, a group who had managed to retain the scientific knowledge of their ancestors but had lost the vigor and fire that are found in active and vital nations.

BELOW them lay the greenish yellow expanse of the Great Sea. Though these electronic flying cars of Moorn traveled with a noiseless smoothness that was the last word in flying comfort, their speed was much less than that of the *Viking* at even minimum rocket power. The pilots were holding the flotilla down to a level of only a few hundred feet. The sight of the vast expanse of rippling waters sliding past so close below them was a strange experience to Gerry Norton, who had spent his life in space-ships that always traveled at the upper levels where everything below looks like a gigantic patch-work quilt.

Scattered islands shouldered their way upward through the sea ahead, and then sailed past below. So utterly smooth and noiseless was the movement of the electronic flying cars that they seemed to be standing motionless, while a strong wind blew against their glass shields and the surface of the planet unrolled beneath them. It was well into the afternoon before the familiar mountain ranges bordering Savissa came into view ahead.

Closana was leaning forward on her seat, her eyes eager and youthful in the shadows of the steel helmet with which she had been fitted out from the *Viking's* stores. Then, as the coast line became clearer with every passing mile, she suddenly pointed ahead and down to two black dots on the surface of the sea. The pilot took one glance at them, and then his hand moved to the dimensional control lever.

When they first entered the flying cars, Gerry had noticed that each one bore a very realistic appearing metal bird at the end of a sort of flag-staff that protruded upward at the bow. At the time he had thought it was simply a form of decoration. Now he realized that the metal bird fulfilled a much more useful purpose. It was outside the zone of invisibility, and gave all the pilots something to indicate the locations of the other cars and avoid collisions. When he glanced back, all he could see was a flock of birds following them in a wide V. The flotilla was keeping formation.

AS they soared closer to shore, the two black dots gradually took shape as a pair of good-sized surface craft. A black-hulled raider, manned by a crew of the Scaly Ones, was hotly engaged with a wooden Savissan patrol boat. Companies of Amazons crouched behind the high bulwarks of their warship, loosing their arrows in stinging flights. Explosive bullets crackled around them as the Scaly Ones replied with their gas-guns. The boat was equipped with a big charging-tank, for reloading the gas-guns, equipment too heavy to be carried by land raiders but possible here. The tide of battle was definitely setting against the Amazons. The bodies of many of the golden-haired feminine warriors lay sprawled in the scuppers or scattered on the riven decks.

Closana's fists were clenched as she peered down at the battle on the seas below. The decks of the Savissan craft were beginning to smolder, and her arrow fire was weakening. Closana threw Gerry an agonized glance, and he turned to the pilot beside him.

"Is there any way we can strike at that raider below?" he asked. The Moornian pilot smiled faintly, and then handed Gerry a long metal rod that was equipped with gun-sights and had a sort of rubber stock. A wire trailed away from it and was attached to the car's power plant beneath the control boar. It looked like an odd form of rifle, but the metal rod was solid instead of hollow.

"Aim—then press the button!" the taciturn Moornian said.

Gerry brought the strange-looking weapon to his shoulder and sighted through a line of rings set in the top. He centered the cross-hairs amidships on the black-hulled Reptilian craft, then gently pressed the switch button set in the stock.

There was a blinding flash of lightning. An instant later came the crashing roar of thunder. Momentarily the flying car rocked under the buffeting of the disturbed air masses, then it steadied down again. On the sea below, the battle had come to an abrupt end. That single blow was enough.

The lightning bolt struck the sea raider amidships, with a blinding flash. The metal hull glowed red hot. Water steamed about it. The dark shapes of Scaly warriors went spinning off into the sea. Then the tank of gas amidships exploded, sending a sheet of blue flame high into the air.

The Savissan war-craft rocked violently on the waves created by the lightning bolt and the explosion. The surviving Amazons clung frantically to bullwarks and rigging to avoid being washed overboard by the sheet of foam-flecked water that spread over the decks. Then as their craft steadied down again, they looked up into the sky. All they could see was a flock of small birds speeding rapidly inland. They lifted their weapons to the sky in salute, a tribute to whatever dark Gods had sped the deadly bolt that wrecked the enemy craft.

Gerry gingerly handed the deadly lightning caster back to the pilot.

"That's an effective weapon," he said. "If these flying cars can only stay with us for a few hours after we arrive at the city of Larr, we can probably break up the attack of the Scaly Ones and . . ."

"We return to Moorn immediately, as soon as we have landed you in Larr," the pilot said with cold finality. "Those are the orders of the Council of Elders."

DUSK caught them just as they passed over the Savissan coast line. They saw the gleaming lights of various scattered towns and hamlets below them. An hour later the lights of Larr itself came into view. At first they were only a glow along the horizon. Then, as the flotilla of flying cars swept nearer, the lights of the city began to take on definite form and shape. Closana was again leaning eagerly forward.

"The lights look strange!" she said, "so many of them are unsteady and flickering!"

Gerry Norton peered ahead through the night. His own eyes were narrowed and thoughtful.

"Those flickering lights you see are ray-guns," he said at last. "The city is already under siege."

Before attempting a landing as they came to the Golden City of Larr, the flotilla of flying cars swept in a wide circle over the city and its surrounding suburbs. Great fires burned in braziers along the walls. Other fires had been kindled by the besiegers. Dozens of cottages outside the circuit of the city walls were also aflame, blazing furiously. The whole place was suffused with a ruddy and uneven light, and the observers in the flying cars had a clear view of the scene below.

Behind the battlements and bastions atop the city's walls crouched the Golden Amazons of the garrison, loosing their storms of arrows at the swarming besiegers below them. Other tawny-skinned crews worked the alta-ray tubes that belched blasts of blue flame at regular intervals. Wherever the blue beams struck, the ground was blackened while the twisted and charred shapes of Scaly Ones writhed in brief agony. The myriad brazen trumpets of Larr sounded hasty rallying calls, or else tossed staccato signals from one part of the defences to another.

The hordes of Lansa had invested the city on three sides, the marsh-land on the far border of the city protecting that side from direct assault. Groups of Scaly Ones took shelter behind tree trunks and mounds of earth and any other possible cover, firing their gas-guns up at the battlements in an effort to lessen the arrow fire. Others crept forward behind movable metal shields. Heavy-caliber gas-guns inched slowly forward behind wooden mantlets that bristled with arrows, and hurled their larger explosive bullets up at the walls. Wherever they struck there was a puff of yellow dust and a scarred place on the stones. Reptilian trumpets beat with a staccato thunder as Lansa kept in touch with his various divisions. Not all the advantage was with the besiegers, however. Even as Gerry watched, a blue heat-ray struck full on one of the big gas-guns and blew it up with a shattering crash.

In all but one particular the battle was a large-scale edition of the type of assault that the Scaly Ones had often tried against various barrier forts in the past. The difference was that they now possessed the supode ray, which Lansa had been able to prepare for his forces. Long beams of the familiar murky, reddish light were continually playing upon the walls of Larr.

The effect of the supode rays seemed to be less serious than Gerry would have expected. Perhaps Lansa's ray-guns were lacking in power because inefficiently made. Perhaps the yellow stones that formed the walls of Larr contained some radioactive substance that partially neutralized the rays. The walls were crumbling into powder in dozens of small spots as the searching beams of the rays found a weak point or flaw in the stone, but there was none of the wholesale collapse that Lansa had probably hoped to achieve.

The whole scene below was like a macabre nightmare. The fires flashed and crackled, and the explosive bullets of the Scaly Ones twinkled like fire-flies through the drifting smoke. Red light glinted on the points of flying arrows. Savissan trumpets blared defiance to the thunder of reptilian drums. Most dramatic of all, silent but terribly deadly, was the duel of the ray-casters as the red beams of the attackers and the blue rays of the defenders darted back and forth through the night like the rapiers of fencing giants.

THE flotilla of flying cars darted down to the plaza in front of the Tower of the Arrow. The pilots kept them invisible until they had landed, lest the nervous crew of a defending ray-machine blast them before their identity was known. As soon as the dimensional-control was switched off there were cries of alarm, and a few hasty arrows glanced harmlessly off the Earthmen's armor. Then Closana shouted reassuringly and they were recognized.

A little later Gerry and a few of his officers stood with Rupin-Sang on one of the balconies of the Great Tower. The aged king of Savissa wore full armor though in the shadows of his gilded helmet his face looked old and gray and tired. Beside them, a squad of the Golden Amazons worked a long-range ray-tube that was firing at the rear areas of the Reptilian position. The muscles of the feminine warriors rippled beneath their tawny skins as they swung the heavy controls of the big ray-machine.

"They came against one of our barrier forts from the rear, in great numbers," Rupin-Sang said wearily. "I cannot imagine how they had managed to get so many men in behind our lines. . . ."

"Probably brought them under water in that submarine they used when they took me captive," Gerry said. "Brought them through in relays. I should have sent you warning to block the river channel against that craft, but I never thought Lansa would strike so quickly."

"At least we had enough warning to prepare for the defense of the city after they broke through the frontier," Rupin-Sang said. "We called in all the surrounding troops. We sent the very young and the very old, the ill and the crippled back to comparative safety in the hills by way of secret trails through the swamps. If the walls will stand against the new rays the Scaly Ones are using, we should be able to hold out for a long time."

"The armor of my men is proof against either rays or explosive bullets," Gerry told him, "and our ray-guns are superior to those that Lansa has been able to make. We'll use my men as shock troops to beat back any particularly pressing attack. Between us, we can hang on until Lansa gets tired of the siege."

"I hope you're right," Rupin-Sang said gloomily, "but I recall the old prophecy. It is in my mind that the end of the Golden City of Larr is at hand, and that the sands of my nation run very low. However— we will fight to the end."

"No bunch of half-lizards led by a white renegade is going to lick me!" Gerry rasped.

A WEEK later Gerry Norton was less confident. Haggard and unshaven, he stalked into an inner room and tossed his helmet clattering on the table. His armor was badly dented by the impact of many explosive bullets, and one forearm was burned where a supode ray had momentarily pierced between the chinks of the armor.

"All right, Steve," Gerry said wearily, "it's your watch. Go up on the walls and take over."

"Anything new?" Steve Brent asked, sitting up on the cot where he had been sleeping and running both hands through his tousled crop of sandy hair. His freckled face was as lined and drawn as Gerry's own.

"Another of the bastions on the west wall came down under the rays, but we're holding the breach all right with archers and a portable ray-caster. Hurry and get up there, like a good fellow! I left Portok in charge, and he's dead on his feet."

"I am not so damn much alive myself!" Steve muttered, but he put on his helmet and went clanking off up the corridor.

Gerry sat down heavily on a bench, at the moment too tired even to take off his armor. The city of Larr still held out—but that was all that could be said. The Scaly Ones still pressed the assault day and night without ceasing. The once mighty walls of yellow stone were crumbling under the constant attack of the walls while the defense of the steadily widening breaches put an added strain on the dwindling numbers of the garrison.

If only the *Viking* would come! Her duralite hull would withstand either rays or explosives, and her own powerful ray-tubes should be able to blast the attacking artillery out of existence ad thereby raise the siege. But he could not raise the spaceship on the radio! That was the thing that worried Gerry most of all. Tanda had been trying at hourly intervals for days, but he could not get any answer from McTavish.

At last Gerry stretched out on the cot that Steve had quitted, and almost instantly went to sleep. It seemed only a moment later that he awoke to find Portok the Martian shaking him by the shoulder. Gerry laboriously raised himself up on one elbow shaking his head to clear his brain. So strong were the bonds of sleep that several seconds passed before his brain grasped the meaning of the words that Portok was shouting in his ear.

"Chief! Can't you hear me? The whole western wall has come down, carrying all the ray-tubes with it. The Scaly Ones are in the city!"

GERRY seized his helmet and weapons from the table where he had thrown them, and dashed out of the room. From one of the balconies of the Arrow Tower he could see the swift disaster that had come upon the City of Larr. The ceaseless, unrelenting play of Lansa's supode ray machines had finally weakened the city's western wall until the whole rampart had collapsed.

The once towering wall was now only a long mound of rubble. The companies of Scaly Ones nearest the wall had been buried in the débris when it fell, but fresh hordes were pouring forward with a shrill yelping. The Amazon archers defending the wall from above had been mainly crushed in the wreckage. Reserve regiments were hurrying into place at the double, bow strings twanging and long golden hair streaming out behind them but there was one loss that could not be replaced. All the alta-ray machines on that wall were shattered and broken.

The despairing courage of Larr's feminine defenders was not enough to hold that mile-long pile of rubbish whose sloping sides could be easily climbed by the swarming hordes from Giri-Vaaka. The Amazons were falling back all along the line. The retreat was a slow and stubborn one, but it was steady. Such of the alta-ray machines as could be brought to bear upon the shattered wall from other portions of the fortifications swept the advancing Scaly Ones with blue blasts that tore gaping holes in their ranks, but there were not enough of them. The firelight gleamed on the armor of a few of the *Viking's* men who were fighting with the rear-guard, their ray-guns stabbing viciously into the Reptilian ranks as they fell back. The drums of the Scaly Ones took on a deep-mouthed bellow of triumph, and the brazen trumpets of Larr were the voice of a forlorn and fading hope.

Rupin-Sang appeared on the balcony beside Gerry, leaning his gnarled old hands on the rail. He was smiling, as though final disaster had at least brought a relief from strain.

"This is the end of the City of Larr," he said. "The ancient prophecy of Jeddah-Khana comes true after all. Save yourself and your men while you can, my friend."

"Can't we all escape through the swamps and put up a better fight in the hills?" Gerry asked. Rupin-Sang shook his head.

"No, my friend. The last survivors will do that when all is over, but we will defend Larr to the end—street by street and house by house—as is the tradition of Savissa. We are the last descendants of the Old Ones. We may die, but we will do it with honor."

The swift advance of Lansa's men bit deeply into the city, halfway from the shattered wall to the central plaza surrounding the Great Tower, before it was checked at a line of hasty barricades. There was bitter house-to-house fighting all across the city. Gerry knew that the stand at the barricades could not be sustained for very long. The advance of the Scaly Ones had at the moment outdistanced their supode ray casters and their heavy caliber gas-guns. For the present the Amazon arrows held them checked. The advance was sure to resume as soon as Lansa's heavy weapons could be brought up again.

IT was a hopeless fight—and yet Gerry could not bring himself to leave. Partly it was his affection for the grief-stricken but indomitable Closana that held him there. Partly it was the sheer courage of the Amazon's gallant fight against such heavy odds that kept him in the battle line. By some standards the affair was none of his business but he could not quit now. However—he had not the right to hold his men in the stricken city if they wished to leave. As he located the various members of the *Viking's* crew in the disorganized Amazon ranks, he gave each one permission to escape from the city through the eastern marshes. Portok's reaction was typical.

"Run from these snake-skinned devils?" the little Martian panted hoarsely, his ruddy face gaunt and his eyes sunken deep in their sockets. "Not while I can still stand. I'm staying with the rear guard— as long as there is one!"

New fires had been started by the victory-drunk Reptilians, fires within the walls. The lurid glow of burning houses made the night hideous. Fully a third of the city was in flames by now, and only the easterly wind kept the flames from driving the defenders away from those portions of the city that they still held.

By noon the next day the tale was nearly all told. The Savissans now held less than a third of their city, a V-shaped sector with the Arrow Tower at its apex. The murky beams of supode rays were now continually playing against the walls of the Great Tower itself, and small cascades of pulverized rock kept sliding off the face of the stone work as the weaker parts began to decompose under the steady impact of the rays. And still the fight went on!

Gerry had forgotten what it was like to lie down and rest. He was leaning in an angle of the wall, actually asleep on his feet, when Chester Sand from the *Viking* hurried across to him.

"Rupin-Sang wants to see you down in the garden right away, Chief!" Sand panted. "You and Steve Brent both."

"All right. Get Steve," Gerry growled. He sighed, and tightened his belt, and went wearily down the steps to the lower floor of the tower.

THE pleasant walled garden behind the tower was a very different place from the stop Gerry had seen when he first came to Savissa. The explosive bullets of the Scaly Ones had ripped up many of the trees, and shattered the marble statues. A heap of débris fallen from above lay along the base of the tower wall, while more was constantly trickling down as the murky beams of the supode rays criss-crossed overhead. The bodies of dead Amazons were scattered here and there on the trampled grass. Dense clouds of acrid smoke from the burning city swirled down over the garden wall.

Closana was waiting in the garden, her armor dim and battered. Her left arm was heavily bandaged, but she still carried a naked sword in her right hand.

"I was told that you wanted me," she said. Gerry shook his head.

"No, it was your father who sent for *me*." Just then Steve and Chester Sand came across the garden. A faint suspicion began to stir in Gerry's mind.

"Where is Rupin-Sang?" he demanded.

Sand hesitated, and cleared his throat. His eyes were shifty. Then Gerry heard a slight sound behind him. He spun around—and looked squarely into the muzzle of a ray-tube held by Lansa himself!

They had been neatly trapped! Lansa and a dozen of his men had come up through the sewers and slain the Amazon guards posted there.

"Drop your weapons!" Lansa snapped. Gerry shrugged and obeyed, and the others followed his example. There was a triumphant smile on the renegade's saturnine face. "I am glad you were not killed in the fighting, Norton," he said, "because you and Brent and the girl will make very valuable hostages for me when your spaceship eventually returns."

Gerry turned and stared at Chester Sand. The *Viking's* Safety Officer was pale, but he met the other man's glance with a sort of weak defiance. Gerry's lip curled.

"So *you* are the rat who slugged me that time I caught Olga in the radio room!" he said. "I should have known it. I seem to have left several loose ends I should have watched, but I'll fix you for this some day and . . ."

"You won't be fixing anybody any more, Norton," Lansa said grimly. "After I've used you to get possession of the *Viking* you'll die in the torture chambers at Vaakahausen. Thanks to my good friend Sands, I also know the location of the invisible city. That, too, I will attend to. But all in good time. Guards! Bind and gag the prisoners. . . ."

He never finished the sentence. There was a sharp hiss, and a thud. A narrow steel point stood a hand's breadth out beyond his throat. A wondering expression came into his eyes. Then his knees buckled, and he went down on the trampled grass. Across the garden, still holding the airgun from which he had shot the long steel slug, stood Sarnak of Luralla!

THE Scaly Ones went for their weapons, but a vengeful throng of the outlaw brood of the Dragon came pouring up from below on the heels of their leaders. There was no thought of quarter between these hereditary foes. There was a short, sharp fight—and then the last of Lansa's raiding party died in the shadow of the wall. Sarnak came striding forward, his hand outstretched and a cheerful smile on his broad face.

"It seems that I came in very good time, my friends!" he said.

"Perfect," Gerry grinned. "But what does your coming mean?"

"It means that the hour of deliverance is at hand. When Lansa brought his full force eastward against Savissa, it gave us the opportunity we have been needing for generations. We of the Dragon's Teeth rose against the scanty garrisons he left behind, and put them to the sword. The mass of the people joined us then, when the chances of victory looked so strong that hope overcame the despair born of generations of oppression. Now the Green Folk of Giri have thrown off the yoke of the invader at last, and thousands of them are marching this way to take the army of the Scaly Ones in the rear."

"But how did you come to arrive in the garden at this particular moment?" Gerry asked.

"The forces of Giri have forded the river and are marching overland, but I came ahead with a hundred picked cavalry mounted on swift saddle-dolphins. We saw a crude type of under-water craft moving in this direction, and followed it at a distance. You know the rest. After bringing down the sentries that Lansa had posted below, we left our dolphins and our water helmets down at the main drain and crept up through the passages to this place."

"When do you think the rest of the Green Folk will come?" Closana asked.

"Within a few more hours, Princess. They will not be in time to save your city, but they will be in time to protect the survivors."

"If there are any of us left by then!" the girl said bitterly. Gerry suddenly pointed upward.

"Look there! The worst is over now!" he shouted. The *Viking* was streaking across the sky in a burst of yellow rocket flame.

The big space-ship dropped down over the beleaguered city, her powerful ray-tubes flashing. Other murky beams stabbed up to meet her, but her duralite hull was impervious to the rays and Angus kept her high enough so that the helicopters were protected by the curve of the hull. One after another the ray casters and heavy gas-guns of the Scaly Ones went out of action. When the ship's beams had silenced the artillery and commenced to rip black holes in the ranks of the Reptilian warriors themselves, they suddenly broke and fled.

THE war drums of the Scaly Ones were silent at last, while the trumpets of Savissa raised a long-drawn paean of vengeance. Out of the ruined and flaming city fled the Reptilian men, while troops of swift-footed Amazons hung on their flanks and rear with twanging bows. Back across the plains toward the border they fled—and ran squarely into the grim thousands of the Green People who tore them apart with the savagery of an oppressed race just finding their souls again. The few that survived, out of the powerful army that Lansa the mad Earth-man had brought eastward to attack Savissa, were a handful who fled back across the land of Giri and vanished into the desolate Vaaka marshes from which their people had first emerged generations before.

The Golden City was hopelessly afire, past saving, and the survivors gathered on a level field outside the northern wall. Gerry and Sarnak and Rupin-Sang were standing together as the *Viking* dropped down to land on the edge of the field. McTavish stepped out, red bearded and jovial but showing the effects of sleepless nights himself.

"Sorry we couldn't get here sooner," he said, "but we've been working night and day to make proper repairs with that queer metal the people of Moorn gave us. We got your radio messages, but couldn't reply because the ship's sending set is broken and I figured the helicopters were more important repairs."

In a few brief words Gerry told McTavish of the fight in the garden. The big Scot beamed his pleasure. "An' did they get that slinking she-devil of an Olga along with the rest of the carrion?" he asked.

Gerry shook his head. "No, she wasn't there. At least, we didn't see her. It wasn't likely though that she would come. She probably remained back in Vaakahausen."

McTavish frowned his disappointment. "Ah, weel," he shrugged, "ye canna' have ever'thing."

"Don't worry, McTavish," Sarnak

grinned, "we'll probably have her in a few hours. A force of Savissans and Green Men have already left to clean up Vaakahausen."

Gerry grinned. "Good. There's one thing I would like to suggest. I loathed Lansing as much as any of you, but he is a white man, and I dislike thinking that he may be hauled off and tossed into a common grave with the rest of the Scaly Ones. Let's go to the garden, and see that his body has at least a half-way decent interment."

The rest of the party agreed to this, and they made their way back to the garden. They went down the steps leading to it, then all stopped in surprise. The bodies of the slain Scaly Men and Lansa were gone!

McTavish rubbed his eyes unbelievingly. "What kind of devilment is this?" he whispered. Sarnak shook his head slowly. "I don't understand. Unless the retreating forces found them, and carried them along with them. They were all dead, of that I'm sure."

"Lansing, too?" inquired McTavish suspiciously.

Gerry laughed. "Lansing never walked away from here, unless as a ghost. I saw him go down. And men with an arrow transfixing their throats don't do much walking."

But the big Scot didn't seem entirely convinced, and as they walked away, he was still shaking his great, shaggy head in doubt.

With the strain of the siege over at last, many of the garrison had simply dropped to the ground and gone to sleep where they fell. Gerry was watching the flames sweep over the last of the city. For a long time the Arrow Tower remained standing above the sea of fire, but then it began to tip. Faster and faster it fell, till it came down in a shower of sparks. Closana dropped her head in her hands, but old Rupin-Sang touched his daughter on the shoulder.

"Save your grief, girl," he said. "It is true that the Golden City of our fathers no longer exists, but there was a second part to the prophesy. That, after the great disaster, the people of Savissa would have a re-birth. A message that just came through from those of our people who are hidden in the hills tells me that—of ten children who have been born since we sent all the non-combatants out of the city—seven have been boys! The curse has been lifted from our race."

TWO days later, even before the ashes of Larr were cool, working parties of Amazons began to clear away the ruins to prepare for the building of a new city. Sarnak of Luralla had already returned across the river Giri to supervise the rebuilding of his own land. Angus Mc-Tavish came up to where Rupin Sang and Gerry stood in front of the king's tent.

"Tests all complete, Chief," he said. "That material we got in Moorn is all right."

"I don't suppose there's any way of thanking them for it."

The big Scot shook his head slowly, tugging at his beard. "The city isn't there any more."

"What do you mean?"

"Just that it's gone. We heard the bells a few hours after you left, and then we never heard them again. You can walk clean across the plain where the city stood. Sand from the beach is drifting into the holes that held the wall foundations, and grass is already beginning over the rest of the place. . . . It's gone, that's all."

"They were queer folk, the people of Moorn," Gerry said moodily. "I suppose they were afraid they might get dragged into the affairs of the planet in spite of themselves, and simply moved the whole city off to some distant and unknown planet."

"But how could they do that?" Mc-Tavish said. Gerry shrugged.

"Ask me another! How could they make the place invisible? We know they did that, we don't know how much further their science went. Anyway—I'm going to be glad to get back to Earth for a while. I guess we're ready to start."

He turned to look at Closana for a moment. The girl had laid aside her battered armor for her customary bright loin cloth and golden breast plates. She shook back her long golden hair and faced him with a smile.

"Want to come back to Earth with me, Closana?" he asked.

"Either that—or the ship goes back without its captain," she said quietly. Gerry laughed.

"Darling, I feel sorry for any Earth-woman who ever concludes you're some shy little stranger she can patronize. Well —the trails of interplanetary space are long and we'd better get going. All aboard!"

Expedition to Pluto

By Fletcher Pratt and Laurence Manning

Within the *Goddard's* hurtling hull Captain "Steel-Wall" McCausland, hero of the space fleets, nursed his secret plan for an Earth reborn. Reuter the scientist cuddled his treacherous test-tubes. And Air Mate Longworth grappled an unseen horror that menaced a billion lives!

"*N*OW *passing Phobos, the second moon of Mars. From this point to the orbit of Jupiter we are in the planetoid belt, the* most *dangerous portion of our voyage. This ship's armor of twenty-inch beryll-steel may be perfectly adequate to keep meteorites out, but let just one of those* *planetoids, little worlds, hit us and this broadcast would end right now. Here we are! Phobos at our left and down, if there is any up or down out here in empty space. It's a little red moon, cracked and seamed, all rock; it has no atmosphere and no weather. The rocks stand up, jagged and sharp. There she goes! Good-bye Phobos—we're making 9,250 miles an hour past Phobos, accordinig to a message from Captain McCausland which has just been handed to me. The Captain doesn't look well this morning. He seems depressed and the difficulties of this expedition are weighing on him. That's all for today. This is 7-LOP, the interplanetary expedition ship* Goddard, *on the exploring expedition to Pluto. Your reporter, Paulette de Vries speaking. Interplanetary time 0–six–0–0, May 24, 2432."*

The girl snapped the key of her microphone off and turned angrily to the young man who had tapped her on the shoulder. "What do you mean by interrupting my broadcast, Adam Longworth?"

The tall young man was frowning at her. "You know the crew listens in on these broadcasts, don't you?"

"Well, what am I supposed to do about that? Give three cheers?"

"Listen, Paulette. On an expedition as dangerous as this, is it right to let the crew know the Captain is feeling depressed or doubtful? I didn't mean to make you sign off, though."

"I signed off because I was through. Don't flatter yourself! Trouble with you is you try to run everybody's business. I thought you might have got over that in the ten years since I knew you in school, but you haven't. Trying to keep me out of the control room so I wouldn't hurt myself! Wake up, Mr. Longworth, this is 2432; you're still living back in the nineteen-hundreds when woman's place was in the home."

Longworth glanced at a bandage around the girl's left wrist. Paulette reddened.

"All right, I slipped and sprained my wrist. So what? So you have my things moved to another cabin, where I'll be more comfortable. You're an interfering old woman, Mr. Longworth. You're hopeless!"

Longworth reddened uncomfortably.

"Very well, Paulette, I'll stop interfering as you call it. But really, you ought to stop referring to the Captain in such a manner as to break down the morale of the expedition."

The girl glared at him. "I'll take orders about that kind of thing from Captain McCausland and nobody else. And I don't think the man I'm going to marry will censor what I have to say."

Adam Longworth's face set as he stood for a moment irresolute. Then, as Paulette said nothing more, he turned and left the cabin. Outside he paused, gazing down the long main corridor of the space ship toward the open fo'castle lock, where the crew lolled in the month-long idleness of space-voyaging. He frowned, strode off to find Captain McCausland.

CAPTAIN McCAUSLAND — "Old Steel-Wall" as he was known in the League of Planets Space Service — was poring over the course plotted on the chart table. The handsome, saturnine face and straight back were those of a youth; but he was forty-five and had twenty years of service behind him and had won the honor medals of three planets. He was so absorbed that he did not notice the Mate till Longworth touched his arm.

"Yes?" he said, turning round with a pair of dividers in his hand.

"It can wait sir, if you're busy."

McCausland looked at him out of cold, efficient eyes. "Speak up."

"It's the crew, sir. You know how these long runs are. Months with nothing to do, nothing to see."

There was a flicker around the Captain's mouth that might have been amusement. "Trouble?"

Adam looked startled. "Oh, no, nothing yet. I just wanted to head off trouble before it started, sir. You heard Miss de Vries broadcast just now?"

Captain McCausland nodded, and this time the smile of amusement was definitely present. "I think the word was 'depressed' wasn't it? And you're afraid it will throw the crew into a panic, and they'll turn the ship around on us and head for home. Is that it, Mr. Longworth?"

Adam, wishing he were anywhere but just there, and wilting visibly under the sarcastic gaze of the Captain, plunged desperately ahead. "Well, sir, I took the liberty of asking her not to do it again. . . . She said she was taking orders only from you . . . that is . . . I'm sorry, sir, I didn't know you were going to. . . ."

"To be married, you mean? Well, why not?" He smiled again. "The ceremony will take place as soon as we come back from this expedition. That gives her a certain amount of privilege you understand." His face turned suddenly grave and his voice a trifle sharp. "Moreover, Miss de Vries is here as radio reporter for the Interplanetary broadcasting. I want you to understand, Mr. Mate, that I'll have no interference with her. Instead of chasing bugaboos, suppose you check the course through the planetoid belt. I'll leave you with it; that will give you something real to worry about for a change."

Adam stared hopelessly after his retreating back. Damnation! Everything had seemed to go wrong since the beginning of this voyage. The harder he tried to prove himself worthy of the appointment as second-in-command to "Old Steel-Wall" the worse things went. With a shrug he turned doggedly to the chart work.

Two hours later he stepped over to the chart-room port and gazed out into the velvet blue-black of space where the thousand suns of the Milky Way burned across the horizon. It was no use. He was going to have to make a fool of himself again.

But could he help it? Captain McCausland had certainly asked him to check the course through the planetoid belt. Perhaps he would forget now, and not ask about the checking operation. But if he did? Certainly Walter McCausland couldn't have been wrong. Yet the figures—? Adam studied his work sheet again, shaking his head.

"Finished the checking, Longworth?" The voice startled him so that he jumped.

"Yes, sir. Shall I take over the watch, sir?"

"Little early, aren't you? What do you think of the course, Mister?"

Adam hesitated.

"It seems . . . likely to get us there, sir."

McCausland's eyes became points. "Are you by any chance evading my question? I'll repeat it. It was—what do you think of the course? What is your opinion?"

Adam gulped. Here it was.

"There seems to be a fault in it, sir. I'm sorry."

"Indeed?" The tone was sarcastic. "Elucidate, Mister Mate."

"It takes us up out of the plane of the ecliptic, then back again beyond the planetoid belt. That's very good, sir, and quite safe, but didn't you omit the fuel consumption factor? The course as plotted gives two shifts of forty-five degrees each, or half a complete stop, as far as fuel is concerned. It would cut down the amount of fuel available for exploration on Pluto to—well, here are the figures as I've worked them out. We'd have about enough for two or three landings. But if we went right through the danger belt of the planetoids as originally planned, we would save enough fuel to really explore the planet. We have to explore thoroughly if we're going to find beryllium there. It won't lie on the surface. Why, it's hardly worth going on at all if we can't do any more exploring than that. . . . That's my opinion, sir, and I didn't volunteer it, and I ask your pardon in advance."

THE great space captain smiled easily. "No need to beg my pardon at all. At first glance one would think you had the right of it, but I just happen to have gone into the matter a little deeper. You understand the reasons behind this voyage? Well, suppose that after having been away for two years we come back right on schedule, but without a load of beryllium, without having found any trace of it. What will happen? The League of Planets simply orders out another expedition, better equipped, and we go down as having failed."

"But Captain! In two years there may not be enough light alloys left on the three planets to build another ship as big as this! The service to Mars will have to be stopped long before that. The lithium mines there can't operate unless the water supply from Venus is maintained."

"Well, what of it? Nobody likes to work in that Martian colony."

Adam caught his breath.

"But how are the atomic motors that do all the work going to operate without the lithium from Mars?"

"And what of that, even? It would be temporary. Just a few months or years till another expedition could be sent out. You take things too seriously. What is there to prove that some other method of armoring space-ships won't be found? Beryllium may not be necessary after all."

"Perhaps you're right." Adam was still skeptical. "But is it likely, sir? You've been on the space run so long you haven't kept up with chemistry. The armor against meteorites now is so thick that any metal but beryllium would double the weight of the vessel, and even with these seven million horsepower Buvier-Manleys we couldn't make the run from Venus to Mars. Why, sir, it would mean the end of the lithium mines, it would mean the end of atomic power, and we'd have to go back to the barbarism of the twentieth century, when they ran everything by electricity from waterfalls!"

Captain McCausland raised an athletic hand. "Spare me that, Mister Mate! I have heard it at approximately a hundred banquets before starting out on this expedition. Yes, we carry the fate of the world and all that. We have to find beryllium or else the Mars mines can't be run and the atomic motors stop. I could sing it in my sleep. But suppose we do take chances and get this ship wrecked. Won't the world have to go back to 'barbarous' electric power after all? For my part, I think some of those people in the twentieth century probably had a good time."

Adam was silent. There was something in the Captain's reasoning, he felt. Yet he, Adam Longworth, could not but feel that the issue was a desperately serious one for every inhabitant of the three worlds—Earth, Venus and Mars—belonging to the planetary league. The entire known supply of beryllium, the precious light, strong metal that was alone suitable for the armor of space ships, had been exhausted. All that remained was in the hulls of the few dozen ships carrying water from Venus to Mars, and from the arid deserts of Mars, bringing to earth the equally precious lithium which was the only material with which atomic motors could be powered.

Every year, in spite of the best of care, one or two space ships would be wrecked—caught in the sun's gravitational field, or lost through some small error of navigation. Soon there would be no more space ships; and no more could be built. Each of the outer planets had been explored in turn—each but the last, the outermost and most distant; Pluto. They were on their way there now; if they could not make it—

"Very well, sir," he said aloud. "I see your point. Will you take over the controls at the change of course?"

"I'll take over now. Report in two hours. . . . One more thing, Longworth. You're young, damn young, to be first mate on this expedition. You know you were a last-minute choice, because of an accident to a much more experienced, and from what I've seen so far, a much better man. Make the most of your chance, but don't forget I'm captain here. I can't go into my reasons for everything I do. That's all, Mister Mate."

"HELLO, EARTH! *This is Paulette de Vries speaking, aboard 7-LOP, space-ship* Goddard. *For the last two days we have been running along the first leg of the angle that will lift us over the dangerous belt of tiny planets thirty million miles beyond Mars. In a few minutes, the ship's motors will be started to turn our course again—straight for Pluto. I'm going to turn you over to the microphone in the motor compartment and let you listen as the seven-million-horsepower atomics take hold. Jake Burchall is in charge down there at the motors. . . . Ready, Jake? Take it away!*

. . . "That's all, folks. We're on the new course, with the engines shut off, and we'll coast along for eight months at a speed of two miles a second, 120 miles a minute, 7,200 miles an hour toward Pluto. Nothing for anyone to do—a nice vacation for eight months. We're giving a costume ball, folks; it's all we can think of. It won't be much of a ball, though, as I'm the only woman aboard. I'm going to lend

some of the space-men some of my dresses—" (CRASH!)

"What was that, quick—!"

She got the answer, and went on.

"It's all right, just one of the incidents of interplanetary navigation. Hit by a meteorite. Out here above the planetoid zone and close to Jupiter meteorites are more common. Here's Mr. Wayland, one of the junior officers, with a report. What's the damage, Mr. Wayland? It is! Folks back on earth, we surely got it that time! The meteorite penetrated! Right through the twenty-inch beryll-steel armor of our hull into compartment eighteen. The whole wall of the hull is crushed in there, we've lost a few hundred cubic feet of air, but the doors are closed and our air supply is safe. Here's First Mate Longworth, just back from compartment eighteen. He says they'll leave the compartment as it is, and build a tunnel of thin metal through it to reach the five compartments toward the stern.

"Folks, can you imagine the shock of that meteorite? It's only a foot through and weighs five hundred pounds. If it had been one of the planetoids our whole hull would be crushed now. Captain McCausland turned our course to avoid the planetoid zone entirely and does that prove he was right? It does, and how! Well, folks, it's been a long day and an exciting one. This is 7-LOP, space-ship Goddard, signing off. Paulette deVries speaking. O-nine-two-seven, May 27, 2432."

A DAM had returned from the damaged compartment in time to catch the close of the broadcast as he was stripping off the space-suit in which he was making the examination. Dog-tired, he had just switched off the light preparatory to turning in when the light and buzzer flashed at the door.

"It's me, Jake," came a voice.

The First Mate switched on the light, and called: "Come in."

A small man, his face seamed by a thousand wrinkles, slipped through the door almost furtively and stood, twisting his hands in the audition helmet which enabled him to hear in the engine room above the noise of the motors.

"Didn't think you'd be in bed so soon,

Mr. Adam," he apologized. "But you always was an early retirer. I remember when I had you on the training ship—he—he—he." He ended on a kind of nervous little giggle, and Adam looked at him sharply.

"Yes, I remember. I couldn't cork off for a minute without hearing someone pounding on the door and you yelling, 'It's Jake Burchall! Time to get up'" His face sobered. "You didn't come here to talk about old times, Jake. What's on your mind?"

"Well, you know how one thing and another gets around on a long run like this. I didn't know but maybe there was something I could help you about, sort of, he—he—he."

"Afraid not, Jake. Everything on hand is up to me. You can tell me one thing, though. I was just in from the Mars run when I found my name posted for this expedition, and I never did hear whose place I got as First Mate on this trip. Do you know who it was?"

"Didn't nobody tell you that? It was Blagovitch."

"Why, he's one of the most cautious men in the service! What happened to him?"

"Bruk his foot. He-he-he. There was some said he did it on purpose."

"But what could Old Steel-Wall—that is, why did the Captain pick him in the first place?"

"Well, Mr. Adam, there's a lot of things about this trip ain't the same as an ordinary run. I wonder myself sometimes. The Cap'n, he picks a course way out of the ecliptic to dodge planetoids he didn't stand one chance in a million of hitting anyhow; and he picks him a mighty cautious mate, and then he picks him a young mate when the other one can't go. What's he 'fraid of?"

"He's afraid of failing, that's all, Jake."

"He-he-he. Well, maybe I'm a old fool. I'd say it was more like he was 'fraid of succeeding."

"H ELLO, EARTH! *This is your radio gal, Paulette deVries, speaking from 7-LOP, space-ship Goddard. Interplanetary time two-two-0-three, or just three seconds behind sched-*

ule for entering the atmosphere of Pluto. We're falling rapidly toward the planet. I can only see half of it, filling the entire horizon. The color is almost exactly that of a pearl in moonlight, white with blue lights and absolutely featureless. Sunlight out here is indescribably weak. Our spectroscope, handled by Professor Reuter, shows the atmosphere is high in fluorine, with traces of argon, and outside that a thin belt, a very thin belt of helium and hydrogen. I told you all that the other day. We have accurate temperature readings now, folks, and what they say is 200 degrees below zero, which is plenty chilly. You could drive a nail with a butter hammer at that temperature, folks, and it means we will have to do our exploring by diving, since the whole surface of the planet will be covered, perhaps miles deep, by liquid gases. Can't tell till we get there. Once we do get in, however, these talks will temporarily cease, folks. I'll be sorry, because I've enjoyed them, and I've enjoyed hearing from all of you back on earth, so many million miles away. But I'll be back, and so will all the crew and its heroic captain. You may remember— Stand by! We're in the hydrogen layer now. It's misty, streaming past the ports, so I can hardly see anything. I must sign off now. This is 7-LOP, space-ship Goddard."

Adam Longworth crouched motionless. The muscles bulged along his arms, shoulder and neck quivered with tension, and perspiration stood in tickling beads on his skin. His eyes were fixed on the control panel before him; on either side was a quartermaster at a set of controls and behind the three stood Captain McCausland, calm and watchful.

Adam's hand moved rapidly and a quivering needle stood still on a dial.

"Three gravities insufficient."

The Captain's finger found a red button on the portable signal panel that made a three-inch medallion on the left breast of his uniform. Throughout the ship there was a flash of red lights; loudspeakers echoed his "Stand by for five gravities."

THE quartermasters flung long levers; the motors boomed, braking the speed of the *Goddard's* fall toward the surface.

Captain McCausland slumped to the acceleration and recovered; the air-speed indicator crept toward the bottom of the dial, and had almost reached it, when a loud-speaker twanged nasally. "Visibility fifty feet, liquid surface. Forty feet—going down—afloat, sir."

Adam killed the motor with a plunge of his finger and his ears rang in the sudden stillness.

"Thank you, gentlemen," said the Captain. "Perfect landing, Mister Longworth. Relieve the navigation watch and report to the chart-room in ten minutes."

Adam saluted, said a few words to the quartermasters and went out with them to the fo'castle. The men off watch were just unstrapping themselves from their bunks. Jake Burchall stepped up.

"Do I take up the new watch, Mr. Adam?"

"Two hours from now. Look here, Jake, there's something I wish you'd do."

"Yes sir."

Adam lowered his voice.

"Did you hear the report? Fluorine all through this planet. Our ports are glass, and fluorine acts on glass. They're thick, of course, and have layers of plastic, but it will wear them through eventually. We've got to think of something to do about it, and I think I have the answer. Remember compartment eighteen? She'll be flooded. Suppose when you're posting that watch you get into a space suit and slide in there. Don't go outside, but cut loose some of the mica lining around the break. When you get it, you can make some mica sheets for the helmet viewports of your space suit. Then get into compartment eighteen again, and try it out. I'm no chemical expert, but mica should insulate the view-ports on the helmet, and if it'll do that, it will insulate the view-ports of the whole ship. Report to me privately. I don't want to make a fool of myself if Professor Reuter already has some other scheme worked out."

Jake grinned in understanding.

"Yes sir. He—he—he. Hope he hasn't."

In the chart room, when Adam arrived, he found a small gathering. Perkins, the chemists, was there; so was Professor Reuter, the astronomical man, a couple of assistants, and Captain McCausland, looking extremely grave, thoughtful, but ruffled.

"Well, Longworth," he said. "You're just in time to order out the navigation watch and set the course back to earth."

Adam was aghast. "Not really?"

"Ask these gentlemen." He indicated the scientists.

Professor Reuter cleared his throat, but it was Perkins who spoke. "At least we cannot remain here. The fluorine here will gradually, but certainly, cut through the glass in this ship."

ADAM flushed. He burst out: "But you knew there was fluorine a month ago! Didn't anyone—?"

Captain McCausland raised his hand. "Please."

Professor Reuter explained. "To tell the truth there was some discussion at that time. I am afraid I must confess myself considerably at fault. Dr. Perkins at that time urged that the expedition return and install quartz ports on the *Goddard*. At that time I judged the temperature would be about what it is, minus 200, and at that figure fluorine would not be present in the liquid portion of the atmosphere, but would exist as a gas, and therefore would not make contact with our ports while diving."

"I warned you it would be in solution," remarked Dr. Perkins.

"Yes." Professor Reuter, a big man, with folds of fat hanging from his cheeks, pursed his lips and blew through them. "At the time, I must confess, I really must confess, that I failed to consider the fact that the enveloping upper atmosphere of the planet would cause the surface temperature to be lower than that in the atmosphere itself. As a result, it is just cold enough to hold a certain amount of fluorine in solution in this cold ocean—"

"And, in a nut-shell, we must turn back," said Adam. He appealed to Captain McCausland. "Isn't there anything aboard ship with which we could insulate the ports?" Scientists always made difficulties, he thought; an old space captain like McCausland would not be so hard to down.

"We can try putting divers in spacesuits with double-thickness glass in the ports. That would last a couple of hours

at all events. I don't doubt but we could get volunteers in *this* crew."

Reuter blew through his thick lips again. "Dangerous. As scientific head of the expedition I will permit nothing of the kind. Naturally, Captain, we are under your orders, but if you take such a step it will be without my authority."

McCausland made a gesture of hopelessness. "Have you any other ideas to suggest, Mister Longworth?"

Was "Old Steel-Wall" giving up this easily? Adam's thoughts wheeled, but he schooled himself to inquire mildly, "Have you thought of trying mica windows, sir?"

"That would do it!" cried Dr. Perkins excitedly. "Fluorine doesn't attack mica— at least at earth temperatures. I don't know about these sub-zero atmospheres, but it ought to work. Have we the mica?"

"The ship is lined with it," remarked McCausland. "But we can't very well take the ship apart."

"Compartment eighteen, sir!" Adam burst out.

"Try it by all means: Hurry though, for we'll have to shutter the ship's ports within an hour or get out of here. I congratulate you, Mister Longworth. That was well thought of."

Was there a touch of irony in the voice? As Adam saluted and withdrew, he wondered. Nobody else appeared to have noticed it, to have noticed that there was something in the Captain's voice that didn't somehow sound quite right.

THREE men were grouped around the air lock at eighteen, and they looked up as the First Mate approached. "He's coming out now, sir," said one of them. "Been in already once, and Bjornsen fitted a mica shield over one of his helmet ports. He's trying that and the straight glass shield in comparison."

Adam nodded wordlessly, watching the lock handle. Presently it turned and out stumbled a figure like a gnome, cased in hairy hoar-frost. "Pretty cold out there," said one of the men, as with gloved fingers he labored deftly at Burchall's helmet.

The little wizened face came out of it, grinning like a monkey's. "It works, sir! I was in a good five minutes. Look here— the glass lens is all pitted and scored, but the mica isn't touched. Something funny out there in that ocean, though."

"What do you mean?"

"Something with legs, only they weren't exactly legs, either—"

"Careful with that space suit there, Jake. Material's brittle after that cold."

Adam raised his voice. "Look here men. We have a job on our hands. We must make and install port covers for every port on the ship. You know, the regular collision covers—beryll-steel. Jake, go up forward and get a dozen men, while you, Bjornsen, fix those mica covers on a dozen space-suit helmets. Make it snappy, for Heaven's sake. We have just one hour to work in."

"Beg pardon, sir, but wouldn't it be easier to do it outside this atmosphere?"

"Haven't the fuel. Hurry!"

The ship rang with orderly disorder, as man after man of the off-duty watch reported, received the space-suit with the new mica windows, and passed out through the air-lock in compartment eighteen to join the others who were adjusting protective collision-shutters over the big ship's ports. The last man through, Adam embarked on an inspection tour of the ship. Compartment 23 checked—all ports shuttered; compartment 22—

A bell rang violently, and the loudspeaker system shouted: "First Mate Longworth wanted in the Captain's cabin at once. First Mate Longworth wanted—"

"First Mate Longworth reporting," Adam remarked into his chest phone, and hurried along the corridor.

Captain McCausland was seated at his desk, drumming on it with his fingers. "Mister Mate," he burst out, as Adam entered, "do you know what time it is?"

"No, sir."

The Captain indicated the space-chronometer set in the wall. "Your hour is up. Call your men in. We're leaving."

"But, sir, they're nearly finished—"

"Mister Mate, I have taken the trouble to explain my orders to you once before. I'll do it once more, so there will be no possible mistake. I'm responsible for the safety of this expedition and the lives of the people aboard. In the present case it's my responsibility to see that this cold fluorine ocean doesn't eat through the

ports and put everyone to a horrible death, corroding as it freezes them—including Miss deVries. Call in your men. That's an order!"

Adam's mind filled suddenly with the picture of Paulette struggling vainly to beat back the hideous icy wave of acid at a temperature lower than anything on earth, of. . . . He lifted his chest phone and spoke slowly. "Working party outside; abandon work and return at once. Enter by lock in compartment eighteen."

THE sound of hammers and the grind of wrenches on the outer hull went on uninterrupted. An expression of surprise spread across Adam's face; Captain McCausland's darkened with anger. "First Mate Longworth speaking! Did you hear me? Burchall, answer at once!"

Again that pause, punctuated only by the sound of tools. McCausland lifted his own phone. "Burchall! Heinstatt! Captain McCausland speaking! Answer at once." Again no reply but the mocking tap of hammers. The Captain's face flushed darkly.

"Longworth, if this is more of your officiousness, I'll have your badges! Mister Longworth, you will get into a space suit at once and bring those men in. Knock them out if necessary."

Adam ran down the corridor toward the compartment eighteen air lock thinking to himself that if this was a mutiny it came at the most fortunate time for the success of the expedition. He took his time donning the space suit, his time about entering the air lock and turning on the pressure jets that would clear the way before him into the icy ocean outside. Just as he was about to throw open the outer door of the lock, the indicator on it moved, it was flung open from the outside, and the first of the divers stumbled in, accompanied by a rush of the icy sea that began immediately to vaporize in the warmer space of the compartment. The clang of hammers outside sank to a tap, then ceased altogether. The work was done! They could float on that Plutonian sea for as long as necessary without danger.

When they were out of compartment eighteen's air lock again, with the helmets off, Adam turned to Jake Burchall.

"Why didn't you answer me or Captain McCausland just now? Didn't you know you could be sent to the mines on Mars for disobedience?"

"Didn't hear you, sir. You see, we was in such a hurry to get out that we kind of forgot to put our radiophones on the helmets."

Before Adam could put another question the bell clamored for lunch.

ABOARD the space-ship *Goddard* the fiction of keeping up the normal twenty-four-hour early day was maintained, and it was not till after the meal called, by courtesy, lunch that Adam again faced Captain McCausland across the desk of his cabin. Paulette deVries was on the Captain's other side as Adam entered and saluted stiffly.

"Your report, Mister Mate? I am anxious to learn why my orders weren't obeyed."

"No radiophones on the suits, sir."

The Captain stared, taken aback. At last he nodded his acceptance of the wholly reasonable explanation.

"Very well. . . . Glad you got the shutters installed in time. As matters stand, then, we can remain here for some time. Professor Reuter reports we are near one of the poles of this planet. We might as well start exploring here as anywhere. Will you take the detail?"

Adam's face lighted. He hadn't expected a chance like this. "I'd be delighted, sir," he began, and then, catching sight of Paulette's slightly disdainful smile, broke off short.

"Very good. Take at least one good man with you. Professor Reuter says the depth here is about sixty feet, which is the equivalent of thirty feet on earth, due to the difference in gravity. That is, the pressure ought not to bother anyone in a space suit provided the depth is constant. I'm sending you because you made good on that mica stunt. Now here's your chance to do something bigger. You'll have complete charge of whatever party you take."

"Mr. Longworth will enjoy that very much," remarked Paulette. "He likes to take complete charge of things."

"I've noticed that," said McCausland, drawing down the corner of his mouth. He reached into a drawer, and producing one of the ugly, ungainly rocket-pistols, shoved it across the desk. "This thing fires the new atomic shells. Pretty dangerous, as you probably know, but it's about the only thing that will work in these liquid densities, and you can't tell what you'll run into out there. Good luck!"

Adam saluted, and was just turning away when out of the corner of his eye he caught sight of Paulette's face. It had gone suddenly rather white, and her lips were slightly parted. He turned back to speak, but the moment had passed, and contenting himself with an awkward repetition of the salute he made his way out of the cabin.

JAKE BURCHALL, responding to a call over the loud speaker system, found him changing into the electrically warmed clothes used in the depths of outer space.

"Want to come with me, Jake? An hour or so scouting along the ocean floor. We'll be the first men to land on Pluto."

To his surprise, the wizened little man, instead of bursting into his habitual giggle, looked thoughtful.

"What's the matter, Jake?"

"Nothin', Mr. Adam. I was just wonderin', that's all, if maybe you volunteered for this, but I don't s'pose you'd care to tell."

"I don't mind telling you. Captain McCausland assigned me."

Burchall scratched his head, evidently seeking to choose his words.

"You think a mighty lot of him, don't you, Mr. Adam?"

Adam stopped dressing with a zipper half closed, his mouth open. "Why sure! Ever since I was a kid—I remember being brought up on the story of how Steel-Wall McCausland saved the Venus mail rocket, the time—"

"Yes, I know, Mr. Adam. But looky here, I'm goin' to tell you for your own good, there some folks think Old Steel-Wall is a little bit too smooth outside and too hard inside, and I ain't satisfied. There's some mighty funny things goin' on. I don't like the way he called us in from that port detail—and that there navigation around the planetoids—and this here exploring trip—I'm just maybe a old fool, but I got my ideas."

"Bunk, Jake. Captain McCausland has other people to think of, too. . . ." Adam's sentence trailed off as he remembered the Captain's willingness to give up the expedition when they had landed on the wet surface of Pluto. Could it be possible that the hero of his boyhood, the man Paulette was going to marry—?

"What have you got there?" Jake Burchall's voice interrupted his chain of thought. "I s'pose the Captain gave you that, too?" inquired the old engineer, picking up the rocket pistol, and when Adam nodded. "Not for mine, Mr. Adam. Them things is twict as dangerous to you as to whatever you shoot 'em at. Come back there with me to the engine room. I got some of those marble bombs stuck on long rods back there. When you poke something with them, you know the explosion isn't going to blow you into the middle of next week."

Cased like lobsters in their space suits the pair waddled clumsily up the spiral ramp to the main outlet lock. The pair of duty men at the lock swung the handles in a bored manner, and just as he was entering Adam thought he caught another glimpse of Paulette around the corner of the corridor, and raised one sheathed arm to wave her farewell, but she did not answer.

"All right, Jake?" called Adam through the chest phone. There was a series of clicks. "All right, Mr. Adam."

Adam swung the lock control and felt the grip of the pale ocean, colder than anything on earth, sliding up around his legs, to his waist. Another spin of the handle, and side by side the two were settling gently through the opalescent depths toward the surface of Pluto.

INSIDE the ship, the lock attendants had gone off duty and the corridor was for the moment empty. Paulette glanced at the pressure gauge, saw that it registered a blank, which meant that the two had left the lock, and then turned swiftly to look along the corridor. No one in sight.

"At least," Walter had said to her, "wait till those two come back. You don't know what may be in that ocean out there—an ocean of liquid air and fluorine. Dr. Perkins says we don't know a thing about the climates of these extreme cold planets, and what forms of life may exist. Think of those horrible quick-acting fungi that destroyed the explorers of the first Uranus expedition."

"But you practically ordered Mate Longworth to go," she had retorted.

"That's different. Danger is his business."

There was no point in arguing. She left it at that, and promising Walter to rejoin him later, strolled down the corridor and up the ramp to the outer airlock. But danger was her business, too, she told herself, as she swung back the door to the compartment in which the space suits were kept, and hastily took down the smallest on the rack. Yes, the eye-pieces were mica-covered.

Danger was her business, she told herself again, as she turned on the pressure jets to clear the lock; she was Paulette deVries, the radio gal, chosen for her part in this expedition out of all the radio recorders of three planets for her utter fearlessness. And besides, that snip of a First Mate, Adam Longworth, had intimated that she needed protection. The lock snapped to behind her, and as it did so, she thought exultantly that Captain Walter McCausland might as well learn now as any other time that he couldn't order his prospective wife around, even if he could make everyone else aboard the *Goddard* jump.

THE water was very dark, the color of bottle glass, splotched here and there with darker, purplish shadows. Far above her, Paulette could see the faint shimmering line of light that marked the space ship. It looked to be hundreds of feet above her. Five steps in any direction, she knew, would blot it out completely. She had no great fear of getting lost, as the compass guide at her belt was tuned to the ship's control compass and would always point to it. Somewhere down here in the dark around her Adam and Jake were also exploring the bottom. Although she couldn't see them, the thought gave her courage. She stepped tentatively forward. One—two—three—four—five—at each step floating a little before she came down. She could no longer see the faint, comfortable lights of the ship somewhere above her, and for a brief moment, panic tore at her throat. She fought it down. Silly! She peered around her, as though the thought of Jake and Adam would make them materialize. There! There they were. She could see them dimly, like shadows, to her left. She turned and walked as swiftly as she could in the direction. How Adam would laugh at her for her fears. What a little coward—. She stopped suddenly, and cold, clammy fingers of fear rippled along her spine. The dark shadow before her wasn't Adam or Jake! It was something tall and thin. Something that seemed alive, weaving back and forth, and about the same color as the water. It seemed about ten feet high and six inches through, and was made up of sections like a string of sausages. Then over to the right she saw more of them—a regular forest.

Like the snapping of a brittle icicle, the tension broke. They were plants. Some form of natural flora, swaying to and fro in the icy currents of that dark sea. She laughed hysterically, and relief flooded her, bathing her in perspiration. But the experience had nevertheless unnerved her. Coward or not, she decided she had had enough, and turned to find her way back to the ship. Then she saw it! Behind and a little above her. Something big, whiter than the color of the water, hovering, drifting. She tried to hurry. Tried to tell herself it was just another surprising but inanimate form of life to be found in this strange planet, but as she glanced back and up, she saw the thing was keeping perfect pace with her. Horrified, she watched as it settled slowly toward her. Huge. White. Hideously opaque. She couldn't move. She could only stand, rooted as in some frightful nightmare, staring with bursting eyes as the thing drifted gently toward her. Then panic took her. She opened her mouth to scream, but no sound came from her strangling throat, and her tongue clove tightly to the roof of her mouth. She

put her arms up, like a child trying to push aside a horrible dream. Her hands touched a soft, white pulpy body. Touched it, then to her utter horror *passed through into the body itself!* They were gripped in that opaque substance. And still the thing settled lower, like a great hideous, white cloak. It would cover her completely. *Absorb her.* As it had absorbed her hands. As it was even now absorbing her wrists—her arms . . .

ADAM and Jake Burchall had set out with the idea of tracing a circle of some 300 yards around the ship. In spite of the weak gravity, the pressure was against them, and at each long, floating step they paused while Adam probed into the silt of the ocean floor with a long rod. Rock surface was only inches down; what kind of rock he could not tell. At each step they encountered the same sausage-like chain-weeds Paulette had met, and twice Adam attempted to pull up one of the singular Plutonian plants, only to find it breaking into sections at a touch.

"I suspect," said Adam through his phone, "that these are some very low form of life. Look how they break along the joint, Jake. They probably reproduce in that fashion, breaking off to form an entirely new plant."

"Funny we haven't seen any other form of life."

"Yes. It would be more usual to find a couple of hundred on an ocean floor like this."

A surge in the water round them nearly swept the explorers from their feet. Adam looked up. Scarcely ten feet above him, a huge brownish globe shot past, twice his own height, its smooth surface studded with countless tiny arms that beat the water in unison. As he gazed at it, a paler, whitish mass soared through the twilight to leap on the brown globe, and twisting in each other's grip, they passed from sight.

Jake's gasp came through the earphones and then his giggle, "He—he—he, Mr. Adam, there's two more forms of life and we make another one, if we stay alive till we get back."

Another three steps, and they halted again at the sight of a shapeless, almost white mass looming through the fog of green ahead. It was alive; it moved, but flowing, rather than swimming, and as nearly as they could make out in the dimness was without eyes, mouth or visible organs of any kind, a huge, shapeless jelly. Adam reached for the rocket pistol at his belt, but Jake's eye had caught the motion and his voice came through the earphones, "Don't use that thing, Mr. Adam. It ain't—Holy catfish!"

The huge colorless jelly had sidled toward them through the water, then sheered off, revealing as it did so, a core of some darker color through its translucent sides and three shapeless legs whose motion propelled it. As it made the turn away from the explorers it bumped one of the curious segmented weeds and Jake had cried out.

FOR where the animal had bumped the weed a huge dent appeared in its rounded forward end, growing rapidly till it was a cavern, a cavern which engulfed the chainweed. Instantly the lips of the cavern closed; Adam could see that the surface had become as smooth as before, while inside the translucent structure of the animal the outline of the weed was faintly visible.

"I've seen things like that before," said Adam softly, as though fearful of attracting the monster's attention.

"Where? I ain't never seen nothing like that. And I'm telling you, Mr. Adam, I been around a lot. Even in those dinosaur swamps on Venus."

"Ever look through a microscope, Jake?"

"Can't say as I have very often, Mr. Adam."

"That's just what you see in a microscope, Jake. That brown thing was just like a rotifer. Those big white lumps, that can turn themselves into mouths anywhere they want to and then close up and turn themselves into stomachs, they're amoebas. Amoebas as big as whales! They're the most savage animals in the whole created kingdom—and just about the most dangerous for their size."

The engineer's voice was doubtful. "You mean we're sort of in a microscope?"

Adam grunted.

"Microscope my left foot! Those things are real! They're dangerous! They're the lowest form of life, but what happened is probably that they couldn't develop into any higher forms on this cold planet, so they simply grew to gigantic size. Let's get out of here."

He took off in a long soaring step that carried him jerkily six feet through the water, Jake following. They had progressed perhaps three leaps, when the engineer's voice was suddenly loud inside Adam's helmet—"Look! On the left there!"

Adam checked himself in mid-leap and saw a dark figure in the green gloom of the undersea world, with one of the giant amoebas swooping toward it. "A man!" came Jake's voice. "It's attacking one of the crew. Stand still you, we're coming!"

THERE was no answer; the other diver only put up his arms to ward the thing off, and they saw his hands were empty, weaponless. Another leaping step carried them almost within reach of the hideous thing that at the first touch of the other diver's hands had suddenly formed itself into the huge ingestion funnel. Adam swung his arm back to stab the amoeba with his explosive spear, but Jake's voice came through the earphones.

"Too close, Mr. Adam. He's right on top of that man; you'll blow him to pieces. Let me try to attract him away."

Jake was holding out the harmless end of the spear. He prodded the giant amoeba briskly, and he did so, the jellylike creature again opened a huge funnel and swooped with a speed surprising for so large and formless an object. Jake dodged and flattened to the sea-bottom, shouting "Give it to him!"

Adam jabbed, pressing the button of his spear as he did so. There was a violent shock; Adam himself went down from the impact of the compressed water and as he fell saw the diver they had rescued tumbling also. Above them a cloud of milky silt boiled up, then whipped away in long ribbons as some obscure current of that strange sea caught it. The giant amoeba loomed through the murk, with a great ragged hole in its side—but the hole was closing, healing before their very eyes!

As he tried to rise and draw the rocket-pistol again, Adam's ears caught Jake's growl of fury, and he saw the engineer lunge with another of the bomb-spears. Again there was the violent shock and murky cloud, half clearing to show Adam the strange diver, who took two staggering steps toward him and then collapsed against his supporting arm. At their feet the giant amoeba lay, a whitish, shapeless mass, injured beyond the power of a second restoration—but no! As he watched, a foot long bud suddenly projected from the side of the mass, swelled, detatched itself, and then slithered off into the dimness.

"Holy catfish!" ejaculated Jake. "You can't kill the thing! Who is it you got there?"

"Don't know. Hello there, hello! Doesn't answer."

"Better get him inside. I'll help."

Together they half dragged, half lifted the diver toward the air-lock, leaped, caught it, and in a few minutes more were in. The lights in the corridor were blinding bright; Jake and Adam snatched off their own helmets, and worked feverishly on the gears of the stranger, to reveal the pale, half-unconscious face of Paulette deVries.

SHE grinned feebly and licked pale lips.

"Hello, Adam! Oh, boy was I glad to see you a few minutes ago! I thought that thing had me. It was like a bad dream."

"Are you all right? How did you get there?"

"I'm all right now, thanks . . . I walked." She got up, a tottering step, and slipped out of her space suit. "I don't need help—excuse me, I'm being ungrateful. What was it?"

"Giant amoeba, I think. He might have found that space suit of yours a little hard to digest, but you would have smothered, waiting for him to discover that. What ever persuaded you to go out there without your headphones connected up or any weapons?"

"Adam Longworth, are you going to lecture me again?" she began, then her face broke into a smile. "Oh, I suppose you're right this time, though. The main reason was really to show Walter that I could do my own thinking, to be honest. And—thank you again."

She held out her hand in gratitude. It lay cool in his for a minute, returning the friendly pressure, and then she was gone.

"I think," said Captain McCausland, "that we can evade any more incidents with these animals of yours by having the digging parties work in an air-lock attached to the ship's entry lock. Diving suits won't be necessary in that case."

"Of course, sir, that would be safer. Won't it use up a good deal of fuel to move the ship for each separate dig, though, sir? We're very low on fuel. May I suggest we pump into storage the amount necessary to make the return voyage? Whatever is left over we can use for exploration from a special tank. When that tank's empty, we're through and we have to go."

"Good suggestion. Give orders accordingly, Mister Mate."

"What would you think of sampling parties, sir, say three well-armed men, chipping off the surface rock wherever they can find it?"

"Waste of time. Beryllium will have to be dug for."

"Where shall we dig, sir? Right here? I understand that beryllium would be closer to the surface near the planet's equator—if there is any."

"You understand? What gave you to understand anything of the kind? Are you the geologist? We'll dig right here. Professor Reuter has made a very exhaustive study of the question and he thinks the pole is much the likeliest spot."

Adam stared. "Professor Reuter! I thought he was an astronomer."

"Reuter is an eminent scientist—which is more than you'll ever be, Mister Mate. You have your work to attend to, and if you do it you'll have no time for doing mine or Professor Reuter's. Now detail an engine-room party to pump fuel for the return trip. Allow ten per cent margin for safety. . . .What are you staring at me like that for? Do you realize you are impudent! Allow ten per cent. Then report to me how much is left for exploration. Next watch, have the mechanics begin work on the digging lock. By the way—may I have my rocket pistol back?"

Adam remembered that he had handed the pistol to Jake Burchall and had seen it disappear in his capacious pocket. At another time he might have said as much; but in his new-born suspicion of the Captain he merely replied:

"Sorry, sir! Must have dropped it in that fight with the giant amoeba—"

He stopped. For just an instant there had flashed across Walter McCausland's face an expression of fierce, snarling hatred. Then a smooth mask seemed to be drawn across it, and the Captain's voice was serene. "Of course. If it turns up, return it to me. That's all."

"BUT Adam! That's absurd. What possible reason could he have for wishing to make the expedition fail?"

Paulette looked anxiously from Jake Burchall's face to Adam's and back as the three sat in the girl's cabin.

"I know," said Adam. "I don't understand myself, Paulette. Why, he's been a hero of mine ever since I was big enough to know what a space ship looked like! But—"

Jake's wrinkled visage contracted in a frown. "I don't know much about the rest, Miss, but I do know I could have navigated through that planetoid belt myself, and I'm only an engineer. But he certainly used up an awful lot of fuel jumping over it."

"Yes," Adam broke in excitedly, "and he knew there was fluorine in the atmosphere here, but he landed right into it without making any preparation to shutter the ports, though he knew very well fluorine eats into glass like water into sugar. Then he wants to turn back. Then he gives us an impossibly short time to shutter the ports and tries to call in the men and leave before they get it finished. I won't mention—"

The girl burst in on him. "Adam, you're frightfully unfair. There's a perfectly sensible explanation of everything you've mentioned." She held out one hand. "Really, you saved my life down there and I don't want you to think I'm ungrateful, but you're letting things get you. You mustn't

think you're running the whole expedition."

Adam's face flushed. He swallowed twice as though about to speak, but before he could say anything, Jake Burchall slowly produced from his pocket the rocket-pistol and laid it on the table before the three.

"Look here, Miss," he said. "I don't want to say nothin', but when I got into my own bunk, I took one of the shells out of this thing. The others are in the magazine. Now I want you to look at this."

He snapped back the catch at the side of the pistol, and two atomic-power shells dropped out—the most powerful and terrible weapons yet invented by the scientists of three planets, ugly little things in their gleaming metal cases. Jake picked up one of them and handed it to Paulette, indicating a spot on the side of the shell with his finger-tip. The girl bent and gazed; there was a tiny pin-prick, a puncture entering the side of the shell.

"Do you see that little hole there?" said Jake. "Do you know what would happen when the trigger was pulled with that shell in the gun? Instead of firing the bullet toward the giant amoeba that hole means the whole force of the charge would have gone off in the gun itself. And that's the gun Captain McCausland gave Adam. . . . I'm sorry, Miss, I didn't mean to—hurt your feelings."

Paulette had collapsed suddenly across the table, her shoulders shaking with sobs, her face buried in her hands. "Go away, please go away," she cried, as Adam touched her shoulder.

"HELLO, Earth! This is Paulette deVries reporting progress aboard the Goddard by recording for later broadcast. The first dig ended in a failure this morning. Fifty feet down, and Dr. Perkins reports the composition of the rock strata remarkably uniform in character, but no sign of beryllium in them, nor any formation that looks as though it might contain beryllium. We're on our way from the North Pole of Pluto to the South Pole, where Professor Reuter thinks we stand the best chance of finding the metal we need. Just reached the half way mark. . . . Hello, the motors have stopped! I'll find out what the reason is for you in just a minute. What's going on, Rossiter? . . .*

Hello, Earth! Our motors have stopped, the fuel in the special tank we had set aside for exploration purposes is exhausted. We seem to be somewhere near the equator of Pluto. . . . No, the fuel didn't run out, they've found a leak, a leak in the fuel tank. It's all right, folks, we've set aside enough fuel to ride home to earth on, but we'll have to dig here instead of at the South Pole. I'm going to ask—"

"Isn't it a curious coincidence, Mister Mate, that this leak should bring us down over the equator—just where you wanted to dig all along?" Captain McCausland's voice was biting.

"Yes, sir."

"Curious coincidence, too, wasn't it, that when those shutters were being put on the workmen's radiophones went out of order? Listen here, Mr. Mate, there have been too damned many coincidences around here here to suit me. A few more and you're going to find yourself working in the engine room. That's all. Get out of here and get the digging lock rigged."

Adam saluted mechanically and left the cabin. He knew with sickening precision what the captain meant. Demotion to the engine room would mark him forever in the space service as an inefficient mate. He could never hope to obtain a command of his own, and throughout the rest of his life, wherever he went the record of it would follow him. Even now, the unfavorable report McCausland was sure to turn in when they returned to earth would block his way to any higher command, any other rating. He felt sick at heart as he joined the group at the main lock, helmet in hand, as they were about to launch themselves into the green ocean below—six men, armed with the bomb-spears Jake Burchall had provided.

He was surprised to note that Paulette deVries was standing waiting with the others, helmet in hand and her face deathly pale.

"Paulette," he begged, "do you really think you should go? Remember what happened last time. Does McCausland—"

"He knows I'm going."

"All right. But keep with the men please. For my peace of mind if not for your own sake. All ready? Close lock!"

The green waters rose about them in the lock and they swung off. Adam's voice came clearly through the earphones of the party.

"Be careful everyone! This is a regular jungle of those chain-weeds."

Paulette's voice answered. "Look, Adam! Where I'm pointing. There's something different over there, little round things, dark red, with a few yellow ones."

"I see them, Paulette. I don't think. . . . Jake, I don't like this. Let's test that bottom and get back as soon as we can."

The men stooped and scraped in the silt with their metal tools, reporting results. "Not over six inches to rock here." "Eight inches here." "Just about as shallow here as before."

"Take a few samples, then. Make it as quick as you can. As soon as you get your samples move back, be ready to ascend to the main lock."

ADAM could see nothing but the cloudy liquid around him, stirred to green milk as the sampling of the silt raised a murk around him. "Paulette," he called, "what's your compass reading?"

"Nineteen-0-thirty south. Sixty-three—seven, west."

"I can't see you. Move due east two long steps and stand still. I'll reach for you."

She complied and called out to him. "What's your reading now?" he asked, and she thought his voice sounded strange as she replied, "Same south reading. Sixty-three—six, west."

"Jake! Where are you and what's your reading?"

"I'm right here, Mr. Adam. Can't see you? This silt doesn't seem to settle down. There's a current of some kind carrying it; I can just stand against it. My reading's eighteen-forty—forty-two south; sixty-two—fifteen west."

"Bjornsen, Rossiter! Report and extend hands. If you don't touch anyone, reach out with the safe ends of your bomb-spears and swing them in a circle till you do. . . . Ah, who's that who just touched me?"

"Rossiter, sir."

"That makes three of—"

The words were suddenly cut off by the shock of an explosion that nearly tore them from their feet and a heavier cloud of the milky silt came eddying past, fragments of chain-weed moving through it. Burchall's voice came through the earphones. "Attacked! New kind of animal! Eighteen-forty—twenty-one south. Twenty—thirty-two west!"

"Never mind the bearings!" cried Adam. "Rossiter, Paulette! Hang on to the ends of these spears, and take three steps with me, don't lose contact!"

The three leaped as one, then again and again, through the murk in which everything was invisible. As they touched bottom at the end of the last leap, Adam saw a long writhing arm, with a barbed tip at the end of it, swing past his helmet viewports, caught a gasp from Jake through his earphones, and then felt Paulette at his side pull free from his gripping hand and reach up with the bomb-spear.

There was the shock of another explosion. Down he went, and saw something murky with whirling arms fly past the view-ports. Then Paulette's voice came through, clear and triumphant.

"I got rid of it, Adam, and here's Jake. He's all right, I guess."

"Everyone attention," said Adam, picking himself up. "Make toward the direction where that explosion came from. Then join hands and get back into the ship, quick!"

A few moments later, when the space suits had been put away, and the men were dispersing along the corridors to their cabins, Paulette touched Adam's arm.

"What was the idea of keeping asking for those compass bearings?" she said. "We found the main lock all right, didn't we?"

"Yes," replied Adam shortly, "thanks to your compass. And thanks to you, too, Jake's life was saved. But didn't you hear the reports from those others? Every one of those compasses was wrong, sometimes wrong by a whole degree, and every one was different."

"I don't understand," replied the girl. "Didn't you have the compasses checked before you started?"

"That's just the point. I did have them checked and adjusted. And Professor Reuter was the man who adjusted them. If you hadn't been with us—"

"*HELLO, earth! This is Paulette deVries, speaking to you from Pluto. In about an hour or more we'll be through, one way or another. The digging has gone down to a depth of fifty feet, sheathed in its steel casing, and there's no sign of beryllium yet. We haven't enough fuel to try another dig. I've just been down in the well the men have sunk, looking it over. They're working at the bottom with the new atomic power diggers, that compress the material taken out of the well into a fused, rocklike substance with which the walls of the well itself are lined as they go down, making it safer the deeper they get. One strange thing about the digging so far is that the temperature has advanced sharply as we go down. The ocean from which we're working is two hundred below zero as you know. Down there they struck rock colder than any ice on earth at the start and had to work in warm air supplied from the ship. Now the temperature has gone up at least a hundred degrees, and its rising faster with every foot. Just a minute. People are hurrying past me, there's been some kind of an accident at the dig. I'll have the details for you. . . ."*

The girl snapped off her key and hurried down the corridor to the open lock. Above her the loudspeaker system was booming: "All watches. Summon all watches. Second Mate Wayland report to Captain McCausland. Diggers have broken through into a cavern. Seven men have fallen. All watches."

Two or three men were standing at the edge of the air-lock, gazing down the spiral staircase that wound its way into the digging.

"Who's down there?" asked Paulette.

The man saluted. "First Mate Longworth," he replied. "Six men with him. We're trying communication by radio, but haven't got in touch with him yet."

An icy hand gripped tightly at Paulette's heart.

"Adam!" she cried and was surprised to discover there were tears in her eyes, as a touch fell on her shoulder, and she looked around to see the face of Captain Walter McCausland.

"What's the matter, my dear?" he asked.

"Your dear!" she half shrieked. "I'm

not your dear, and I wouldn't marry you if you were the last man on earth! You did this!"

The captain's mouth curled in a sneer. "So that's it, is it? He's persuaded you he can run you as well as the expedition. Well, I hope he can run things down where he is as well as he can everything else." He turned on his heel and walked away without another word.

IT seemed useless to go any deeper, but Adam, driving the digging machines hard at the bottom of the excavation, was determined not to give up till he was called back. There would be no more excavations; there was no more fuel to take the *Goddard* to another spot. The lights, led down from the ship, flared about them, the tongues of the atomic power rasps worked against the rocks with an annoying, grating sound, discharging their take of powdered rock into the machine that fused it, and worked slowly around the circular wall of the excavation behind them, plastering it with white-hot material that cooled rapidly into the smooth, stony cylinder that towered far above to join with the ship.

Suddenly, one of the diggers took on a new, high-pitched note. Adam turned; and as he turned felt himself slipping, clutched at something, and the next minute was sliding down, down, a long slant it seemed into total darkness. A weight gripped him around the chest; he rolled over, but his hands caught only loose stones, and when the slide came to a stop as abrupt as its beginning, he found himself lying on his back, the weight across his legs, looking up, far up toward where a speck of light from the ship seemed miles away.

He reached out one hand and touched something as smooth as though it were polished and gently warm. "Mr. Adam!" said a voice suddenly, and he recognized it as Jake's. "Are you all right, Mr. Adam?"

"I think so, but my legs are caught."

"I'll get you free in a minute. Anybody else?"

"I got hit in the belly," came a voice. "Where's Flack?"

The engineer was lifting something. "Can you get out there now, Mr. Adam? We'll be all right in a minute." Adam

gave a heave, felt his entangled legs slide free and pulled himself onto a pile of debris just as a light glared on like a star from one of the other men.

"Are we all here? Where's Flack?" There was a counting of noses and a general feeling of bodies for bruises. Above them, where the wall of the cylinder stopped, they could make out that the sudden break through had carried them down some twenty feet. "Here he is. Just an arm sticking out. I'm afraid he's done for. Come here, everyone."

One of the digging machines was brought into play and they labored to get the prisoned man free, but as they cleared the broken stone and rubble from around his face, it became evident that the effort was useless. The eyes were glazed, the head hung limp. Adam stepped back against the wall of the cave-in around them, and as he did so his hand touched it. Once more he noticed it was both smooth and warm. He turned, and in the light of the atomic lamps now blazing across the top of the cave-in examined it. It was not only smooth and warm, but polished; and just over his head he could see where the rock stopped and metal began—a clean-fitted job, a manufactured wall!

"Jake!" he called excitedly, "bring that digging machine over here for a second. The one with the cutting head."

The little engineer turned, and bounded over in a couple of steps, digging machine in hand. "Why, that's a metal wall," he cried, and applied the head for a moment in a brief surge of power. The bit cut out an inch-deep circle of metal, dropping it on some of the rubble with a tinny clang. Jake bent to pick it up.

"It's light enough to be beryllium," he said, handing the disc to Adam, and turning back to the wall, drove his cutter into it with renewed energy.

"What are you doing?" demanded the mate, hefting the disc of metal.

"This wall sounds hollow. Here goes!" He had driven the machine deep in, and stepping back, pulled the handle marked "Split." There was a sudden rending clang; a crash and a six-foot section of the wall fell inwards. The two men stared into the hole it had left, heedless of the fact that the other members of the excavating crew were crowding up behind them.

They were looking into a low square room, perhaps twenty feet across. At the far side was a doorway, and in the doorway stood a man!

To be sure he was such a man as none of them had ever before seen. He was not over four and a half feet tall, yet with arms as long as an earthling's hanging down below his knees, tremendously broad shoulders, and a head that seemed permanently pushed forward and downward above them. Below that head the creature was wrapped from neck to toe in some shimmering blue material with a metallic luster, banded around the arms and legs with red metal.

As they gazed in astonishment, the man took two steps forward, his head bobbing on his neck at each step, opened his lips, and uttered "Wahwahroo!" in a voice thick with gutturals.

ADAM glanced around at his own men, then once more at the Plutonian dwarf, whose face, as far as he could judge, bore an expression of intense interest rather than of fear or anger. The remark, he judged, would be a greeting.

"Wahwahroo!" he replied amiably, but the Plutonian continued to stare in a manner that indicated Adam's first lesson in this unknown tongue was far from a success.

"Stand by," he remarked to the crew. "I'm going in and try to talk to this bird. May be trouble." Catching the sides of the split in the wall, he jumped down in a small cascade of pebbles that rang on the floor below in a manner which assured him this also was metal.

"I don't understand what you're saying, old man," he remarked to the Plutonian, who had remained standing in the doorway, and touching a finger to lips and ears to emphasize the point. "I don't understand, but maybe you'll be able to get it from a picture."

From one of his pockets he produced a piece of paper, and with one of the new print-pencils that had just been developed, sketched rapidly at a crude drawing of a rocket-ship with little men issuing from beneath it into the waves of an ocean.

The Plutonian accepted it from his hand, looked at it with a puzzled expression, then returned it, nodding violently, but with an expression on his face that bespoke complete lack of comprehension.

"Mr. Adam!" It was Jake's voice from the door. "I'm sending the others back with Flack to get some weapons."

"All right. Just stay there to keep up communication, Jake," Adam called back. "I'm trying to get over the idea to this guy that we're civilized."

He stepped over to the wall of the room and with his print-pencil tapped on the metal "Ping!" then twice "Ping-Ping" and then three times, "Ping-Ping-Ping."

The Plutonian watched him attentively, grimaced with thick lips, and then catching Adam's eye, tapped with his foot, once, then twice, then three times in quick succession. Adam smiled approval; the Plutonian reached out, took the drawing again and studied it gravely for a moment, then pointed at one of the little figures, at Adam, and smiled.

Adam did his best to signify that the Plutonian had grasped the point. The dwarf held up one hand, palm out toward Adam, then turned to the door behind him. Adam watched without moving, and a frown spread across the Plutonian's face.

"I got it, Mr. Adam," called Jake from the rent in the wall, "all the signals are different here. He holds up his hand to stop you because he wants you to come along."

It might be. Adam took an experimental step toward the Plutonian, and saw the latter's face clear. They reached the door together, and Adam noticed it did not open on hinges, but slid. The Plutonian touched some kind of lever or contact in the frame, uttered something in his deep voice, and stood waiting. Beyond the door, Adam noticed, was another room, perfectly dark, but as the Plutonian stopped speaking, there was a rustle of feet within and a file of half a dozen dwarfs emerged, each an exact duplicate of the first as nearly as Adam could judge. They formed a circle, staring at Adam and at the torn wall with Jake gazing through. Each in turn stepped forward, examined Adam from head to foot and having emitted a few expressive grunts took his place in the circle again. All seemed friendly, but after the last one had looked over Adam, one of the Plutonians produced some kind of weapon with a hammer-like head and a handle set cross-wise, and waved the earth-man back toward the tear in the wall.

Adam looked around at Jake, saw that he had one of the digging machines in his hand, and decided that retreat toward this protection was the best policy. But it was not the Plutonian's intention to dismiss him, evidently. One of them, whose metallic armbands were more numerous than the rest, stepped forward, reached for Adam's print-pencil, and when Adam added to it his piece of paper, was busy for a moment.

ON the paper, when he handed it to the earth-man, were seven groups of dots, one in the first, two in the second, three in the third, regularly up to seven dots in the seventh group.

The dwarf pointed to himself, then to the single dot; and followed by indicating each of the other six Plutonians, in turn with one of the lines of dots.

When this effort at communication had been executed, he pointed to the single dot again, then to Adam, and finally to the wall.

"What does he want?" asked Jake. "What's he trying to get at?"

"I think I know," replied Adam. "See these numbers of dots? He's trying to tell me he's the number one man here, and he wants to talk to our number one man."

He turned to the Plutonian, saluting, and laughed to see the dwarf returning him a carbon copy of the movement.

"I'll stay here," he said to Jake. "As soon as they get that emergency ladder in position report to Captain McCausland and ask him whether he can come down. You might take along those metal samples you routed out. Ask Dr. Perkins to test them for beryllium. They're light and strong enough to be the stuff."

"GENERAL staff assembly in the mess room! Time one-two-four-five. General staff assembly in the mess room! Time, one-two-four-five. General—"

The ship's loudspeakers were carrying the message all through the big hull, and even down into the base of the tunnel where the spiral stair of alloy had now been carried to the spot of the cave-in, and Second Mate Wayland was superintending the job of fusing some of the debris into place to strengthen and lengthen the cylinder.

Coming down the corridor toward the mess room, Adam almost ran into Paulette. She took his hand impulsively. "I'm so glad for you, Adam," she said. "You wanted this expedition to succeed so much, and you've worked so hard on it."

He smiled wryly. "Lot of good it'll do me now. The captain's going to turn in an unfavorable report and he's even now threatening to demote me to the engine room."

The girl's eyes flashed. "Never mind. You forget that I'm the power of the press. When Paulette deVries, the radio gal, lets go, Captain Walter McCausland is going to be good and sorry for some of the things he's done."

Adam stopped and stared at her in amazement. "Why, I thought you were going to marry him!"

"Him! I wouldn't marry him if he were the last man on—on Pluto." She gave a laugh that was half a sob.

"Then—then, there's a chance—"

"Sssh. Here we are."

The scientific staff, Dr. Perkins, Professor Reuter, three assistants, the medical staff and a geographer, were at the front of the room, with the second and third mates, and the other officers of the expedition, Captain McCausland in their midst. As Adam and Paulette, the last to enter, came in, McCausland glanced at them sharply under lowered brows. Adam realized suddenly that he was holding the girl's hand and dropped it; someone laughed, and McCausland's hard, thin face was etched in a sneer.

"Miss deVries," he said. "I called the entire staff together to listen to this report on the sample of metal brought from below, because it is very important. Would you be good enough to open your key and make a record of this report?"

The girl obediently snapped the switch on the device that hung at her chest, and spoke briefly into it. "Hello, earth! Paulette deVries speaking. We are about to hear the report on the metal found in the digging on Pluto. Dr. Perkins, our chemist, will speak first. . . ."

Perkins' report was brief. "I have made spectroscopic tests on the metal brought from the digging, and which is used by the inhabitants of the interior of Pluto. It registers as certainly beryllium."

PAULETTE was about to speak again, when McCausland held up his hand. "I would like to hear from Professor Reuter," he said. "He conducted the chemical and physical analyses of the metal after Dr. Perkins had finished his spectroscopic tests."

Professor Reuter's oily voice boomed out. "I regret to say that although this metal responds to the spectroscopic tests for beryllium, it will not do for our purpose. It is, in fact, an isotope of beryllium, a metal which resembles it spectroscopically but not physically. The weight is wrong; the metal is much too heavy and will not do for making armor for space ships."

"But—but——" babbled Adam. "I didn't weigh it, of course, but it seemed very light to me."

"And to me also," remarked Dr. Perkins. There was a frown of puzzlement if not of suspicion between his brows.

"Miss deVries, you will not make a record of this useless argument," snapped McCausland. "Professor Reuter will explain——"

"I will explain that the sample in its original form was full of air particles, like a fine sponge," remarked the professor easily, but with his mouth working. "The Plutonians evidently have some process of lightening in this fashion."

"Isn't there any way of treating it?"

McCausland turned to Dr. Perkins. "Will you explain to our young but over-enthusiastic friend about that?"

Dr. Perkins shook his head. The frown still persisted. "Not if it's a true isotope. That would be the same thing as transmuting elements. But I still confess I do not entirely understand."

McCausland took up the word swiftly. "Meanwhile, since it is certain that the metal used by these Plutonians will not do for our purpose, I think it important that we at least look into the composition of their civilization to some extent," he remarked. "I propose to investigate them with Professor Reuter's co-operation. Mister Longworth, you will take charge of the ship guard."

Paulette spoke up suddenly. "Captain McCausland, I think it is important that I go with you on making this contact with the Plutonians. Certainly everyone on the three planets will want to know about them."

The captain's mouth writhed a moment, and Adam noticed the glance he shot at Professor Reuter, but his voice was smooth. "To be sure, Miss deVries. I think, then, this is all that comes before the present meeting. Dismiss."

THE space in front of the metal wall that shut off the Plutonian domain had been cleared. As Paulette, accompanied by Professor Reuter, McCausland, and Bjornsen of the engine-room staff, reached the bottom of the dig and stepped over to it, they noted that although the wall still showed part of the jagged break, a door had been fitted to fill most of the gap.

The four stepped over to it, and McCausland tapped at the door. There was no answer at first, then from the other side there came an answering tapping—one tap, then two, then three, as though for a signal. McCausland answered in the same fashion, and after a moment the door slid back, revealing one of the strange ape men of Pluto. He saluted in a strange copy of the movement Adam had made at the time of their first contact, and McCausland, returning the salute, stepped through the door, and producing a piece of paper from his pocket began to make sketches, while the dwarf watched with interest, his face working rapidly to indicate comprehension.

After a moment the captain beckoned to Reuter and both stepped down into the Plutonian room, leaving Paulette and Bjornsen on the heap of rubble at the base of the digging. The girl looked round, then in a low voice, said to the engineer:

"Will you do me a favor?"

"Sure. What is it?"

"I'd like a souvenir. See where that part of the wall is torn? Could you break me off a little sliver of that metal to take back with me?"

"Simple." The giant mechanic stepped over to the wall and twisted at a rag of metal. It tore loose with a little ping! The other two were absorbed in their pencil-and-paper conversation with the Plutonian and did not appear to notice as Paulette slipped the fragment into the pocket of her skirt.

Bjornsen's eye looked along the crack and the fitting of the door, and he was shaking his head, clucking despondently. "These people," he said. "They are bad mechanics. Look at that joint. I'll fix it for them."

He bent and picked up one of the atomic power drills that had been left at the foot of the dig, and applying it to the wall, turned on the power. As he did so, there was a commotion; a dozen or more of the Plutonians, all dressed in the same wrappings, but with varying numbers of metal bands, came pouring through the back door of the room. McCausland turned fiercely. "Drop that!" he shouted. "Do you want to bring them all down on us?"

"I was just repairing this break for them," replied the engineer.

"Don't touch anything that doesn't belong to you," replied the captain, and turning, began to draw rapidly on his paper.

THE crowding Plutonians, gabbling in their guttural language, were examining the work that Bjornsen had done, gazing at him admiringly and then at the power drill he had used. Three or four of them attached themselves to him, while another picked up the machine, and pulled him along as though to lead him through the rear door of the room, while their chief made a rapid drawing for McCausland.

"They want you to go with them and work for them," explained Reuter, peering over the Plutonian's shoulder as he sketched. "Just disengage their hands, gently, Bjornsen. We'll explain."

"Yes," said McCausland, "and go back up to the ship. You and Miss deVries both. I don't care how important this is for purposes of record. That's an order. Go!"

Adam was on duty at the head of the spiral stair when they arrived. "Did you get it?" he asked.

Paulette put a finger on her lips and

glanced at Bjornsen, then as though referring to some previous arrangement, said easily, "Do you suppose Dr. Perkins will explain the matter now?"

"I think so," he replied, catching on quickly. "I'll leave Burchall in charge of the watch and we can go up and see him at all events."

A few moments later they had reached the top of the ship where the scientific laboratories were located in a series of outer compartments. Dr. Perkins looked up from his desk as the pair entered.

"Hello, Miss deVries," he said. "Glad to see you, Longworth. What's on your mind?"

Adam spoke. "I just wanted to ask you two questions."

"Go ahead."

"Well, the first is—what did you think of that isotope business?"

The chemist's face gathered in a frown.

"I think it was rather a tragedy. After so much effort and such high hopes! The world can go back to barbarism again now, and it will be barbarism, too. All the machinery will have to be built to use crude electric power, the standard of living will have to be reduced, and only a few people will profit—the people who own the electric plants. . . ." He glanced at Paulette. "Is this an interview for the press?"

"No," replied Adam slowly, "and that wasn't exactly the answer I wanted. But perhaps you'll understand from the second question. Why did Professor Reuter make the test on that beryllium instead of you? I understood you were the chemist of the expedition."

PERKINS glanced at him sharply. "I might say that you take a good deal of interest in a good many things, young man. Captain McCausland remarked about that already. But for your information, Professor Reuter is the head of the scientific staff, and is perfectly adequate to conduct so simple an examination. You aren't insinuating he isn't capable, by any chance?"

An irritated retort rose to Adam's lips, but before he could make it Paulette laid her hand on his arm and broke in: "Mr. Longworth, of course, doesn't mean to insinuate anything, Dr. Perkins. He came with me, because as press representative I felt that we ought to be perfectly sure in a matter that so vitally affects the future of the world. There are going to be quite a number of questions asked when we return and I thought we ought to have a confirming test made by you."

A curious expression flashed across Perkins' face. "Reuter should have allowed me to make one in any case, I think," he said. "Where can I get a sample?"

"I have one here." The girl produced the fragment Bjornsen had wrenched loose for her.

"You needn't mention this to anyone till we get back to the earth," said Dr. Perkins, sawing the sample in two. "I wouldn't want to appear insubordinate. Now, let's see, we'll leave the spectroscope test out —that was made on the other sample." He sliced off a shaving, set it on the viewing table and adjusted the light. "That's odd," he remarked after a moment. "There's no sign of the air bubbles Reuter found in the other sample."

One of the other fragments he dropped into a crucible, set the dial at 900 degrees and flicked on the little motor that would melt it by atomic power heat.

Adam watched breathlessly as the oven was opened, the little molten globe of silvery metal quenched in acid, then dropped into an open-ended pipette and the container filled with liquid.

"The difference between what that pipette held and what it should hold," explained Dr. Perkins as he adjusted a scale to weigh the liquid, which had been poured off, "will be the displacement of the sample. See—2.4 cubic centimeters. Now the weight. We read it directly by putting the displaced weight in water on one arm of the scale and the sample of metal on the other. Now, when they balance the pointer—my God! Longworth!"

There was a ghost of a smile around Adam's mouth; Paulette gripped his arm. "Yes?"

"Longworth, the specific gravity is 1.93! This is more than important, it's vital! I'm going to call in my assistant and make that test over again, spectroscope and all. This is no isotope. This is perfectly genuine beryllium. How could Reuter have made such an error!"

Adam and Paulette left the chemist feverishly ringing for his assistant.

"I TELL you, Walter, I don't like it. We've got to get out of here." Professor Reuter's usually smooth voice had an edge of worry and his fat face was haggard.

"What's the matter, losing your nerve?" taunted Captain McCausland.

The professor slapped the table of the cabin to which they had returned from their visit to the subsoil of Pluto. "I tell you, Walter, I'm risking everything by going on. My own men are wondering about that fluorine fiasco, and Perkins was just able to swallow my analysis of the beryllium and no more. I have a scientific reputation to keep up, you want to remember; it won't do me any good to succeed if I go back with my reputation for accuracy in tatters."

"Reputation!" McCausland's voice was mocking. "Just like a school girl, afraid to be caught out with the boys. Why, you old goat, if anything went wrong now, do you suppose anyone would blame me? No, they wouldn't. I only acted on the advice of my head of science. You're in this right up to the neck, Reuter, reputation or no reputation, and now you're going to see it through—on the lines I mark out for you."

The professor's weak anger collapsed. "Now, now, Walter, don't be angry. I had no intention of falling down on you. But it seems to me that I'm taking a good deal of the risk, while you—"

"While I'm going to get all the profit, I suppose? Now, listen; you have as many shares as I have. Anyway, we can settle such details at a later date. What we've got to work out now is details. That young Longworth suspects, I'm sure, and he's got the girl onto his side."

The professor's voice became smooth and unctuous again. "It was too bad about that rocket-pistol. You're sure they didn't suspect anything about that?"

"Wouldn't Longworth have mentioned it? He's just the sort of hot-headed young busybody who would burst out with the whole story. No, he lost it all right. The main thing now is to keep any of the rest of them from getting a sample of that unalloyed beryllium wall down there."

"In which you are fortunately aided by the Plutonians' interest in Bjornsen. You can give orders now that the thing isn't to be touched for fear of provoking them. They're amazingly strong, physically, by the way."

"We might—" What it was that Mc-Causland was going to suggest they might do was never finished. The buzzer at the door sounded at that moment, and as the captain said, "Come in," the pair of conspirators looked up to see a little procession, composed of Dr. Perkins, his two assistants, Adam and Paulette coming in. The face of the chemist was alight.

"Gentlemen!" he exclaimed. "I am glad to say that our expedition is a success after all. I have found another sample of beryllium and tested it. There is no indication of isotope; the weight is correct, and it has been checked by these two gentlemen. We're saved."

There was a rasping sound from Professor Reuter's throat, but McCausland's saturnine face never altered.

"And where did this other sample come from?"

"From a different portion of the wall," replied Paulette. "I found it."

"Probably beryllium exists in both forms here," remarked the captain easily. "But in any case, I hardly see how that affects our problem. What do you propose to do?"

"Do! Load up with beryllium and head for home," cried Adam.

"Unfortunately the beryllium belongs to the Plutonians. They use it in these partitioned compartments to keep out the intensely cold ocean that surrounds their planet. I do not well see how we can deprive them of it, especially over their opposition." He gathered a sheaf of papers from his desk. "Here are the notes of a picture-conversation I have had with them. They naturally decline to part with their metal. I had the idea of taking some of this isotope beryllium back with us."

There was a moment's silence in the cabin, through which came the wheezing sound of Professor Reuter's breath, heavily indrawn.

"I know that," said Adam after a moment. "Because I have just been down

to the bottom of the dig, and held a picture conversation with the Plutonians. Would you be good enough to look at these, sir? The Plutonians say that they are only anxious to have these compartments built against the entrance of the ocean. When I offered to replace any beryllium we took with walls of our stronger steel alloy, they agreed at once to give us all we wanted. We can use the steel from compartment eighteen."

"Why . . . that's fine, Mister Mate." Captain McCausland seemed to be drawing his breath in with some difficulty. "I congratulate you. You may start work at once."

"Oh, my Lord!" said Reuter softly.

"HELLO, Earth! This is Paulette deVries, recording for later broadcast. This, folks, is our last day on the planet Pluto—our last day by earth time, though the Plutonians wouldn't recognize it. They seem to have no sense of time or time-telling instruments. I told you in our last record how the ship has been loaded with beryllium. We have her full now of as much of the metal as we can carry. Compartment eighteen has been cut away, and the ship neatly joined together along the line of the cut, the metal that armored the compartment has been worked over into partitions to replace the beryllium from Pluto.

"The entire crew has been given shore leave for this last day. Only Captain Mc-Causland and Professor Reuter will remain aboard the ship, with your radio gal, Paulette deVries herself. I have to work up my description of the interior of Pluto, gathered on my trip a few days ago.

"Just for the present I'll tell you it's a wonderful world down there—four thousand miles in the center of a planet, filled with streets and houses, plants grown by artificial chemical fertilization. Never any bad weather. The Plutonians who live here have told us in their picture language that this planet was the center of life in the solar system. Millions of years ago, when the sun was much larger, they sent out expeditions to the other planets, of which earth was one. We may be descendants of theirs. . . . Just a moment, there's someone at my door. Signing off."

She flicked off the key and opened the door to reveal Captain Walter McCausland.

"Oh, hello," she said.

"Paulette—Miss deVries," he said earnestly, "can you come to my cabin for a few minutes? I want to say something very important to you where we won't be interrupted."

"If it's important."

"It is." He stood aside for her to pass and they moved silently down the empty corridor to his cabin. When they were seated he looked at her seriously for a moment.

"I never asked you why you took it upon yourself to break off our engagement in so dramatic a manner.

"The reason was sufficient for me. It doesn't matter otherwise."

His lips drew back. "I suppose it has something to do with that young puppy of a mate."

"That, Captain McCausland, is none of your business."

He leaned forward. "Paulette, stop fencing with me. I'll be frank. You know that not everything has gone smoothly on this expedition. You may think you know the reason; perhaps you do. And then again, perhaps I know a lot more about it than you do. You think that the expedition is a great success so far, but I want to remind you that we're not home yet. We haven't even left Pluto and those queer people down there. I think—that is—if you really want to be certain that we will get back to earth with our load of beryllium, it might be an extremely good idea if you reconsidered your breaking the engagement."

She spoke with acidity.

"Captain McCausland, I still wouldn't marry you if you were the last man on earth. Anything else——"

The buzzer whirred and a voice spoke through the loudspeaker system. "Professor Reuter requests Captain McCausland's presence in the laboratory. Professor Reuter requests——"

The captain snapped his key, said, "Coming," and then turned to Paulette. "Wait here. I haven't finished. There's something more important——" and was gone, leaving her there.

IT was a chance for which she had long hoped. Perhaps she could discover why he seemed to be intent on wrecking his own expedition. She glanced about her noting every possible location for hidden things. There was the chart rack, full of rolled maps. Not likely. Then the bookcase, rows of neat bound volumes. There remained the desk and the safe. Methodically she examined drawer after drawer, feeling sure that nothing very important would have been left so loosely about. There was nothing—but what was this? A slip of paper on which were written four numbers and the words, "Changed 4/14/2432."

She pocketed it quickly.

Hastily she went to the safe and tried out the simple number locks—to find the handle swing instantly open! Its contents were two bundles of papers. The first consisted of ancient stock certificates. Her eye glanced at the name on one, one thousand shares of Niagara Hydro to Walter McCausland. Worthless old things . . . but *kept in the safe!* Then the light broke. She pieced together a dozen slight references from remembered conversations— Walter's warm liking for the ancient days of electricity and steam, his hatred of modern things. He had plotted to turn the world back four centuries; to destroy the whole system that had been built on atomic power. And, she realized as she explored the thick pile of stocks that he would be the richest man in that restored world. It was a wild dream, an insane one, yet she shuddered as she thought how nearly he had succeeded.

Idly she glanced at the other slab of paper—the drawn conversations with the Plutonians. Nothing else. But why were they also kept in the safe? She glanced hurriedly through them, frowned at one, and then gasped in sheer horror as she understood it. It was an incredible drawing of dwarf men who thrust taller humans into a tank of water, while other dwarfs bowed in a strange ritual. But the horror was for the vague thing drawn inside the tank—it was impossible, yet what mistake could there be? . . . She must hurry . . . hurry . . . yet she banged the safe shut and locked it, before leaving and rushing down the corridor with the bundle of drawings hugged to her gasping breast.

McCAUSLAND'S face was drawn with some nameless thought, but his eyes narrowed shrewdly enough when he saw the girl had left. Hastily he tried the safe and found it locked. Reuter came in and asked, "Where's the girl?"

"Gone back to her cabin, most likely."

The professor's eyes glanced idly over the floor and grew large. McCausland looked where he pointed. There between desk and safe lay a stock certificate!

Reuter was the first to recover his speech. "Left her alone here, eh? Try the safe. . . ." But McCausland was already opening it and together they stared at the empty space where the Plutonian drawings should have been.

"Search the ship!" snapped the captain. Then, "Well, Reuter, why are you looking like that?"

"You don't think she's," he licked his lips furtively, "gone down there with the others . . . trying to save them. . . ."

Captain McCausland, gray in the face, was shouting into the loudspeaker, "Paulette! Paulette!"

"She won't answer you, if she's seen those drawings," reminded Reuter.

Cursing, he rushed down the corridor to the open lock that connected with the Plutonian world below. Far down on the bottom he glimpsed a familiar tiny figure as it vanished from sight.

"Paulette! Come back." His voice was a hoarse scream. He leaned against the side of the lock and groaned.

"Walter," Reuter arrived panting, "she's gone. We can't help it. She turned you down anyway, didn't she? Let's get the ship out of here quick."

Walter's face was ghastly pale, but he straightened his back. "Do you think I'd leave *her!* Those other fools, yes! But not my girl, you old goat. She's *mine*, I tell you."

Reuter groaned.

"But they'll get you, too . . . you can't leave me alone here!"

The captain turned back, snarling. "That's right. I won't leave you. You'd start the ship and leave us all, wouldn't you! Very well; you're coming, too!"

A heavy hand dragged the screaming, protesting professor into the lock-door and pushed him savagely down on the rungs of the ladder.

ADAM herded the forty-six sight-seers from the *Goddard* into the room. He was a little puzzled. The Plutonians now, on the last day, not only permitted but actually suggested that the crew visit their sacred temple. He looked hastily around the ante-room, trying to keep the men in order. The half dozen scientists were everywhere, poking about into things with cries of excitement. Two strangely dressed guards began throwing open the temple door and everyone surged forward. Inside, they gazed open-mouthed. The huge room was three times as high as the usual low Plutonian ceiling, on which the earthmen frequently bumped their heads. At one end was a large gallery, ten feet off the floor, and here, tier on tier, were hundreds of the dwarfs. They rose at the moment and began reciting a sonorous chant.

In the center of the room, twenty feet square, milky blue, lit from unknown depths below, was a glass tank. Adam saw, with a gasp of horror and dread, the thing that floated in it—it was a huge Amoeba. He looked shrewdly about and noted the reverent attitude of the gallery. Could this horror be the Plutonians' deity? The Great God Amoeba? Nervous now, he glanced behind and shouted. The temple doors were closing!

"Wayland! Jake!" he cried, leaping to the doors. A dozen men turned and came on the run, but they pushed and battered in vain on the smooth metal as the doors clanged shut.

"We're prisoners!" snapped Adam. "Anyone bring a weapon . . . anything at all? Even a spanner, Bjornsen? A bomb-spear, Rossiter? Don't use it, fool, you'll kill us all! Well, we're in a hell of a fix! Our bare fists! Let's get at those dam' dwarfs on the balcony, anyway. Each fellow boost his neighbor up. Ready?"

They rushed in a mob, and though the ten-foot wall meant incredible height to the dwarf Plutonians, their front ranks drew back nervously, and the rearmost made for the exits. When they saw these earthmen climb on each other's shoulders and actually drawing themselves over into the gallery they broke in a panic and milled about the exits. Great Bjornsen was among the first and while the others turned to aid their companions, he charged roaring. But a dozen of the dwarfs, dangerous as trapped rats, threw themselves on him. Three went down with pile-driver blows, skulls cracked like egg-shells, but the giant was pulled down by sheer numbers and would have been killed on the spot had not a cry from the rear of the balcony saved him. The Plutonians were through the doors, which were held open until the engineer's assailants rushed through, whereupon they closed shut. The earthmen charged and raged against them five minutes before Adam called them back.

"Save your strength, men. This is a good place to keep together and wait. It's all we can do . . . they'll have to come at us some time."

MINUTES passed, slowly, watchfully. Nerves were tense to the breaking point. Then, on the ceiling low over their heads at the back of the gallery the familiar whining snarl of one of their own atomic drills broke out. Adam crouched, muscles ready for whatever might offer. The drill droned on and the point showed through. There was a pause and with a clang a great section of the ceiling was wrenched up and fell over on the floor above. And the opening framed the face of Paulette deVries!

"Come up!" she cried softly. "Oh hurry, hurry!" and into Adam's ear she poured her story, as soon as he had crawled on Bjornsen's shoulders to her side. Adam's voice immediately broke into action, urging the men to greater speed. He lay on his stomach reaching down to aid the climbers from below. Bjornsen was the last man, and as the strain of his weight fell on Adam's muscles he saw the door of the temple open and a vast mob of Plutonian guards rush in. Bjornsen was up now and Paulette tugging at Adam to come, too, but Adam had seen something—could it be! Yes, no mistake. There were two humans, still struggling, being carried across the temple floor to the great tank. A dozen dwarfs bore the leading man to its brink and with a great heave and a shout from the mob, he fell into the milky water. "It's the captain," groaned Adam, half-lowering himself as though to attempt a rescue. But Bjornsen's great arm gripped his leg. "The dirty rat," growled that giant, "he's gettin' what he planned for us. Anyway, it's hopeless, sir."

And as he dragged Adam away from the hole in the ceiling, he caught one last glimpse of Walter McCausland, frantic staring eyes pressed to the glass under water, as the great white Amoeba closed its flesh around him and the man's form became cloudy and, after a moment, ceased struggling.

"Oh Adam, hurry!" moaned Paulette.

They were in a low space, which extended in all directions, supported by squat pillars. "It's a sort of bulk-head space above their hollow world—separates them from the water above," explained the girl. "I broke into it from the dig-tunnel and if we hurry. . . ."

"Mr. Longworth, sir," a member of the crew broke in excitedly. "I've still got this bomb-spear. I can set it and time it to go off. Why not leave it here behind us, and blow this damn bulk-head to pieces. Wipe out that lousy nest of murderers." He gripped the missile in his hands, and bent over to place it against the bulk-head wall. Adam turned to him flashingly. "None of that, Rossiter. These people are only protecting themselves. And if we flood their world, we can never come back to it for more beryllium. Come along, we've got to move. . . . Did you hear me, Rossiter? I said to pick up that bomb and come along."

Rossiter looked at Adam with red, fury-filled eyes. "To hell with what you said," he screamed. "These lousy freaks killed Captain McCausland. They're not going to kill me! Do you hear? They're not going to kill me! I'll blow them all to hell first. Yes, and us, too. Let me go! They'll kill me, you fool! Let me go! Ah—a-a-a-ah!" He collapsed inertly to the floor of the tunnel.

Adam sucked his bruised knuckles, his eyes like bits of flint. His gaze stabbed at the silent circle of men around him. "Anyone else feel the same way?" he asked quietly. "No? All right, we'll go on. Petersen, pick him up and carry him along. He'll be all right. He cracked, poor devil."

They raced along the bulk-head, crouching in the confined space. After what seemed ages, Paulette gasped. "Just ahead of us . . . see it . . . there!"

The jagged hole in the wall appeared before them, but even as they tore madly toward it, it filled with a horde of seamed, wrinkled faces, and squat, ugly bodies. Adam knew there could be no hesitating. If they stopped now, they were lost. "Don't stop," he shouted. "Keep going. Right through 'em!" With a thudding shock the earthmen met the dwarfs. Bare fists rose and fell, flailing like sledge-hammers. The brown horde fell back before the onslaught. Countless numbers were down, skulls crushed like egg shells. Then suddenly the crunch of Bjornsen's fists cleared a gap, and the desperate crew plunged into it. Ahead of them was the dig-tunnel, with its ladder leading upward to the precious safety of the space-ship. The way was clear, for the astounded Plutonians had not had time to rally their scattered forces.

But Adam knew it would not be long before they did. Across the intervening space the little party dashed, straight for the opening of the dig-tunnel. Fifty feet. Just fifty feet above them was safety. But climbing the ladder with an unconscious man among them was torturingly slow work. Adam was the last to go up. As he passed the quarter mark, he heard the enraged shouts of the dwarfs behind him. He risked one quick look over his shoulder. They were already pouring into the tunnel, and the first ranks had started to swarm the ladder. "Hurry," he gasped. "They're coming up!" Like a snail he climbed. Rung by slow rung. Time stood still. There was no sound except the panting of the earthmen above, and the ever-nearing swish of small slippered feet below. Then Adam saw that the first of his crew had reached the ship, and were clambering through the port. He saw Paulette enter, and hands reached down to help Petersen and his unconscious burden. They could go up faster now. Another moment or two and they would be safe. Adam gasped in relief as he saw the open port close above him. Three more rungs. Two! One!

Something gripped his foot. Something

that pulled, and clung like a vise in spite of his frantic kicking. He looked down. Two of the Plutonians had grabbed him, and bracing themselves were pulling frantically. Helplessly he watched while long, powerful arms went out, closed about his other foot. He felt it pulled from the rung, and now he hung there, held only by his arms that grasped the rung above him. Arms that creaked in their sockets, until darting streaks of pain shot across his eyes. Hands that were wet with sweat, slipping . . . slipping. . . .

"Quick sir. Here!" Adam's staring eyes saw the huge figure of Bjornsen leaning from the port above him. But so far above him. The man could never reach him. Then he felt strong huge hands that gripped him by the arm-pits and pulled. Pulled until he thought his body must tear in two. But he was going up! With the last of his strength he kicked his feet viciously, trying to dislodge those straining, sinewy hands that gripped his legs. Then suddenly, they let go. Like a limp bag of sand he was hauled through the port, and lay gasping on the flooring. "Quick!" he croaked. "The door. Close it." With the clang of metal against metal he heard it shut, and lay back, drawing in great lungfuls of cool, refreshing air. After a moment he clambered rockily to his feet. His eyes met those of Bjornsen. His hand went out, and was clasped in the Norwegian's great paw. "Thanks," he said quietly. "I shall never forget that." He shook his head, and passed an aching arm across his eyes. Some measure of strength returned to him, and with it the realization that as officer in command, there was much to be done. "To your stations, men. Prepare to ascend immediately. Close the inner hatch. We're not safe yet. They have our atomic drills, and if they start to use them on the ship, we're lost. Mr. Wayland, come with me. Jake, to your engines."

With Paulette at their heels, Adam and Wayland hurried along the passages of the great ship until they reached the control room. "Engines ready, Jake?" he asked into the radiophone. "Stand by. Very well, Mr. Wayland. Six ascensions please."

Wayland gasped. "Six, sir! Why that'll

tear the ship to pieces. She won't stand it, sir!"

Adam fixed him with cool eyes. "I said six ascensions, Mr. Wayland."

Wayland opened his mouth to protest further, then closed it with a snap. "Very good, sir. Six ascensions, sir." He seized a lever to the left of the control board, moved it to neutral, then shoved it hard over. Six red lights glowed suddenly on the board. For a moment nothing happened, then deep in the bowels of the great ship a low, almost inaudible whine started. Like a siren it rose in pitch and tone, until it sounded like a hundred banshees screaming and wailing. A great shudder passed through the ship from stem to stern. Like a wounded beast struggling to rise she strained upward from the bottom of the icy ocean until it seemed she must tear herself to flying, screaming fragments. Wayland's eyes were filled with fear. Paulette stared unblinkingly, breathless, at Adam. Little beads of sweat stole out on his forehead, but with a calm he didn't feel he forced himself to keep his eyes on the panel before him. "Let me know the moment we're clear," he ordered. For a long minute no one spoke. Then from the control board a voice: "We're clear, sir."

Wayland's eyes lost their wild look. A great sigh heaved from his lips, and he slumped to trembling relaxation. Paulette uttered a single, glad cry, then sank gently to the floor, while great sobs racked her bowed head and trembling shoulders. "Reduce to two ascensions, Mr. Wayland." Adam's voice was hoarsely unsteady. "In two minutes plot your course and shift your engines. We're heading home." Then in two steps he was beside Paulette, was bending over to pick up the sobbing girl. He held her close, with her arms curved tightly around his neck, and her head buried in his broad shoulder.

IT was a quiet group that gathered some two hours later in the main cabin of the *Goddard*. Every member of the crew was there. Deep within the great hull the engines were running smoothly. Outside the glassed ports the dark blue heavens stretched away on all sides. Like the shimmer of a thousand diamonds against a velvet backdrop the suns of the Milky Way danced and glowed. At Adam's side sat Wayland and Paulette. Adam looked at those before him. "At ease, gentlemen. With the grace of good fortune we are on our way home. The expedition is a success. A success, that is, materially. As you all know, we have lost Captain McCausland and Dr. Reuter. If I am correct, you all know also the reason, and the manner in which we lost them. Perhaps Captain McCausland is not entirely to blame. Perhaps it is given to every great man to fail once. Whatever the reason, he has always been—up to this trip—a hero to all of us, and to the world. I must of course make a complete report of his death. That report will be: 'Killed by the Plutonians in defense of his ship and his crew.'"

For a long moment no one spoke. Then Paulette, with tears of happiness dimming her eyes, turned and gripped Adam's hand in her own. "My dear," she smiled, "thank you." As Adam turned to her, he felt Wayland gripping his other hand tightly. "I understand, sir. Nothing will be said." Adam smiled tenderly at Paulette, then his eyes turned anxiously to search those of his crew. On every face was a commending grin of approval. In every pair of eyes was a promise that had been given, and would be kept. With a suspicious huskiness in his voice, Adam drew himself erect. "Thank you gentlemen," he said softly. The crew filed out.

With his arm around Paulette, he drew her gently to the starboard port, and pointed to a dim, fast-receding, silver-green orb. "There it is, darling. I don't know whether to curse it or bless it." He grinned at her quizzically. She came close to him, and her arms stole gently about him. "I'll bless it as long as I live," she breathed.

He held her close. His head bowed to meet her soft, red lips.

"Beg pardon, sir." Wayland's voice sounded far away.

"Yes?" Adam did not turn his head.

"The course it set, sir. Any further orders, sir?"

"Yes, Mr. Wayland. One."

"Yes, sir?"

"Get out, Mr. Wayland."

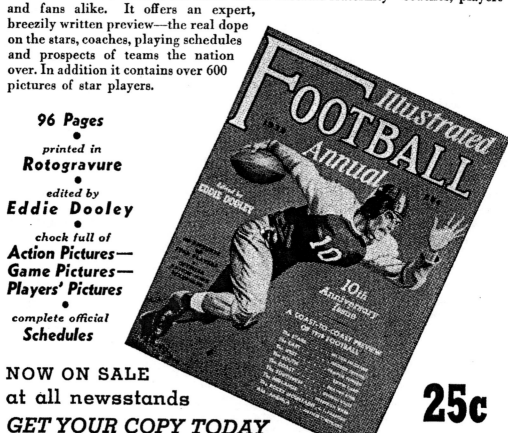

War-Lords of the Moon

By LINTON DAVIES

Bruce Ross, on the Earth-Moon run, asked a simple question, "How are the stars behaving, Harry?" But Harrell Moore could only stare at him in horror. For the stars had run amok—cosmic engines of destruction in the hands of the twisted genius of the Moon!

A FAINT quiver ran through the great hull of the rocket ship, and passed. The harsh drumming of her motors died to a singing drone. Flight-

Commander Bruce Ross nodded absently. The ship had shaken off the Earth-drag, and the speed indicator climbed fast. Eleven, twelve hundred miles an hour, the flagship of the rocket-ship fleet sped on its way to the Moon.

He moved to the forward telescope at the side of the control cabin and squinted at their objective. The pale circular bulk of the Moon loomed larger than when he had last observed it. He twisted to look through the rear telescope, and saw with satisfaction that the other seven ships of his fleet were following in echelon, each a mile and somewhat to the right of the one before it.

Ross grinned with pleasure. It wasn't his first trip to the Moon, but on that earlier occasion, when Magnus, King of the Moon People, had pledged a truce with the Earth's Council of Seven, he had commanded only the flagship. Now he had his own flagship, larger and more powerful that that outmoded rocket ship of five years ago, and seven more fighting ships besides. He strolled over to stand behind his navigator, plump, bespectacled Harrell Moore, who was squinting strainedly through the star-scope.

"How are the stars behaving, Harry?"

Moore's forehead was corrugated with concern. Without taking his eye from the scope he muttered softly, "Something funny going on, Bruce."

He moved back to let his chief step to the eye-piece. But before the flight-commander could take the seat a sliding door opened with a bang. The two turned, startled.

In the opening swayed a white-faced clerk. "Sir," he gasped, "there's trouble with communications!"

"Well?" snapped Ross.

The clerk brushed sweat off his brow. "The ray-type machine's gone dead, sir, and the ray-phone's crippled. We get only a weak muffled voice from the Council of Seven Headquarters!"

"How about the blinkers from the other ships?" snapped Ross.

"Blinkers are working, sir—" The clerk stopped short as Ross jumped to the rear of the control room.

"Jorgens!" snapped Ross. "Signal each ship, and ask if they've—they can get Seven Headquarters on the ray-type!"

"Aye, sir!" The signal chief hastened to the blinker buttons and began to rap out the message. He was half through it when a dull boom echoed like a sigh through the control room.

ROSS and Moore exchanged startled glances. Jorgens, white of face, looked up, his hand poised as if paralyzed over the buttons. Then Ross jumped to the rear telescope, which commanded a view of his following seven ships.

There were only six. Where the seventh—the last in the staggered-line—should have been, a faint glow filled the air. Ross stared at it, heart-sick. Was that blow the last sign of his rear guard? A rocket ship blotted out—destroyed! But how? How?

"Jorgens!" he snapped. "You had the Moon on the ray-type a while ago! Try to get that Peak One station again!"

"Aye, sir," breathed Jorgens shakily. He tapped the black key, rattling the call signal feverishly, then snapped on the receiver. The prong-like type fingers made no move.

"The ray-phone!" rasped Ross.

The signal chief plugged the yellow cylinder into its gray socket, and flashed the light beside it. "First Fleet, calling Peak One!" he chanted. "Peak One, answer First Earth Fleet!"

Ross, Moore and Jorgens held their breath. No sound came through the ray-phone trumpet. Jorgens lifted a gray face toward Ross.

The fleet commander smiled wryly. "Let it go, Jorgens. Check all the batteries and connections before you try again."

As Jorgens nodded and disappeared to trail the snaky coils of insulated ray-tubes to their battery reserves, Ross turned to Moore. "Number Eight's gone," he said softly.

Moore blinked. "Gone? Where?"

"Where the woodbine twineth," said Ross.

Moore's breath came faster. "Wiped out?" He whipped off his spectacles and polished them absently, his jaw working on his half-forgotten chew of tobacco. "Gone," he muttered dazedly.

A sudden thought struck Ross. He gripped his navigator's shoulder. "The stars! You said there was something funny going on!"

Moore's eyes flashed. "Yes!" He slapped his glasses on. "Come on! Let me show you!" He led the way to the star-scope.

Ross, following, stopped as a signalman approached with a typed message — the answer to the blinker call that Jorgens had started. The first sentence was short and blunt. "Number Two reports ray-type dead, ray-phone weak." Messages from the other five ships were identical except in the case of Number Seven. An added sentence from the last ship of the line stood out on the page and Ross felt sick inside as he read it. "Number Seven also reports explosion on right quarter where Number Eight was flying. No sign of Number Eight."

AT the star-scope Moore hovered as Ross applied his eye to the powerful lens. "That's Denabola you're on." The navigator's jaw worked, his eyes glittering.

"Dim," muttered Ross. "Clouds?"

"No!" exploded Moore. "Denabola was bright as ever, then suddenly went dim!"

Ross sat up quickly, a question in his staring eyes.

"You mean—the way the red stars go dim when we drain them of the red rays that power our ships and inter-planet communications?"

"Just that way," said Moore, blinking in excitement.

For a long moment their glances were locked. Then Ross heaved a stifled sigh. "This may mean a lot, Harry," he murmured. "I wonder if it might not even mean—"

"Whatever happened to Number Eight?" asked Moore quickly.

Slowly Ross nodded. "Let's see. Denabola's a blue star. Have you checked on any other blue stars?"

Moore took the seat at the star scope. "Only Vega. She's dim, too. Let me get Sirius." He twirled a knob at the side of the telescope barrel, then another, then straightened, with an explosive gasp. "Look at Sirius!"

Ross looked and caught his breath.

Sirius, the brightest star in all the firmament, was a dull lackluster thing.

Flight-Commander Bruce Ross sat back at the star-scope and pushed his space helmet off his head. He ran a steady hand through his unruly blond hair, smoothing out the tight wrinkles in his broad forehead as if to silence the urgent question that hammered in his brain. Something was happening in the heavens, and all his lore of flying and fighting might be none too much to set against the celestial puzzle.

"Harry," he asked finally, "the Moon Men know all about our red-ray work. Do you suppose they've gone to work somehow on the blue stars?"

Moore screwed up his face, blinking behind his glasses. "Well," he said finally, "there's Horta."

Ross nodded. "I was thinking of Horta," he admitted grimly. He had never forgotten Horta, Lord of the Moon Caverns, the darkly hostile savant who had held out so long at that fateful conference when the Council of Seven, rulers of the Earth, had made their all-or-nothing flight to the Moon, there to lay the question of peace or war before Magnus, the Moon King, and his lords. The Seven had won Horta over finally by offering him all the Earth secrets of the red rays that had made Earth-Moon travel possible. They had even set up a ray reservoir in Horta's great cavern, and had shown him how the harnessed rays could provide power for ships and explosive for sky-torpedoes. Yet Horta had never succeeded in building any but tiny ships that could barely circle the Moon, and he had denied any success with the torpedoes. Only on the ray-type and the ray-phone, essential to Earth-Moon intercourse, had he followed instructions with real results.

"BLUE rays, then?" muttered Ross, staring at Moore. He turned as Jorgens appeared hesitantly. "Well?"

"Garbled message by ray-phone from our Earth station, sir. From Censor Trowbridge, apparently." Jorgens handed over a sheet of paper. "We put it down as we heard it."

Ross and Moore bent over it eagerly. "...trouble...Moon...Four ..Magnus killed. . . ." It ended with ". . . bridge."

Ross wheeled on Jorgens. "Magnus— killed? Is that what you heard?"

Jorgens shook his head. "That's what it sounded like," he insisted. He flicked a hand at the ray-phone. "And that's all we got. She went dead on us. But," he added hopefully, "the ray-type seems to be coming to life."

"Good! Work on it, Jorgens. And try for the Peak One Moon station, or Peak Four." Ross watched Jorgens join the little group of signalmen toiling over the ray-type machine, and shook his head. "Did you get that, Harry? Magnus killed."

Moore blinked inquiringly. "Do we go on?"

"Go on?" Ross hesitated. He read the mangled dispatch, then squared his shoulders. "Nothing here about turning back. So on we go. Heaven knows what we'll find."

"Magnus dead." Moore shook his head. "Who takes over?"

"On the Moon? I happen to know, because it came up at the conference five years ago. Queen Boada and the two chief lords form a Council of Three. That'll be Boada, Horta and Artana, Lord of the Peaks. You remember him?"

"Sure." Moore wagged his jaws, chewing reminiscently. "Nice kid."

"Well, he was sixteen then. He'll be twenty-one, grown up. And say! Remember the Princess? Illeria. She was fourteen, she'll be nineteen now. Sweet kid."

"Skinny," grunted Moore.

"Yes," Ross agreed absently. "Well, we'll get a welcome from Boada and Artana. Maybe Horta will kick up a fuss, but he's the minority."

The ray-type machine came to life with a faint rattle. Jorgens watched it critically, then stared as the words ran out on the page. He waited for the sentence to finish, then snatched the sheet from the machine and held it out in trembling fingers to Ross.

The message was brief. Ross read it, shoved it at Moore, and grasped the orders tube. "Gun crews!" he sang out. "Load fore and after torpedo tubes and stand by!" He waited for the "Aye, sir!" to sound from both gun stations, then turned back to Moore.

The navigator was standing with jaw agape. He repeated the message word for word as if in a hypnotic spell. "Nagasaki destroyed. Purple Death."

Ross shook his arm. "Harry, snap out of it! We've got to fight!"

"Fight what?" asked Moore dazedly.

"I don't know," rapped Ross savagely. "But at a guess, I'd say the Purple Death, whatever that may be!"

II

THE assistant navigator looked back from his post by the helmsman. "Coming in to Peak One, sir," he called.

"What's our speed?" asked Ross.

"Two thousand, sir."

"Cut her down to a thousand," commanded Ross. "Any signals from the Peak?"

The navigator shook his head nervously. "None yet, sir. Shall I cut speed if they don't signal?"

"Yes," Ross decided. "Slow up as you see fit, and hover at fifty miles if they show no signal." He gestured to his chief navigator. "Come on, Harry, let's inspect ship."

The two passed from the control room to the gleaming engines. Here the silent engine crew hearkened to the pulse of the powerful rocket engine, and kept steady eyes on the gauges that showed the compressed ray fuel was feeding steadily into the discharger. Out of the engine room they passed to the after gun station. Ross tapped one of the six-inch torpedoes, and slapped one of the slim three-inch cylinders in the number two torpedo rack. "We may need them all soon," he told the station chief.

The gunnery chief's eyes widened. "We'll be ready, sir. Can you—is there anything I can tell the men about—Number Eight?"

Ross shook his head. "She's gone," he said briefly. "Might have been an accidental explosion—but I don't think so. We're landing soon. Just be ready, that's all."

He swung away to the forward gun station, saw that all hands were alert, and led the way back to the control room. Jorgens was pulling a sheet from the ray-type. He handed it over quickly.

It was from the Moon. "Warning to Earth Fleet!" it began. "Peak One wrecked. Come in on Peak Four." And it was signed "Artana."

Ross strode forward, his blue eyes blazing. "That's all, Jorgens?"

"No, sir. More coming now." He waited until the flying keys had rattled out two more lines, then ripped the sheet off. This message told more.

"Peak One wrecked by rebels who assassinated King Magnus. Signal systems at Peaks One, Two and Three destroyed. Greetings to Commander Ross. Artana."

"Rebels!" exclaimed Ross.

"Horta!" murmured Moore.

The chief signalman caught the name. "That louse!" he exclaimed in disgust. "Pretended we couldn't teach him anything, the time we set up his systems for him. He's raising hell on the Moon, Commander?"

Ross frowned. "That's just a guess, Jorgens," he reproved the signalman. "We only know this much for sure." He tapped the two sheets.

"Huh! Ten to one that blue-nosed devil's in it," grumbled Jorgens, turning back to the ray-type. "Want to answer, Chief?"

"Yes." Ross thought rapidly. He spoke in a low tone to Moore. "This might be a trap."

Moore blinked. "You mean, Artana sent this to decoy us in to Four and smash us?"

"Not Artana," corrected Ross. "Horta."

"Gosh, yes!" Moore fumbled his glasses off. "I hadn't thought of that! No reason why Horta couldn't send a message in Artana's name!"

"It's a possibility," Ross grinned sourly. He turned to Jorgens. "Send this: 'Greetings to Artana, Lord of the Peaks, from Ross. Coming in to Peak Four.' Repeat it, too, in case they aren't getting it any too clear." He wheeled to the helmsman, noted the speed was cut down now to six hundred miles, and nodded approval. "Change course for Peak Four."

Moore laid an urgent hand on his chief's arm as the helmsman obeyed. "Say," Bruce, this is risky!"

"Risky!" Ross laughed shortly. "Of course it's risky."

"Wouldn't it be better to stand off and wait for more news?"

Ross shook his head. His eyes blazed. "Harry, there's a lot of hell breaking out on the Earth and on the Moon, too. We're in the middle. We can't be in both places, but we can find out—I hope—what's going on up here. And if we do, maybe we can put a heavy foot on what's happening to the Earth. Do you remember what Trowbridge's message said?"

Moore's ordinarily placid features tightened. "The Purple Death," he whispered. "You're the boss, Bruce. All I want is to get in on whatever happens!"

THE Earth Fleet slid slowly down to the craters. The pale surface of the Moon gleamed dully, phosphorescent, lambent where the rays of the sun struck crater tops. Off to the left the High Peak, Peak Number One to the Earth visitors, loomed dark and sinister.

But Peak Four showed all its lights, bright and steady. Ross ordered the six following ships to stand off and await orders, or act on their own judgment if the flagship came to harm. Then he took his place beside the helmsman. "Take her down slow," he ordered.

The rocket ship glided straight and sure for the brightest light. Slowly the pinpoint of white fire became a circle, then an oval. Then it broke up into hundreds of lights surrounding a platform. The helmsman muttered an order, and the rocket ship, answering the urge of her flippers, dived briefly and straightened out into a glide. From the control windows the shape of the platform took form, and dim little figures could be seen scurrying on its edges.

Moore fidgeted uneasily. "We'll be duck soup for them if it's Horta," he muttered.

Ross chuckled. "Where's your sporting blood?" he jibed. "Bet you even money it's Artana."

"That's an easy bet for you," retorted Moore. "You won't live long enough to pay off if it's Horta."

The crew of the ship seemed to share his fears. Every man hunched tense at his station. The ship glided lower, to three hundred feet. Two hundred. She lost way almost entirely, and grounded with scarcely a jar.

"Nice set-down," Ross complimented the helmsman.

Instantly the crew sighed in unison. Tension was broken. They peered through the windows.

"Back to your stations!" rapped Ross. He glanced through the control port and immediately saw a group advancing toward the ship. For an instant he held his breath. Then he whooped. "It's Artana!"

The crew cheered, briefly, knowing nothing of the importance of that single identification. Two artisans stood by the gangway, waiting.

"Secure your helmets, men!" shouted Ross. He adjusted his own headgear, made sure that the thin tubes from his breastplate were feeding their tiny jets of oxygen to his nostrils, and signaled to the artisans. They threw the door wide, and Ross stepped forth to meet Artana.

The young Lord of the Peaks came forward with a glad cry. "Ross!" he exclaimed, and grasped the Earth-man's hand warmly.

"Artana!" cried Ross. He eyed the Moon Lord from head to foot, and grinned. "You've grown, Lord of the Peaks!"

THE boy he remembered was indeed now a man. Matching the six-foot Ross in height, he stood straight and slender, carrying easily the weight of the ray-rifle slung on his shoulder, and the poison-pistol at his belt. He smiled briefly at the Earth-man's sally, then sobered at once.

"You come at a critical time," he murmured, pitching his voice so that his half-dozen followers could not hear. "The Moon People are divided by revolt, and the fate of the Kingdom is not easy to predict." He caught sight of Moore.

"Ah, my friend Harrell Moore!" His hand went out in a warm clasp.

"Hi, Artana," returned the navigator awkwardly. "You're looking great. What's the trouble? I'll guess it's Horta."

"Softly!" Uneasily the Lord of the Peaks glanced about him. "Let us go to the Peak Chamber, where we may speak at ease." He led the way from the platform, halting only to allow Ross to relay an order for his six ships to land. Through a winding subterranean corridor they hastened to the council room of the Peak, which marked the administrative center of one of Artana's provinces. Once inside the great room, Artana led them to low divans of stone, covered and made comfortable with soft cellulose-like stuff that rustled as they moved. He gave them the news bluntly, without preamble.

"Horta has seized power in two-thirds of the Kingdom," he cried, his voice breaking with emotion. "King Magnus was killed, perhaps not by Horta's orders—but who else would have plotted it? The assassination seemed to be the signal for an uprising—and Horta issued a proclamation, as one of the three regents, declaring that he would act to preserve order in the Caverns and the land beyond where the Crater folk live. Three of the Peaks were overrun, and the signal systems were all destroyed. Here at Peak Four, my soldiers were ready, and all the rebels were slain."

"Queen Boada—and the Princess Illria?" asked Ross.

"They are safe." Artana twisted on his couch in his distress. "They were at Peak Five when the attacks were made, and are coming here, escorted by a strong body of my troops. I expect them soon. But you, my friends? How can I receive you, when my people are embroiled in civil war —for that is what it is?"

Ross waved his hand deprecatingly. "Don't worry about us, Artana. Of course, we can't take sides here. We can help to preserve the Regency, since the Truce demands it. But there's one thing I'd like to ask."

"Of course, my friend."

"Have you heard of trouble on the Earth?"

Artana looked up quickly. "We have had no word."

"Or—well, trouble in the sky?"

Artana shook his head, puzzled.

Ross answered his unspoken question. "One of our ships was destroyed on our flight from the Earth. And I don't think it was an accident."

"A rocket ship?" Artana sat up. Then his eyes flashed. "Horta?" he murmured, as if asking himself a question.

Moore leaned forward. "Has Horta been up to anything in the ray business?" he asked eagerly.

Artana shook his head slowly. "Lord Horta and his savants have made progress in employing the R-ray, drawn from the red stars, as you taught him." He knit his brows. "I have heard of nothing else —but wait. He and his most learned men have worked secretly for many moons, I know not to what purpose. You think—"

"We think," cut in Ross grimly, "that it's possible that Lord Horta may be cooking up something new in the ray field."

Artana's face darkened. "If that is true," he murmured, "we may have the explanation of the disappearance of two of my brigades. I sent them out in force to scout Horta's territory. No word has come from them." His hand clenched. "A war of rays—here on the Moon!"

ROSS and Moore exchanged uncomfortable glances. They had fought in the terrible war on the Earth when nations battled with the new red ray, and whole fleets of the ancient steel warships were sunk by the first of the ray-torpedoes, before the Council of Seven was formed to rule all Earthly affairs. And they had served in that first Moon-flight, and had slain with rays the first Moon armies who had resisted the intrusion of the Earth-fleet. Was history to repeat itself—in reverse, with Horta's Moon machines raking the Earth with death? Perhaps that strange Purple Death of the Trowbridge message?

Ross made his resolve. "If your armies can't find out what Horta's doing, Artana, perhaps my fleet can."

"Your fleet?" Artana looked up, a flicker of hope in his somber eyes. "You mean that you would fly over the Caverns?"

Ross nodded. "And study the work he has done. Photograph it, and report to you and the Queen. If you then wish us to try to destroy it, I'll take the responsibility. I feel that the Council of Seven would approve."

Artana stood up, his eyes alight. "Ah, Ross! If you succeed, and bring peace to the Moon people, your planet and mine will do you homage!"

Ross flushed sheepishly. "Well, maybe. For my part I'd rather be overlooked. You know, there's an old, old saying where I come from, 'A hero today, a bum tomorrow.'"

"A 'bum'?" echoed Artana, puzzled.

"A-a sort of—" Ross remembered in time that there were no beggars on the Moon. Nor panhandlers, nor paupers, nor hobos. "Oh, never mind. We'll take off in the first hour of light, and see what we can see."

"In the meantime," Artana hastened to say, "You must sleep." He ushered them into a circular chamber, the elevator that would take them to the spacious underworld of the Moon. Closing the door, he pressed a button. The resultant motion was almost imperceptible, but Ross and Moore knew they were being hurtled toward the Moon's core at hundreds of miles an hour. Almost instantly the chamber stopped, the shock of cessation being oddly cushioned. Artana opened the door, and the three stepped into the great rotunda whence radiated the life and activity of the Province of Peak Four. Moon people hurried to and fro, only a few stopped to stare at the Earth-men. Bakers were hawking the curious brick-shaped loafs of bread, and the fruits that had grown from the seeds from the Earth were stacked on stands. Drapers stood by their gossamer-like fabrics. Soldiers hurried to and fro in squads, and their presence explained to Ross and Moore the inhabitants' disinterest in the Earth-men.

The spacious chamber to which Artana led them was guarded by two tall sentries, and tastefully furnished. The Lord of the Peaks cast a last glance about, said, "I shall call you at the first light," and vanished.

Moore sank gratefully down upon a high-piled bed. "Well, if this is to be my last night's sleep, I'm going to do well with it."

"You're always worrying," chaffed Ross. But he lay, awake, mind racing, long after Moore's even breathing denoted that the chubby navigator's fears had succumbed to his fatigue.

III

ARTANA awakened them as he had promised. His first words were of the widowed Queen. "Boada is here," he told Ross. "She has slept, and will greet you after you have eaten."

They breakfasted in the chamber, on food that Artana had commandeered from the rocket ship, with some of the pale, delicious Moon pears beside the familiar Earth fare. Artana talked fast as the two Earth-men ate.

"Two of the Cavern men came in with the Queen." As the two flyers looked up in plain surprise, he smiled. "Yes, they were Horta's men. But they say they do not wish to serve him longer. They say he plans to rule the Moon Kingdom alone, and will make war with the Earth."

The two leaned forward, food forgotten. "Did they say," asked Ross, "how Horta plans to make war? With what weapons?"

Artana shook his head sadly. "They deny all knowledge of such things. They are star savants, and they say all Horta's war secrets are known only to his war chiefs."

The flyers' disappointment impelled Artana to go on. "They do say that Horta and most of his forces are gathered in the Great Cavern, where all his secrets are kept. And that, too, is where he has set up his ray machines."

Ross narrowed his eyes. "The Great Cavern, eh? Well, that's what we'll have a shot at."

"You would have me accompany you?" Artana asked eagerly.

"Ah, no, Artana. You are needed here. What if Horta were to make a sudden attack? You must give us a guide, though, to show us the Great Cavern. And I will leave my chief signalman, Jorgens, so that we may keep in touch with you."

Artana assented, somewhat cast down. Truly, the Great Cavern held a secret, and the Lord of the Peaks was as eager as any to learn it. But he regained his cheerfulness as they sought out the Queen.

She was in the great chamber where Artana had first received the Earth-men. Erect and haughty, she sat on the central divan, regarding them with brooding eyes as they entered. So much Ross saw before his glance went to the slim figure beside her. He caught his breath.

A dream! A goddess! This girl—ah, yes, the Princess Illeria. But a woman now! Not the scrawny girl of five years ago. Ross tore his eyes from her with a jerk. Artana was presenting him to the Queen Widow.

"—Commander Ross, leader of the Earth-fleet, was a visitor at court five years ago," Artana reminded the Queen.

She extended her hand, surveying him with a softening of her austere expression. As he bent over it she said in a harsh voice that was obviously held steady with an effort, "Commander Ross, you come at an unhappy time."

Ross murmured condolences, then plunged into the subject that was filling him with impatience. "I seek permission from you, Queen, and from the Lord Artana to fly over the Caverns and report on conditions there."

Queen Boada darted a sharp glance at Artana, then averted her head. "I see no occasion for such a flight," she said curtly.

Artana stepped forward. "A rebellion, O Queen? Surely that is occasion enough?"

She met his eyes, frowning. "But these are not our people."

"Yet," argued Artana, "the Earth people are at peace with us."

Ross saw the Princess regarding her mother curiously. Moore, too, was staring in frank astonishment at the Queen. As she sensed their intent regard she relaxed her rigid pose. "Oh, very well. But there shall be no fighting?"

"None, O Queen," Ross hastened to say.

Artana nodded with satisfaction. "There remains, then, the finding of a guide for the fleet. I could send Calisto—"

The Princess spoke for the first time. "Calisto has not the gift of the Earth-tongue. Who guides the Commander Ross must speak the tongue he knows best."

"That's true," muttered Artana, taken aback. "Who, then—"

THE Princess was looking at Ross. Almost hostilely, he thought confusedly. Had she resented his long open stare? She was such a picture, clad in only a single filmy garment, caught at the waist with a gold twisted belt and cut tunic-like at the knee. Bare-armed, with softly swelling contours and a skin like peach down, she was an entrancing sight.

His confused thoughts were set at rest. The Princess had a plan. "I shall go with the Commander Ross," she said.

The Queen turned sharply. Artana scowled. "No, no!" he cried sharply. "If there should be fighting—"

"Fighting?" echoed Boada in a whip-like tone.

"No, no, not fighting," Artana hastened to correct himself. "But danger, perhaps."

Boada's brooding gaze came to rest inquiringly on Ross.

"There can be no danger, I think," he assured her. And wondered why he did so. For if Horta was on the war path, surely the Earth ships would be his targets.

He felt his heart beat faster as he considered the possibility of this amazing girl standing beside him in the control room of his flagship, then a moment of depression as he reflected that the queen would refuse her consent. But to his surprise Boada, after one dark look at the Lord of the Peaks, nodded.

They left at once. There was a moment of delay when Illeria, given an oxygen helmet, demurred at the idea of wearing it until she was convinced that it would save her life if the shell of the rocket ship were pierced in the upper air. She wore it with ease, the straps fitting snugly over the flowing golden locks and the oxygen tubes crossing her face to add to the piquant enigmatic look she wore.

The flagship took off with a rush, the six following ships keeping their distance.

Once in the air, they formed the echelon. Then Ross turned to the princess, and led her to the telescopes trained through the floor of the ship.

She studied the crater surfaces wonderingly, like a child with a strange toy. Then she remembered her duty. "Sail there," she directed, pointing.

Amusedly, Ross gave the order. Privately Artana had given him a full description of the Great Cavern, so that once he had sighted it he could map his own course. But the girl had guided him truly. In a few minutes the yawning chasm lay on their bow.

He called Moore. "All the cameras set?"

"All set," grunted Moore, squinting through a glass. "Going to skirt the cavern?"

Ross nodded. "No use tipping Horta off at the outset. We may get a good look without his knowing we're here."

As the last word left his lips a cry from the port lookout froze the three in their places. They turned, fearfully. The lookout's face was working. As they watched, tears began to stream down his face. He tried to speak, but he could only point.

Ross sprang to the window. The sky was clear, save for the following ships. Number Two, and Four, and Five. Six? Where was Six? And Seven? He whirled on the lookout.

The man gulped, drew a deep breath, and said huskily, "There was a flash, sir, and—and then—nothing! Nothing, where Number Seven was flying! And then Number Six—went the same way!"

Ross and Moore stared frantically at one another. Then Ross sprang to the signal post. "Jorgens! Where's Jorgens?"

A white-faced signal-man spoke up. "He's back at Peak Four, sir."

"Oh, yes." Ross in his agitation had forgotten. "Well, signal Ships Two, Three, Four and Five to sheer off the Cavern and return to Peak Four!"

The man sprang to obey. Ross turned to order the course changed. But the crashing din that followed silenced him. His body hurtled against the stanchion, and suddenly he found his arms about the Princess Illeria.

HER body was soft to his touch, her silky hair caressed his cheek, her breath sweet on his face. But he pushed her aside, and cried out to the helmsman, "How does she fly?"

The helmsman, craning his neck as he curled an arm about the wheel, shouted back, "On even keel, sir, but she won't steer!"

Ross pushed the Princess unceremoniously from him and stood erect. He rushed to the window and saw with relief that the ship was circling away from the Crater. Gauges showed that the ship flew steady except for that odd circling. An artisan, bursting into the control room from the after gun station, explained the mystery.

"One rudder flange haywire, sir!"

"So that's it!" Ross spoke calmly. "Shot away?"

The man's face worked. "Burned away, sir!"

"Burned—" Ross thought fast. He nodded to the artisan, who departed with a scared look about.

Moore had heard the report. He whistled. "Burned away, huh? Sounds like a B-ray."

"B-ray? What's that?" snapped Ross.

"B for blue," explained Moore affably. "Horta's draining the blue stars, or I'm no Harvard man."

Ross eyed the navigator narrowly. "You really think that?"

"What else?" countered Moore calmly. "Horta was a washout on the R-ray—and besides, our red ray doesn't burn like that. I think Horta's got something."

Ross turned to the helmsman, then studied the chart that Artana had provided. "We can circle just like this, and make Peak Four if we can cut that drag a bit. Try reducing the speed."

It worked. At reduced speed the ship flew more truly, with less pressure on the rudder. Ross sighed in relief. "Keep her there." He spied the Princess leaning against the stanchion, and walked over. "Quite a scare, wasn't it?"

She regarded him steadily. "You do not like me?"

He gaped at her. "Why do you say that?"

"You pushed me away from you."

"Oh, that!" Ross was nettled. "A man must fight his ship, Princess."

"Yes." She nodded agreement. "But I was afraid. I thought we were doomed. And I wished you to be with me. It is not given to every woman to die with the man of her choice. And you are the man I wish for."

Ross stared open-mouthed. "Say-ay!" he asked cautiously. "You didn't get a knock on the head, did you?"

She shook her head unsmilingly. "The Earth-girls, they do not speak so to men?"

"I'll say they don't," Ross assured her feelingly.

"Oh!" said the Princess Illeria in a small voice.

Ross didn't know what to say then. "Well," he exclaimed, "we'll soon be back at Peak Four."

He was right. But grim news awaited them at the peak.

IV

ARTANA met them, his face a thundercloud. He handed Ross a ray-typed message. "This came just before you landed," he said tensely.

Before Ross could read the message, the name signed to it caught his eye. Horta! The Lord of the Caverns was coming out of his silence! And with what a greeting! "Know, O Queen," read Horta's message, "that I have destroyed three of the Earth-ships, as I shall destroy all who fly against the destiny of the Moon Kingdom. Know, too, that I have destroyed a second Earth city, the place called Los Angeles, as a warning to the Earth people that their destiny is not ours."

Ross read it with a sinking heart. Los Angeles! A city of two million people, destroyed! Then it was Horta who had wiped out Nagasaki!

Moore pounced on that thought. "Nagasaki, then Los Angeles!" he muttered.

Ross turned to Artana. "Any other news?"

Artana shook his head. "No. But I have a plan. You know that when the rains come we store them in the great reservoirs, so that our under-world may not be flooded. Then why not loose the waters in the reservoirs, and flood the caverns?"

Ross stared in admiration. But he slowly shook his head. "You'd have to kill half your people, Artana, just to dispose of Horta."

"But," argued Artana desperately, "Horta will destroy half our people himself, to seize the Kingdom. And he will destroy the Earth folk, too!"

Moore spoke up. "The reservoirs are full?"

"No," admitted Artana. "The rains have not been heavy. The reservoirs are but half full." He sighed. "Horta might escape the flood."

"That's no good, then," Ross said emphatically. "Tell you what, Moore and I will go and scout the Cavern on foot. We may be able to get near enough to the ray works to smash 'em."

"You would die," Artana said somberly. "Horta guards his Cavern well."

Ross nodded. "Maybe. But there's no other chance. Horta can knock us down out of the air, and he's knocking Earth cities to dust. He must be stopped. If we die, you can hold out on the Peaks, and flood him out when the rains come."

"That's right, Artana," Moore agreed. "But let me go, Chief. I'll take a couple of good men. You stay here."

"No dice, Harry," Ross assured him firmly. "I'm the head man and it's my job. I'd like to have you along, though."

"Sure," said Moore mildly.

Artana regarded them with admiration. "You are brave men! But what can I do?"

"Just sit tight, Artana, and wait for the rain to fall," grinned Moore. "And when it comes, avenge us."

"That will I!" swore Artana.

THEY set out in the dark, Moore and Ross and the guide whom Artana had indicated with a gesture. They had covered only half a mile when Ross turned sharply, suspiciously, to the guide. "Sure you speak the Earth tongue?" he demanded. "If you do, why can't you say something?"

The guide threw back the cowl-like head

covering and Ross caught his breath. "Illeria! What are you doing on this tour?"

"I go to die with you, my lord," said the princess simply.

"My lord!" squawked Moore. "Excuse me!" He walked forward hurriedly.

Ross, his face burning in the gloom, took Illeria's arm roughly. "This is no job for you, Princess! There will be danger!"

"Even death," agreed the slim princess equably. "No matter. And the Lord Artana is agreed that I go."

"Artana agreed?" Ross was taken aback. He looked ahead to where Moore waited, looked back over the way they had come, then shrugged. "Oh, well! Here we go!"

Happily Illeria caught his arm, and they strode forward. Moore chuckled in the dark. "Everything settled?"

"Yes, dammit," grated Ross. "Did you ever see such a mess?"

Moore's reply was sober. "We couldn't have a better guide," he pointed out. "And we know the princess is loyal. How could we be sure of some other guide? A jigger who might sell us out to the first Horta sentry?"

ROSS grunted agreement, and they trudged on. They saw no one, heard no one, until the first of the craters lay behind, and the Moon terrain sloped down and down into the caverns. They came upon the first two sentries suddenly. Both swung their ray-guns up, but Moore was quicker. His gas-pistol spat twice, and the sentries crumpled.

"Are they dead?" asked the princess, amazed.

"Dead to the world—er, I should say, dead to the Moon," Ross assured her. "They'll stay that way twelve hours, which ought to be long enough for us."

Moore chuckled. "Before then we'll be on top of the world—I mean on top of the Moon—or dead heroes."

The way was easy, a steady down slope, for a while. Then the rock formations began. They slipped and crawled. The princess suffered a cut on her knee, but shrugged at the suggestion of a bandage. The second set of sentries were easily overpowered. They lolled at ease against a ridge, and Ross shot twice to gas them to sleep. Here the light was better, and Ross paused to look them over. They were darker than the Peak men, with less color, and their veins stood out against their blue-white skin. They bore the ray-rifle of all the Moon soldiers, and another curious weapon besides, a jagged-edged sword with a hooked point.

"It's the old Moon sword," said Illeria. "Horta worships the old customs, and swears by the beliefs of the astrologers. It's the astrologers who direct his actions, my mother had said."

"It's a dirty weapon," shuddered Moore. "I'll take a ray-gun any time."

He came within an ace of regretting his choice a moment later, when a whole squad of soldiers rounded an outcrop of rock. Ross whispered a warning, and shot fast. Moore went into action then, but not be· fore one of the Horta men had fired. The ray blasted past them and sheared off a half-ton of rock behind them.

"Whew, that was close," gasped Moore as the last of the soldiers fell.

"How about ray-guns now?" gibed Ross. "Do you know, I think we're in luck. This party is evidently supposed to relieve the sentries we met—so there'll be no alarm over their condition."

"You're right!" exclaimed Moore. "Now all we have to do is to get to that ray machine!"

They stood within sight of it when the heavy hand of Horta fell.

IN the shadows of the cavern they had crept from arsenal to foundry, until they had inspected from far or near every establishment in this dim and fearsome chasm. And finally they saw it, a great cylinder nestling deep in the ground and looming high in the cavern, supported by guy beams of gleaming metal.

"A ray-gun!" cried Moore. His incautious exclamation was their undoing. A half-clad foundry worker, looking like a gnome in his eye-shade helmet and drooping gauntlets, gaped at them. Ross shot a split second too late to stop the shout of alarm. The foundryman dropped, but a dozen soldiers came on the run. Moore and Ross fired and fired again, but they went down in a charge of scores of Horta soldiers. The flat of a sword struck Ross a stunning blow on the side of his head.

He came to his senses to find himself in a strange room, bound hand and foot and prone on a stone floor. Beside him was Moore.

"Where are we?" muttered Ross.

"In Horta's headquarters," whispered Moore. "Here's Horta."

Ross twisted his head. He blinked. For Horta was an eyeful.

The Lord of the Caverns was a giant. Fully seven feet tall, he must have weighed four hundred pounds. But he bore his great bulk with ease and a certain dignity. He strode over to the two prisoners, looked them over with curiosity but without visible rancor, and spoke sharply to a guard in the Moon tongue. The guard hastened to free the two flyers.

They exchanged glances of surprise. "You don't suppose he's a pal in disguise?" asked Moore blandly. He looked up with a start when he heard a rumbling chuckle.

Horta was amused. "No, Earthman. You are prisoners. But I have no need to bind you, for you cannot escape. Yet you need not fear death, for if you will stay and serve me you shall have life and all the blessings that will be showered upon a new Kingdom."

"New Kingdom?" Moore blinked. "It's a Regency, isn't it?"

Horta's great laugh boomed out. "Nay! I am the King! And for my queen— well, you have delivered her to me!"

Ross sat up and stared. "You mean— Illeria?"

Horta chuckled as he nodded.

"Illeria!" Ross stifled a curse. His mind raced. The girl was a prisoner, too. He spoke aloud, easily. "Well, I guess we can give Your Royal Highness a hand."

"Hey, Bruce!" Moore expostulated. "You don't mean——"

"Why not?" drawled Ross. Turning to face Moore, he winked. "We know a lot that will pay our way with the new Kingdom."

Moore blinked. "Of course!" he assented hastily. "Sure!"

Horta stared suspiciously at the two flyers. "Make sure, then, that you have no secret longings to return to Earth," he warned heavily. "For henceforth there shall be no intercourse between Moon and Earth. The truce is ended."

Ross ventured a question. "What'll you do with the men of the Peaks?"

Horta smiled grimly. "They will submit, or die." He gestured imperiously, and the guards pushed the flyers forward as Horta strode from the room.

As they trailed behind, Moore whispered, "He doesn't look like a killer."

"Probably a fanatic," Ross muttered.

"What's the play?"

"Watch our chance, and wreck the ray machine."

"And us with it," grumbled Moore.

"Most likely," Ross agreed.

They entered a softly lit room, in the wake of Horta. As their eyes became accustomed to the dim light they gasped. There was Illeria. But beside her was the queen—Boada!

SHE swept them with a glance in which contempt was mingled with a kind of pity. "You did not expect to see me here," she said harshly. "But I serve the destiny of the Moon. The wise men have shown me that the Moon was never destined to serve the Earth, but must stand with the Blue Stars when the Universe is rent asunder. And now the Moon is ready to defend itself, thanks to the new King Horta!"

In the silence that followed Ross heard the girl gasp. The queen spoke softly. "And you, my daughter, shall be the new queen, wife of the almighty Horta the Liberator."

"Not," Ross muttered between his teeth, "if I can help it."

"Me, too," whispered Moore.

The girl said nothing. But her eyes sought Ross with piteous entreaty.

Horta broke the silence. "The nuptials shall be solemnized in tomorrow's full light. You, Earthmen, shall remain under guard until you have given earnest proof of your fealty."

The guards punched the two as Horta rapped an order in the Moon tongue, and they allowed themselves to be led away. Through a dim corridor they passed, and into a stone cell, with oddly fashioned stone bars and a door that slid on a metal base, locking them into their tomb.

Ross circled the cell, then shook his head. "We couldn't get out of this without a ray machine," he muttered.

Moore sat down against a wall. "Guess not. Say, Bruce, did you hear the old girl?"

"The Universe is to be rent asunder," grunted Ross. "Where does that leave us?"

"Behind the eight ball, as I believe they used to say back in the twentieth century," grinned Moore. "That is, that's where we would be if the Universe really were to be rent asunder."

"Oh!" grunted Ross in heavy sarcasm. "So it isn't going to happen?"

"Gosh, no," chuckled Moore. "It's the silliest kind of astrological fake, discredited two centuries ago. Where Horta picked it up I don't know. Probably he got some power from the blue stars by accident, and his faker astrologists strung him along on the big bust-up idea."

"Nice clean fun," muttered Ross. "Well, we missed. Horta's still got his ray machine. He's also got the princess—and the queen for an ally."

"He's also," amended Moore dryly, "got us."

"And how," grunted Ross. "How long do you suppose we'll last if we don't—"

He stopped abruptly. A faint noise came to his ears. "Hear that?" he asked, puzzled.

Moore cocked his head to one side. "Running water," he remarked. "They haven't got a river down—"

A scream, faint and far away, took his breath away. Another sounded, and then a chorus, dimmed by space and the stone walls. Suddenly Ross and Moore whirled to face one another.

"Artana!" cried Ross.

"He's opened the reservoirs!" gasped Moore.

They leaped to their feet. Ross tried the door, savagely. Moore broke the skin of his hands on the stout stone bars of the window. In a moment, water was swirling at their feet.

Moore stared down at it gloomily. "I was two days on a raft in the middle of the Atlantic," he sighed, "and I didn't drown."

The water rose to their knees.

V

ROSS tugged at the door. "You aren't drowned yet. How did this door open?"

"From the outside," grumbled Moore, tugging with his chief. "It rolled—ha! It's opening! We've got it!"

The door was sliding open. A rush of water swept them half off balance, and they splashed into the flood when the Princess Illeria catapulted into them.

"Princess!" yelled Moore. "Good girl!"

Ross gripped her arm. "What's going on?"

"Panic," she panted, clinging to him. "Horta and his steadiest men are at the ray machine, fighting to keep the water out of the ray reservoir. The Queen went with him. I'm—afraid—"

"Cheer up," Ross consoled her. "And let's get out of this." He led the way out of the cell. Water was waist deep in the corridor. Ross pointed up an incline, where the swirling waters ran thinly. "Looks good," he suggested. He whirled then on Illeria. "Where do you suppose we could get some guns?"

"What good would they do?" growled Moore.

"There's that ray machine," Ross reminded him.

"Oh! Yes. But—" Moore shot a glance at the Princess. "Don't forget—the Queen—"

Ross scowled. "I know."

Illeria touched his arm. "If the Queen must die, that the Moon people and the Earth folk may be saved, let it be so," she urged simply.

The two men bit their lips.

"Come!" urged the girl. "There is a guardroom above. There must be weapons."

"I could use one of those antique hook-'em swords on old Horta," growled Moore.

They burst into the guardroom prepared for sudden and violent action. But the great chamber was empty of Moon men.

On the walls hung ray rifles. Ross and Moore each snatched one.

"Now where?" asked Moore.

Ross surveyed the room. Windowed on all sides, it had only two doors, the one they had entered and another opposite. "We'll try that," Ross decided. "What we've got to find now is a spot that commands the square where the ray machine is bedded."

The sloping corridor led them to such a spot. On a balcony they stood and for a moment were content to watch Horta's artisans toiling with sandbags and debris to make barricades against the flood.

"They'll do it, too," Moore said aloud, voicing his chief's thought.

"Artana's trick was probably just to help us out," Ross judged. "He hadn't enough water to flood 'em out."

Moore fidgeted. "Let's do something, Bruce! There's that ray reservoir. Think these pop-guns will punch a hole in it?"

Ross raised his rifle, and lowered it as suddenly. For into sight, beside the giant Horta, walked Queen Boada. Moore exclaimed under his breath, fingering his rifle.

It was the Princess Illeria who, snatching the rifle from Moore's hands, leveled it swiftly and fired. As Ross sought to snatch it from her she faced him defiantly. "Let destiny rule us!" she exclaimed. "My mother is an unhappy woman who stands in the way of peace. Let me fire again!"

Her demand left Ross irresolute. As he held her hand, Moore cried out. "They spotted that shot, Bruce! They're looking for us!"

It was true. Horta stood, legs spread, his fierce glance sweeping the open space. Workers had begun to drop sandbags and pick up guns. Ross loosed his hold.

"Let's fire together, then," he said heavily. "The double shot may pierce that thick metal. Aim at the muddy mark, Illeria! Ready—fire!"

The two rifles spat together. Moore yelled, "You've done it! Duck—fast!"

They could not take cover fast enough. Ross had one glimpse of a tremendous sheet of flame licking out of the hole they had blasted, saw its counterpart high in the sky at the mouth of the ray cylinder, heard a great roar, and seemed to know nothing else.

HE regained consciousness on the platform of Peak Four, where his flagship, now repaired, rested airily. Artana, Moore and Illeria bent over him solicitously.

"What happened?" he asked, fretfully.

Artana spoke soberly. "The Queen is dead." He turned to Illeria, dropped to one knee, and bowed his head. "Long live the Queen!"

Ross glanced at Moore. The navigator winked. "Order is restored, Chief," he explained. "That blow-up finished Horta and all his works. And Earth is on the phone. All serene there, since the Los Angeles disaster. You are ordered to return and report."

Illeria dropped to her knees beside Ross. "You will not go? You will stay—and my people shall make you king!"

Ross looked long into her eyes, and the Earth seemed far away and an unreal world. But he slowly shook his head as he rose and gently lifted her to her feet. "I must go, Illeria," he said. "But—perhaps I shall return. Good-bye, Artana, you will restore peace to the Moon."

The Lord of the Peaks bowed his head. "That I will, farewell, Ross!"

With one last glance at the white-faced princess, Ross nodded shortly to Moore. They strode to their ship without a backward glance. At a curt order the helmsman took her off, and in seconds the two figures on Peak Four's platform had dwindled to specks.

"You can come back," Moore grunted.

"Think so?"

"Sure. When the Council hears what you've done they'll give you twenty years' leave. With pay."

Ross smiled. And the smile lingered as he turned to Jorgens to dictate a message for the Earth. The rocket ship droned on through space.

Cave-Dwellers of Saturn

By JOHN WIGGIN

Across Earth's radiant civilization lay the death-shot shadows of the hideous globe-headed dwarfs from Mars. One lone Earth-ship dared the treachery blockade, risking the planetoid peril to find Earth's life element on mysterious Saturn of the ten terrible rings.

IT was a crisp, clear morning in the city of Copia. A cold winter's sun glinted on the myriad roof tops of the vast spreading metropolis. To the north, snow-covered hills gleamed whitely, but the streets of Copia were dry and clean. There were not many people stirring at such an early hour. The dozen broad avenues which converged like the spokes of a great wheel on Government City in the center of Copia were quite deserted. There was little apparent activity around and about the majestic Government buildings, but the four mammoth gates were open, indicating that Government City was open for business.

At the north gate the sentry, sitting behind his black panel with its clusters of little lights, switches, and push-buttons, glanced upward. There was a faint humming and a man was circling downward about a hundred feet above him. The rays of the early sun flashed off a helmet and the sentry knew that this man was a soldier. The newcomer dropped rapidly, the stubbed wings on his back a gray blur. Then the humming ceased as the soldier switched off his oscillator and landed lightly on the ground before the sentry.

The sentry's swift glance took in the immensely tall, broad-shouldered figure, covered to the ankles in the green cloak. He took in also the pink, smiling face and merry blue eyes, and the lock of bright red hair which showed as the soldier pushed his helmet backward off his forehead.

"Your business?" asked the sentry.

"I have orders to report to the Commander-in-Chief," said the soldier, with a pleasant smile.

"Let's see," said the sentry, glancing at the insignia on the helmet, "you're a decurion of the Eightieth Division. And the name?"

"Dynamon," said the soldier.

"Oh, yes," said the sentry, with a recollective smile, "I remember you as an athlete. Didn't I see you in the Regional Games two years ago?"

"Yes," said the soldier, with pleased surprise. "I was on the team from North Central 4B."

"I thought so," the sentry chuckled. "As I remember you walked away with practically everything but the stadium. Hold on a minute now and I'll clear the channels for you."

The sentry bent over the panels, punched some buttons, threw a switch, and recited a few words in a monotone. He

listened for a moment, then threw the switch back and looked up.

"It seems you're expected," he said, "third building to the right and they'll take care of you there."

Ten minutes later Dynamon stood in the doorway of a large, beautiful room and saluted. The salute was answered by a grizzled, dark-skinned man sitting behind an enormous desk. This man was Argallum, Commander-in-Chief of the Armies of the World. He rose and beckoned to the young soldier.

"This way, Dynamon," said he, opening a small door. "What we have to talk about requires platinum walls."

Dynamon's face was a mask as he followed the Commander-in-Chief into the little room, but his heart was pounding and his mind working fast. The platinum room! That meant that he was about to learn a secret of the most vital importance to the world. He remembered now, that there was a delegation of Martians in Copia. They had arrived about a week before, ostensibly to carry on negotiations in an effort to avert the ugly crisis that was developing between Earth and Mars. But the conviction was growing among the citizens of Copia that the chief object of the Martian delegation was to spy. It was a well-known fact that the grotesque little men from the red planet had a superhuman sense of hearing that seemed to enable them to tune in on spoken conversations miles away, much as human beings tuned radio sets. They could hear through walls of brick, stone or steel; the one substance they could not hear through was platinum. Hence the little room off the Commander-in-Chief's office which was entirely sheathed in this precious metal.

ARGALLUM sat down heavily behind a little desk and gestured Dynamon to be seated opposite him.

"On the basis of your fine record," said Argallum, "I have selected you, Dynamon, to lead a dangerous expedition. You may refuse the assignment after you hear about it, and no blame will attach to you if you do. It is dangerous, and your chances of returning from it are unknown. But here it is, anyway.

"The situation with Mars is growing worse each month. They are making demands on us which, if we accepted them, would destroy the sovereign independence of the World-State. We would become a mere political satellite of Mars. But if we don't accept their demands, we are liable to a sudden attack from them which we could not withstand. They have got us in a military way and they know it. We might be able to stand them off for a while with our fine air force, but if they ever got a foothold with their land forces, then it's good-bye. They have a new weapon called the Photo-Atomic Ray against which we have absolutely no defense. It's a secret lethal ray which far outranges our voltage-bombs and which penetrates any armor or insulation we've got."

"Now, of course, our Council of Scientists has been working on the problem of a defense against the Ray. But the only thing they've come up with is a vague idea. They believe that there is a substance which they call 'tridium,' which would absorb or neutralize the Photo-Atomic Ray. They don't know what tridium looks like, but by spectro-analysis they know that it exists on the planet Saturn. So I am sending you with an expedition to Saturn to find, if you can, the substance known as 'tridium,' and bring some of it back if possible."

"Saturn!" gasped the decurion.

"I said it would be dangerous," Argallum said, bleakly. "No human being has ever set foot on the planet, and very little is known about it. But that's where you'll find tridium, if we're to believe Saturn's spectrum. You will have the latest, fastest Cosmos Carrier. You will have a completely equipped expedition. You will have for assistants the best young men we can find. As head of the expedition, you will be promoted to the rank of centurion. Do you accept the assignment?"

"Yes, sir," said Dynamon, unhesitatingly, "I accept the assignment."

DYNAMON walked thoughtfully out of Government city by the North Gate. The sentry noticed that his helmet was now adorned with the badge of centurion, and came to a smart salute. Dynamon went past him without seeing him, and the sentry glared after the new centurion disapprovingly. Lost in thought, Dynamon kept on walking until he came to with a start, and found himself in the middle of the shopping district.

The sun was getting uncomfortably warm and Dynamon switched off the electric current that heated his long cloak and looked around him. A sign in a shop window said, "Only fourteen more shopping days before the Twenty-fifth of December." Dynamon sighed. He wouldn't be around on this Twenty-fifth and it was going to be a very gay one. It was to be the nine hundredth anniversary of the Great Armistice—from which had come the unification of all the peoples of the Earth. Dynamon sighed again.

The long peace was threatened.

The Earth, in this year of grace 3057, was a wonderful place to live in, and Copia was the political and cultural center of the Earth. For nine hundred years now, the peoples of the Earth had lived at peace with one another as members of a single integrated community. The World-State had grown into something which that war-torn handful of people back in 1957 could scarcely have imagined. No longer did region war against region, or group against group, or class against class. Humanity had finally united to fight the common enemies—death, disease, old age, starvation.

And on this nine hundredth anniversary of the Great Armistice, the people of the World would have a great deal to celebrate. Disease was now unknown, as was starvation. Arduous physical labor was abolished, for now, the heaviest and the slightest tasks were performed by machines. Pain had been reduced, both physical and mental. Helpless senility was a thing of the past. Death alone remained. But even death had been postponed. Human beings now lived to be almost three hundred years old.

All in all, Dynamon mused, as he strolled along the broad avenue, the human race had eveloved a pretty satisfactory civilization. More was the pity, then, that human restlessness and vaulting ambition should have led to the construction of the great Cosmos Carriers. If Man had been content to stay on his own little planet, then communication would never have been established with the jealous little men of Mars, and this beautiful civilization would not now be threatened by a visitation of the terrible Martians and their frightful Photo-Atomic Ray. Dynamon's deep chest swelled a little with pride at the thought that he had been selected by the Commander-in-Chief to take an important part in the coming conflict.

HE turned the corner and found himself standing before an imposing building. Across the top of the facade in block letters was the legend, "State Theater of Comedy." A few minutes later he stood in front of a doorway at the side of the great theater building. The door opened and a tall, lovely girl appeared.

"Dynamon!" she exclaimed, "I didn't expect to see you for another ten days." She stepped out of the doorway, and reached her arms up impulsively, kissing Dynamon.

The tall young soldier gripped her shoulders hard for a minute, and then stepped back and looked down into her soft brown eyes.

"Yes, I know, Keltry," he said soberly. "I had to report on short notice."

"Oh!" said the girl called Keltry, "are you here on duty?"

"Very secret duty," said Dynamon with a meaning look. He twiddled an imaginary radio-dial in his ear and looked around mysteriously.

The smile died on Keltry's smooth brown face, to be replaced by an expression of concern.

"You mean—them?" she whispered.

Dynamon nodded. "Yes, I am being transferred to a new post," he said slowly, "and I thought, if you had no objections, I would ask to have you transferred along with me."

"Do you need to ask a question like that?" said Keltry. "You know perfectly well I'd have a lot of objections if you didn't ask for my transfer."

"There may be some danger," he said, giving her an eloquent look.

"All the more reason why I should be with you," Keltry said quietly.

FOUR days later, a conference was breaking up in the platinum room behind the Commander-in-Chief's office. Argallum stood up behind his desk and carefully folded a number of big charts. He laid one on top of another, making a neat stack on the desk, then he looked keenly at the four young men standing before him.

"Once more, gentlemen," Argallum said, "for the sake of emphasis, I repeat—Dynamon has complete authority over the expedition. You, Mortoch"—looking at a lean, hawk-nosed man in a soldier's helmet—"are in command of the soldiers. And you, Thamon"—turning to a studious, stoop-shouldered man—"are in charge of civilian activities. And Borion"—glancing at a stocky, broad-shouldered figure—"you are responsible for the Carrier. But in the last analysis, you are all under Dynamon's orders. This is a desperate venture you're going on and there can be no division of authority."

There was a moment of silence. Argallum seemed satisfied with the set, determined expressions on the four men in the room with him. "Are there any further questions?" he said.

Dynamon shifted his feet uneasily. "Is the decision—on Keltry, final?" he said huskily.

"I'm afraid it is, Dynamon," said Argallum, gently. "I had the director of the theater over here for half an hour trying to talk him around, but it was no good. He said he would under no circumstances spare Keltry. He said she was the most promising young actress in Copia, and that he would forbid her to go on any dangerous trip. Inasmuch as Keltry is still an apprentice, the Director has full authority over her. I can do nothing."

Dynamon drew himself up to his full height and squared his shoulders. "Yes, sir," he said briefly.

"Very well then," said Argallum, "I won't see you again. You will take off from Vanadium Field promptly at four o'clock tomorrow morning. Every one of the one hundred and twenty-nine people on the expedition has his secret orders to be there at three. Dynamon, you have a hand-picked personnel and every possible resource that our scientists could think of to help you. May you succeed in your mission."

"Thank you, sir," they chorused

Argallum shook hands separately with each of the four men, after which they filed out of the platinum room.

Outside the War Building, Mortoch, the decurion, and Borion, the Navigator, took their leave of Dynamon and strolled away toward the West Gate. But Thamon, the scientist, fell in stride with Dynamon.

"For your sake, I'm sorry," said the stoop-shouldered scientist shyly, "I mean—about Keltry."

"Thanks, Thamon," said the centurion. "It was a nasty blow. I don't know how I'm going to get along without her. I guess I'll just have to."

"Well—I just wanted you to know," said Thamon, "that I sympathized."

IN the middle of Vanadium Field a great gray shape, like a vast slumbering whale, could be indistinctly seen in the soft half-light of the false dawn. No lights showed on the field and no sound was heard. But scores of people clustered around the sides of the Cosmos Carrier, dwarfed to ant-like proportions by its great size. Inside the Carrier, standing near the thick double doors in the Carrier's belly, was Dynamon, near him his three chief lieutenants, Mortoch, Thamon, and Borion. The members of the little expeditionary force filed past the youthful Commander, each one halting before him for a brief inspection. One hundred brawny soldiers, divided into squads of ten, stepped through the double doors, each squad led by its decurion. Dynamon ran a practiced eye over the equipment of each man and then for good measure turned him over to the scrutiny of the Chief Decurion, Mortoch. Then came twenty-five civilians, including ten engineers, four dieticians, five administrators, and six scientists. But for a cruel prank of fate, Dynamon reflected, his own dear Keltry would be a member of the expedition.

But there was no time for regretting that which could not be. Dynamon turned and walked toward Borion.

"Are you satisfied?" he asked the navigator. Borion nodded, and Mortoch and Thamon likewise nodded in answer to Dynamon's unspoken question.

"All right," said the young centurion. "Stations!"

A moment later the great outer door of the Cosmos Carrier swung silently shut, after which the thick inner door was secured and the great ship hermetically sealed. Dynamon followed the navigator into the control room.

"This is a gorgeous ship!" said Borion. "It's absolutely the last word. There's a cluster of magnets underneath our feet that are brutes and yet they can be so finely controlled, I'll guarantee you won't feel a bump at any time. Dynamon, these magnets are so strong that this ship will go at least ten times faster than anything that has yet been built. Once we get up out of the stratosphere, beyond the danger of friction, we can go almost twenty miles a second. You ready for the take-off? If you want to use the loud speaker system just throw that switch."

Dynamon nodded; a moment later his voice was heard in every compartment of the Cosmos Carrier.

"Men, we are taking off. Hold your stations for five minutes, after which you may take your ease until further commands."

"Come and watch the altimeter," Borion said after Dynamon closed the loud speaker switch. "You won't believe we're off the ground, these controls are so smooth." The centurion watched the needle creep gently upward a few feet at a time. But he could feel no trace of motion.

"I'm going to take her up vertically to two thousand feet," said Borion. "Then we'll be clear of all obstacles and can pick up our course horizontally—"

"Yes, good," Dynamon broke in quickly, "but don't tell me your course until we are out of the stratosphere."

"Aye, aye, sir," said Borion with a wink, "little pitchers have big ears, don't they?"

"How soon will we get out of the stratosphere?" Dynamon asked.

"Well, I'm lifting her very slowly," answered the navigator, "I don't want to take any chances on friction. I would say in about three hours from now we will be ready to go."

"I will be with you then," said Dynamon, and walked out the door.

THE young centurion had in mind to make a thorough inspection of the entire ship, but he had scarcely been ten minutes away from the control room when the loud-speaker system boomed forth.

"Centurion Dynamon is requested to come to the control room." Dynamon hurried up a metal staircase and then through a companionway. As he threw open the door to the control room, Borion turned quickly and laid a finger on his lips. Then the navigator gestured Dynamon toward a series of glass panels. There were six of these panels, each about a foot square, and ranged in two vertical rows of three each. One word, "periscopes," was stenciled at the top, and beside each mirror were other labels, "port bow," "port beam," "port quarter." The other three panels were labeled in the same way, designating their location on the starboard side. Borion flicked the switch beside the "starboard quarter" panel and it become dimly illuminated. Dynamon threw a swift glance at the altimeter, and saw that it said two thousand feet. Then he bent over and peered into the periscope panel. A wide panorama of twinkling lights spread out before him, the street lights of Copia. But the pale blue of approaching dawn was creeping fast over the city, shedding just enough light to reveal a dark shape a mile behind the Cosmos Carrier, and perhaps a thousand feet below. As Dynamon stared into the periscope screen, he thought he could detect a faint glow of red in the following shape. He turned questioningly to Borion. The navigator was writing rapidly on a piece of paper. A second later he handed the paper to Dynamon. It said:

"I queried Headquarters and was told that the conference with the Martian delegation is still officially going on. But that Carrier following us is bright red, the color of the Martian Carriers."

DYNAMON held the piece of paper in his hand for a minute and gazed doubtfully into the periscope screen. Then

he took the pencil from Borion and, bending over, wrote the following:

"I don't like the looks of this. Can we outrun them once we get out of the atmosphere?"

Borion nodded slowly.

"As far as I know, we can," he said, "unless—" he reached for the paper in Dynamon's hand and wrote "—unless they have developed a new wrinkle in their Carriers that we don't know anything about."

"Well," said Dynamon, "we won't waste time worrying about things over which we have no control. Proceed as usual."

There followed some anxious hours, which Dynamon spent with his eyes glued to the periscope mirror. In a short time the early golden rays of the sun appeared, and the Martian Carrier followed behind inexorably, glowed an ugly menacing crimson. Once Dynamon instructed his communications officer to speak to the Martian ship.

"Lovely morning, Mars. Where are you bound for?" was the casual message.

There came back a terse answer, "Test flight, and you?"

"We're testing, too," Dynamon's communications officer said. "We'll show you some tricks up beyond the stratosphere."

All so elaborately casual, Dynamon thought grimly. It was fairly evident that the Martian ship intended to follow the Earth Carrier to find out where it was going. Those inhuman devils! Why did the Earth's people ever have to come in contact with them?

Dynamon's thoughts went back to his childhood, to that terrible time when the men of Mars had abruptly declared war and descended suddenly onto the Earth in thousands of Cosmos Carriers. Only the timely invention of that remarkable substance, Geistfactor, had saved Earth then. It was a creamy liquid, which spread over any surface, rendered the object invisible. The principle underlying Geistfactor was simplicity itself, being merely an application of ultra high-frequency color waves. But it saved the day for Earth. The World Armies, cloaked in their new-found invisibility, struck in a dozen places at the ravaging hordes from Mars. The invaders, in spite of their prodigious intellectual powers, could not defend themselves against an unseen enemy, and had been forced to withdraw the remnants of their army and sue for peace.

But the unremitting jealousy and hatred of the little men with the giant heads for Earth's creatures was leading to new trouble. It enraged the Martians to think that human beings, whom they despised as inferior creatures, should have first thought of spanning the yawning distances between the planets of the solar system. It was doubly humiliating to the Martians that when they, too, followed suit and went in for interplanetary travel, they could do no better than to copy faithfully the human invention of the Cosmos Carrier. It was only too evident that Mars was gathering its strength for another lightning thrust at the Earth. This time, with the Photo-Atomic Ray, there was no doubt that they intended to destroy or subjugate Earth's peoples for good. And to that end the Martians had been inventing new bones of contention and had been contriving new crises. A peace-minded World Government had been trying to stave off the inevitable conflict with conference after conference. But to those on the inside it was only too evident that the Martians could invent pretexts for war faster than Earth could evade them.

DYNAMON, watching the blood-red Carrier in the periscope mirror, felt a surging bitterness at the Martians. If they could only be reasonable, he reflected, if only they could be *human,* then he, Dynamon, would not now be floating away on a dangerous mission far from the Earth and the woman he loved. He tried to imagine what Keltry was doing at that moment. In his mind's eye he could see her on the stage of the Theater of Comedy, enthralling audiences with her youthful charm as she played a part in the latest witty comedy, or sang a gay ballad in a new revue.

He broke out of his reverie and tossed a glance at the altimeter. The needle was moving much faster now, climbing steadily toward seventy thousand feet.

"It's about time to go now, isn't it?" he asked Borion.

The navigator nodded. "Just about," he said, and put his hand on a lever marked "gravity repellor."

As the navigator pushed the lever smoothly forward, Dynamon turned back to the periscope mirror and saw the red ship behind suddenly dwindle in size. The new Cosmos Carrier was beginning to show its speed.

Apparently, the Martians were momentarily caught off guard. The red Carrier diminished to a tiny speck against the dark background of the Earth. But then it began to grow in size again as the Martians unleashed the power in their great magnets.

"Borion, how about friction?" Dynamon asked.

"We don't have to worry about that yet," was the answer, "we're not going fast enough. And the temperature outside is about sixty-five below."

Dynamon nodded and glanced again at the altimeter. The needle was steadily climbing, a mile every ten seconds. Once again he looked into the screen of the periscope. The Earth was now far enough away so that the young centurion could begin to make out the broad arc which was a part of the curving circumference of the globe. Silently he said a final good-bye to Keltry and turned to speak to Borion. At that moment the door of the control room burst open and an engineer stepped in and saluted the navigator.

"Stowaway, sir," the engineer said. "Just found her in the munitions compartment."

Dynamon stared out through the open door at the woman who stood out there between two soldiers.

It was Keltry.

IT was a harried and heartsick centurion who, a few minutes later, called a conference in his own quarters. Borion and Thamon sat regarding him gravely, while Mortoch, the second in command, lounged against the wall, a faint, derisive smile on his lean face.

"We are faced with a situation," Dynamon said heavily. "I would like to hear some opinions."

"Flagrant case of indiscipline," Mortoch

said promptly; "that is, if we can regard this impersonally."

"Personalities," said Dynamon sharply, "will have no influence on my final decision."

"In that case" said Mortoch harshly, "it seems to me, you are bound to put back to Earth and hand the woman over to the right people for corrective action."

"Good heavens!" cried Borion, "I hope we don't have to do that. We already have a problem on our hands in the shape of that Martian Carrier."

"What do you say, Thamon?" the centurion asked after a significant pause.

"Well," said the scientist quietly, "you can't altogether regard the situation without considering personalities. Keltry stowed away for a very personal reason, and one which it is hard to condemn entirely. I think we are over-emphasizing the official breach of discipline. I, personally, can't see that it makes so much difference. After all, we on this expedition are on our own and are likely to remain so for some time to come. I am in favor of going along about our business and forgetting how Keltry came aboard."

"Spoken like a civilian," said Mortoch sourly, "and I hold to my opinion. Just because Dynamon was promoted over my head, I see no reason for trying to curry favor with him."

There was an awkward silence during which Dynamon's face grew very pink and his blue eyes grew cold.

"I'm going to forget what you just said, Mortoch," he said. "You are a valued member of this expedition, and you are much too good a soldier to overlook the danger that lies in that kind of talk. Without my participation, you are out-voted two to one. We will not turn back."

He stood up with a gesture of dismissal and the three lieutenants filed out of the door. He paced the floor of his quarters for a few minutes, then walked to the door and gave orders for the prisoner to be sent in.

"Ah, Keltry darling," he said after the guard had left the two of them alone, "you have put me in an impossible position."

"I don't see why it should be that bad," Keltry answered. "It was an inhuman thing to do to separate us and I just wasn't going to permit it."

"Yes, but don't you see?" said Dynamon, "I will be accused of playing favorites because I don't turn around and take you back to Earth."

"I'm not asking favors," Keltry retorted calmly, "I just want to be a member of this expedition."

Whatever Dynamon was going to answer to that, it was interrupted by the loud-speaker booming:

"Centurion Dynamon is requested at the control room."

Dynamon leapt to his feet, crushed Keltry to him in a swift brief embrace and then opened the door.

"Escort the prisoner to the scientist's quarters," he ordered, "and release her."

DYNAMON walked into the control room and saw that Borion's face was gray. The navigator was standing in front of the periscope screens looking from one to another. The centurion walked over and stood beside him.

"The Martians are showing their hand finally," said Borion. "They have decided that we're headed for another planet, and I don't think that they want to let us carry out our intention. See, here and here?" Dynamon peered into the port and starboard bow panels. He could see dozens of little red specks rapidly growing larger.

"They will try and surround us," Borion said, "and blanket our magnets with their own."

"That's not so good, is it?" Dynamon murmured. "What is our altitude from Earth?"

"Forty miles," was the reply, "and I think they still may be able to overhear our conversation."

"Let them," said Dynamon quietly, "We have no secrets from them and they may as well know that we're going to out-run them. Full speed, Borion!"

The Navigator advanced the "repellor" lever as far as it would go. There was a slight jerk under foot. Then he adjusted a needle on a large dial and moved the "attractor" lever to its full distance. There was another jerk as the great Carrier lunged forward through space. Borion smiled.

"I put the attractor beam on the moon," he said, "and we'll be hitting it up close to nineteen miles a second in a few minutes. We should walk away from those drops of blood, over there."

"Are we pointing away from them enough?" Dynamon asked. "What's to prevent them from changing their course and cutting over to intercept us? See, that's what they appear to be doing now."

The navigator peered critically at the forward periscope screens. "It may be a close shave at that," he admitted. "But please trust me, Dynamon, I'll make it past them."

THE tiny red specks in the periscope screens were growing shockingly fast, indicating the frightful speed at which the Earth-Carrier was traveling. Bigger and bigger they grew under Dynamon's fascinated gaze. The centurion darted a glance at Borion. In this fantastic encounter, every second counted. Could the navigator elude the pursuing red Carriers? Borion haunched tensely over the control levers, his eyes glued to the screens. The Martian ships were as big as cigars now and tripling their size with every heartbeat. Dynamon clenched his fist involuntarily and fought down an impulse to shout a warning. That would be worse than useless now —the fate of the expedition was entirely in the hands of Borion.

Dynamon held his breath as a flash of red flicked across the port bow periscope screen. The Carrier heaved under his feet for a second then quickly settled to an even keel again. The sweat stood out in little drops on Borion's forehead.

"Too close for comfort," muttered the navigator. His eyes widened as another huge red shape loomed up in the starboard bow screen. Borion's hands flicked over a dial spinning a needle around. Then he hung desperately back on the repellor. There was a momentary shock. The Carrier seemed to bounce off something. Borion staggered and Dynamon hurled forward and crashed into the forward bulkhead of the control room.

Then Borion shouted, "We're through!"

Dynamon picked himself up off the floor with a rueful smile. "I thought we were *all* through for a minute," he observed.

"Well! That was a bad minute there!" said Borion excitedly. "I thought that one fellow was going to get us, but I kicked him off by throwing the beam on him and giving him the repellor. But you can see for yourself, they are far behind now, and they'll never in the world be able to catch up."

Dynamon peered into the port and starboard quarter screens and saw a group of rapidly diminishing red specks. He looked up with a sigh of relief.

"Good work, Borion," he said, and the navigator grinned.

"I don't think we will have to worry any more about the Martian ships from now on, if we're careful," Borion said. "I'm going to run for the shadow of the moon and from there I'll plot a course straight for Jupiter, avoiding Mars entirely."

THE door to the control room opened, and a smiling, spectacled face peered in. It was Thamon, the scientist.

"That was quite a bump," Thamon observed. "Were we trying to knock down an asteroid?"

Dynamon gave a short laugh. "No, that was merely some of our friends from Mars trying to head us off. But they're far behind now and we don't anticipate any trouble for a good many days."

"Ah, round one to the Earth people," Thamon observed. "In that case, Dynamon, have you decided how you are going to conduct affairs within the Carrier in the immediate future?"

"Not quite," Dynamon replied. "Suppose we discuss that, in my quarters?"

Thamon nodded. "I'm at your disposal, Centurion."

Dynamon led the way down the little stair and into the compartment that served as his office. Once there, he threw off his long military cloak and sat down at a little table, his great bronzed shoulders gleaming in the soft artificial light.

"I suppose the first question," said Thamon, sitting down opposite the centurion, "is whether to institute suspended animation on board?"

"I think we'd better, don't you?" said Dynamon.

"It would save a lot of food and oxygen," the scientist replied. "You see, even at our tremendous rate of speed now, it will take two hundred and twenty-six days to reach the outer layer of Saturn's atmosphere. Until we actually land the ship, there is no conceivable emergency that couldn't be handled by a skeleton crew."

"Quite right," said Dynamon. "I'll have Mortoch take charge of the arrangements, if you will stand by to supervise the technical side."

"It's as good as done," said Thamon. "We have the newest type of refrigeration system in the main saloon. I can drop the temperature one hundred and fifty degrees in one-fifth of a second. By the way, I was a little worried by that outburst of Mortoch's when we were talking about Keltry."

"Oh, well," said Dynamon, "Mortoch is only human. He was a Senior Decurion and I was passed over him for this job. He couldn't help but be a little jealous. But he will be all right, he's a soldier, after all."

"I hope so," said Thamon, doubtfully.

"Why certainly," Dynamon affirmed. "As a matter of fact, I wish he had been given the command in the first place. Between you and me, I'm not too keen about this expedition to a comparatively unknown planet. Thamon, why on earth weren't human beings content to stay at home? Why did they have to go to such endless pains to construct these Cosmos Carriers? Before these things were invented, the inhabitants of Earth and the inhabitants of Mars didn't know that each other existed, and they were perfectly happy about it. But when they both began spinning around through space between the planets, all of a sudden the Solar System was not big enough to hold both Peoples."

"It's some fatal restlessness in the make-up of human beings," Thamon replied. "Do you realize how far back Man has been trying to reach out to other planets?"

"Well, the first successful trip in a Cosmos Carrier was made seventy-eight years ago," said Dynamon.

Thamon chuckled.

"As far as we *know*, that was the first successful trip," the scientist corrected. "As a matter of fact, the first Cosmos Carrier was anticipated hundreds of years ago. Just the other day in the library, I found a very interesting account of an archaeological discovery made up in North Central 3A—the island that the ancients called Britain. A complete set of drawings and building plans was found in an admirable state of preservation. The date on the plans was 1956, and as you will remember from your school history, all of North Central by that time had been terribly ravaged by the wars. The inventor, whose name was Leonard Bolton, called his contrivance a 'space ship.' Wonderful, those old names, aren't they? But the most remarkable thing of all, is, that the designs for that 'space ship' were very practical. If the man ever had a chance to build one, which he probably didn't, it might very well have been a successful vehicle."

"That's very interesting," said Dynamon. "Were there any clues as to what happened to Leonard Bolton?"

"None at all," the scientist replied. "All we know about him is that he designed the 'space ship' and then was presumably blotted out by the savage weapons used in the warfare of those days. But, as I say, the remarkable thing is that when we got around to building a Cosmos Carrier eighty years ago, we were able to use several of Leonard Bolton's ideas. Which all goes to show, I suppose, there's nothing new under the sun."

"I'm not so sure about that," said Dynamon with a smile. "I've an idea that we're going to bump into several things new to us on the planet Saturn."

"As to that," Thamon nodded, "I shouldn't be surprised if you are right. Now I suppose I'd better go and make arrangements for the refrigeration job. Will Mortoch be responsible for providing each individual with a hypodermic and return-to-life tablets?"

"That will be taken care of," said Dynamon. "I'll see you later."

DYNAMON stood beside Borion in the control room, staring fascinatedly at the periscope screens. The images that were reflected in the six panels made up a composite scene that was awe-inspiring and fearsome. The great Cosmos Carrier was finally arriving at the end of its seven months' journey. In front of the Earth-craft, a vast, barren expanse, uniformly dark gray in color spread for thousands of miles. To one side of the Carrier a wide belt of mist and shimmering particles stretched upward from the planet out toward space. Dynamon realized that this was a small section of the great ring encircling Saturn, that could be seen in the powerful telescopes from Earth. Glancing at the stern vision screens, Dynamon saw the sun twinkling. So far away it was now, that it was hardly bigger than a large star and gave off not much more light. Even though they were coming to Saturn in the middle of a Saturnian day, there was no more than a gloomy half-light to illumine their way.

"Saturn revolves on its axis with such speed," observed Borion, "that I should imagine there will be tremendous prevailing winds on the surface. I think I can see a range of steep mountains down there; it might not be a bad idea if we landed in the lee of them."

"Yes," agreed Dynamon, "I think that would be a good idea. As a matter of fact, we may have to dig below the surface entirely to prevent being blown away. How is the gravitation pull?"

"It's a curious thing," Borion replied. "It should be tremendous but the centrifugal force is so strong that it counterbalances to a certain extent. The ship is handling very easily."

"How soon do you think we'll make the surface?" said Dynamon.

"I should estimate somewhere around six hours from now," the navigator answered. "I could make it sooner but I'm feeling my way."

"That suits me," said Dynamon. "That will give us just time to turn off the refrigeration and bring our people back to life. Lucky devils to be able to sleep through this trip—have you ever been so bored in your life?"

"Never," agreed Borion. "But I am not bored now."

Dynamon walked across the control room and threw a large switch in the wall panel.

"Decurion Mortoch and Scientist Thamon," he said into the loud-speaker system. "Proceed at once to remove the suspension-of-life condition in the main saloon. As soon as everyone is revived, stand by to take landing stations."

As the centurion closed the switch and turned away, Borion called him over again to the periscope screens.

"That *is* a range of mountains," said the navigator. "I can see it more clearly now. I think I'll slow up our descent a little bit so that by the time we're ready to land it will be midday again. As you probably know, Saturn makes a complete revolution in only a little more than ten hours."

"That sounds sensible," said Dynamon. "We'll need all the light we can get to make a safe landing."

Borion nodded and reached toward the repellor lever. He pushed it gently forward and then looked at his altimeter. He seemed to be dissatisfied with the altimeter reading and pushed forward the repellor lever a little more. Then he looked again at the altimeter, and an expression of bewilderment came over his face. With a muttered exclamation he jammed the repellor lever as far ahead as it would go, at the same time watching the altimeter. Dynamon sensed that something was wrong as he watched the color drain out of the navigator's face.

"The Saints preserve us!" the navigator cried hoarsly. "Something has gone terribly wrong—the repellor isn't working! We're dropping at a frightful rate of speed—!"

Borion leapt to the loud-speaker system and issued rapid orders to the navigating engineers.

"What's going to happen to us?" Dynamon demanded.

"I don't know," Borion said, his face ashen. "I think it is just a simple mechanical failure in the controls from the repellor lever down to the magnets. I don't know how soon my workers can discover the trouble and repair it. In the mean time—"

"In the mean time," Dynamon broke in gloomily, "we may all be spattered all over that gray landscape."

"Either that," Borion gritted, "or we

burn to a crisp from the atmospheric friction. I can feel it getting warmer in here already."

DYNAMON fought down the sickening sensation of panic that was starting to creep over him.

"How long do you think we have got?" he said with an effort.

"At the most," said Borion staring, white lipped, at the altimeter, "at the most, I should say a half an hour."

The door to the control room burst open and Thamon rushed in closely followed by Keltry.

"I heard you talking to your engineers, Borion," the scientist said rapidly. "Are we in trouble?"

"We are," said Borion, "and it may be the last trouble any of us ever have. Our repellor has gone out for some reason. And we're heading for the surface of Saturn like a metorite."

"Can't anything be done?" said Thamon.

"My engineers are doing all they can to find the source of the trouble," Borion replied. "But until they do, I can't slow the ship up."

Keltry's great brown eyes were enormous as she moved over beside Dynamon and took his right hand in hers.

"As long as I'm with you, Dynamon," she said in a low voice, "I'm not afraid to die. But I hate to see your expedition fail. Perhaps the fate of the Earth depends on us here in this Carrier."

"I know," said Dynamon, squeezing her hand. His eyes followed Borion as the navigator went to the loud-speaker system again. But apparently the news from below was not encouraging, and Borion's shoulders sagged as he turned to face the other three people in the control room.

"They haven't found the source of the trouble yet," he said dully, "and there's not a thing to be done until they do. I'm sorry that, as navigator of this Carrier, I am plunging you all to your death. But it's a case of a simple mechanical failure which I couldn't foresee."

Keltry stepped forward impulsively and laid her hand on the navigator's wrist.

"Nobody could blame you, Borion," she said gently. "It isn't your fault if the at-

tractor or the repellor lever, whichever it is, gets broken. You are already—"

"Wait a minute!" Borion shouted, eyes darting out of his head. "The attractor! In my excitement I forgot!"

The navigator leapt to the control levers, spun the dial and put his hand on the attractor lever.

"If—I'm only—on time!" he muttered agonizedly. "It's just possible—the counter-attraction of Jupiter—Lord it's hot!"

The control room was silent as death as the navigator eased the attractor lever carefully forward. Dynamon whipped a glance at the periscope screens. The ground was rushing up at a terrific rate, and out behind the Carrier, a dense cloud of black smoke was forming. The veins were standing out in Borion's forehead as he inched the attractor lever forward. The girl and the two men watched him with bated breath as he slowly raised his eyes to the altimeter. A wild incredulous expression appearing on the navigator's face.

"It's—it's working! Borion muttered hoarsly, *"the attractor beam from Jupiter is slowing us up!"*

DYNAMON'S heart leapt and he sprang back to the periscope screens. The column of smoke behind them was still there but it seemed to be thinning out. But the surface of Saturn seemed to be rushing upward just as fast as ever. Dynamon twisted his head around to look at Borion. A feverish smile was lighting up the navigator's face as he pressed forward on the attractor lever.

"We may just make it!" he breathed, and Dynamon said a little prayer.

In the screen a range of dark gray mountains stood out in bold relief and seemed to reach claw-like peaks toward the speeding Carrier. But the smoke had ceased to whip past, and only a small black cloud far behind served to remind Dynamon of the fearful friction that the surface of the ship had been subjected to. At the same time Dynamon felt an invisible force dragging him toward the front bulkhead of the control room, and he knew that the Carrier was slowing up its forward speed. Through the bow periscopes the jagged range of mountains seemed so close that Dynamon almost felt he could reach out and touch them. Miraculously, they rose up to one side of the ship. A moment later a voice sounded in the loud-speaker system.

"The magnet room calling the navigator. A break in the control shaft has been discovered and repaired. Throw the repellor lever into neutral and than advance it."

Borion gave a little sob, flicked back the repellor and then pushed it forward again. The floor of the control room heaved for a minute and then settled on an even keel, Dynamon stared unbelievingly at the starboard midship's periscope screens and saw that the great Carrier was resting immobile not more than twenty feet above the gray soil of Saturn.

"Saved!" cried Borion hysterically, "and it was Keltry who did it! In my excitement I would have let all of us plunge to our death, if Keltry hadn't reminded me that there was such a thing as an attractor lever! Dynamon, Thamon, we should get down on our knees and thank our stars that Keltry was in here!"

The door of the control room opened and Mortoch stepped in.

"Do you have to toss us around like that?" the lean decurion said. "I had a near-panic on my hands with some of those people just coming out of their suspended animation. Oh!—" Mortoch smiled ironically— "I begin to see why we had such a rough passage. If beautiful stowaways are given the run of the control room, I should imagine it would be hard for the navigator to keep his mind on his work."

Borion started forward with a snarl but Dynamon's voice cracked like a whip.

"Attention! Both of you! Try and remember that you are modern, civilized men, not twentieth century brutes."

Borion's hands fell to his sides, and he began to laugh.

"You're absolutely right, Dynamon," he said, "I don't know why I should let myself be annoyed by this crude soldier. After all, the cream of the joke is that Mortoch would never have been able to come in here and make sarcastic remarks about Keltry, if Keltry hadn't been here for the past half hour."

"What do you mean by that?" said Mortoch suspiciously.

"I mean," said Borion, "that if Keltry had not been in here, you and everybody else aboard this Carrier would now be dead."

"Now!" said Dynamon. "I think we have had enough of personalities. Suppose we get a little work done. Mortoch, prepare the First Decuria for reconnaissance duty. Each man should be equipped with cloak, oxygen mask, counter-gravity helmets, and a supply of voltage bombs, and each man's radio should be set at eighty-one thousand meters. Have them ready at the main door in fifteen minutes. I will lead them on a short tour of exploration and Thamon will accompany me. In the mean time, Mortoch, you will remain in charge of the Carrier until I get back."

DYNAMON'S heart was pounding with excitement as he and Thamon walked through the main saloon toward the group of cloaked figures standing by the big round door. As far as he knew he was going to be the first human being ever to step foot on the planet Saturn. He mentally checked over his own equipment and made sure that it was all in place, including the hard rubber box slung over his shoulder on a strap. That box contained his supply of voltage bombs—little glass spheroids, smaller than golf balls, which, when hurled at an enemy, burst releasing a tremendous electric charge. There was little likelihood that these bombs would be needed, because the periscope screens had shown no sign of life anywhere in the gray, arid valley in which the Cosmos Carrier was lying. However, Dynamon was taking no chances. He glanced briefly at Thamon beside him. The scientist was unarmed, carrying the light metal staff which was the badge of his profession.

Dynamon stepped forward and ran his eyes quickly over the masked, muffled figures of the First Decuria. Then he signed to an engineer who quickly unfastened the great door. Dynamon then stepped through and his party followed him crowding into the air lock between the inner and outer doors. Thamon stepped forward, maneuvered a lever, the outer door swung open and Saturn lay waiting for the touch of Dynamon's foot.

It was not an especially inviting prospect.

A blast of unbelievably cold air swirled through the open door, carrying with it particles of fine, gray sand. In the dim, murky twilight, tall gray mountains loomed ominously across the valley floor. Dynamon shivered and turned up the heat in his electric cloak. Then with one hand on the knob of his counter-gravity helmet he stepped gingerly out on to the ground.

Instantly he sank to his knees in gray sand that was as light and powdery as fresh snow. With a quick twist of the knob on his helmet he kicked his feet free and stood lightly on the surface again.

"Attention, First Decuria!" he said into the transmitter of his radio phone. "Adjust counter-gravitation to approximately plus ten pounds."

Stepping backward, he turned and watched the masked figures of his command leave the Carrier one by one. Thamon came out first, followed by the Decurion, and after him the soldiers. Mechanically, Dynamon counted them. As the tenth soldier stepped out on the gray soil, Dynamon started to turn away when to his astonishment an eleventh cloaked figure came out of the door of the Carrier.

"Decurion!" Dynamon said sharply into his transmitter, "since when have you had eleven men in your command?"

"Never," came back the prompt answer in Dynamon's ears. As the decurion faced about to count his men, one of them moved over beside Dynamon.

"Forgive me, Dynamon," came a soft feminine voice, "but I had to come with you. It's Keltry. Please don't send me back, I promise not to be any trouble."

Dynamon hesitated, then reluctantly agreed to allow her to come along.

"Stay close to Thamon," he warned, and started off down the valley, the rest of the party following him.

Lightened as they were to keep from sinking deep into the treacherous powdery sand, the humans made fast progress, accelerated by the strong breeze that blew at their backs down the valley. At that, Dynamon realized that the lofty mountains on either side provided protection against immeasurably stronger winds higher up. From the saw-toothed peaks on the left, dark streamers of sand stood out for yards, indicating constant winds of gale proportions up there.

THE valley itself, as far as Dynamon could see in the dim half-light, was barren of any kind of life. There was no sign of a creeping, crawling, or flying creature; nor was there any vegetation, trees or grass. Dynamon led his column nearly a mile down the unchanging gray of the valley and then called a halt.

"Thamon," he said, beckoning the scientist to him, "can you see any possibility of human habitation in this valley?"

"Off-hand, I don't, not on the surface," the scientist replied. "I would have to test the atmosphere for oxygen, but I doubt if there is a large enough proportion. My guess is that there is nothing but nitrogen in this air. That won't support human life, or any other kind of life except possibly certain kinds of plants."

"What about tridium?" said Dynamon. "How do you go about looking for it?"

"Electrophysiological tests of all kinds," said Thamon, "I must say this valley doesn't look very encouraging. It looks like burned out volcanic ash. Say! What's that up the valley?"

Dynamon gazed back in the direction of the Cosmos Carrier, and felt an uneasy prickling along his spine. The desert valley floor behind them seemed suddenly to have sprouted some tall bushes. There were possibly a dozen of them standing at intervals of twenty yards. They were too far away—perhaps one eighth of a mile—for Dynamon to see them very well, but they appeared to consist of a score of leafless branches radiating outward in all directions from a small core. It was as if a basket ball was bristling with ten-foot javelins.

"Where did they come from?" Dynamon gasped. "I didn't see them when we walked over that ground a few minutes ago."

"Nor I," agreed Thamon. "I can't imagine where they came from."

Just then one of the bushes apparently moved a few feet as if blown by the wind.

"Good Lord!" exclaimed Thamon. "Did you see that? One of those things rolled forward!"

Then another of the fantastic bushes started to roll, and another, and another. In a moment all twelve of the extraordinary apparitions were rolling rapidly down the wind toward the humans. Dynamon felt the hair on the back of his neck stiffen, and he sprang into action, commanding his soldiers to converge around him.

"Thamon, what *are* those things!" Dynamon cried.

"I don't know," the scientist replied. "I don't think they can be animals. But they might be rootless nitrogen-feeding plants of some kind. Look! Those branches are covered with long thorns!"

The fantastic creatures were rolling swiftly down on the little group of humans, and Dynamon could see the sharp thorns around the end of each branch. He reached into the box at his hip.

"Decuria, ready with voltage bombs," he commanded, and looking around saw that each man held one of the little glass bombs in his hand. The bushes were only fifty feet away now, rolling lightly over the gray sand on their spindly branches.

"Ready?" warned Dynamon, "throw!"

A shower of glistening glass balls flew through the air into the midst of the menacing apparitions. There was a series of blinding flashes and loud reports. Some jagged white lines appeared among the black branches of the monsters, but they kept right on rolling downwind. Dynamon felt a surge of dismay. Those voltage bombs had been, for years, Man's best weapon.

"They're plants all right!" came Thamon's voice. "You can't kill them with electricity any more than you can kill a tree!"

Dynamon looked at the men huddled about him and thought quickly.

"All we can do, men, is to try and dodge them," he announced. "Spread out and as soon as one of those things passes you run upwind! Keltry! Thamon! Stay close to me."

THE line of rolling bushes was almost upon them as the soldiers deployed in all directions. Seizing Keltry by the hand, Dynamon leapt to one side dragging her out of the path of one of the spiney monsters. Thamon gasped a warning, and Dynamon, turning his head, felt a thrill of horror as he saw another of the creatures almost on top of them. Acting instinctively, Dynamon snatched the metal staff from Thamon's hands and flailed frantically at the black, thorny branches. To his amazement, they shivered and snapped under the metal rod like matchwood. Hardly daring to believe his eyes, Dynamon struck again and again at the horrible creature, until in a few minutes it was nothing but a pile of scattered, broken faggots on the gray sand.

But cries for help and screams of anguish sounded in Dynamon's ear phones, and he saw that five of the soldiers were on the ground impaled on the cruel thorns of others of the monsters. He ran toward them and beat them to pieces with the rod but too late to save the lives of the men. They lay pierced in a dozen places by long, black thorns. The rest of the Decuria had managed to dodge the whirling branches of the other bushes and now stood safely up wind of them. Dynamon summoned the survivors around him.

"What do you think, Thamon?" he asked. "In your opinion are there likely to be more of these horrible things around?"

"There may easily be," the scientist replied promptly. "But since the only defense against them is this one metal rod, I recommend that we leave our unfortunate comrades here and head immediately for the mountains over there. Those poor fellows are beyond our help and we should be able to find better protection from these blood-thirsty thorn-bushes among the foot hills. When we get there we can work upwind until we're opposite the Carrier again."

"That sounds like good advice," said Dynamon. "And we'll act on it. It's getting so dark now that we couldn't see to protect ourselves if any more of those creatures came rolling down the wind. Everyone join hands and follow mè."

AFTER a nerve-racking march of about twenty-five minutes through the gathering darkness, the party of nine humans felt the ground rising beneath their feet. Dynamon halted and hurled a voltage bomb forward and upward. As the bomb exploded, the momentary flash revealed to the party that they were at the foot of a steep, rock-strewn declivity. Dynamon led the party upward, feeling his way over the great boulders. After a few minutes of climbing, he called another halt and again threw a voltage bomb.

"We'll stay here for a few hours," the centurion announced, "until it gets light enough to see our way. We will be safe in the lee of these big rocks, so make yourselves comfortable."

Nine dim figures spread out on the slopping ground. Then one of them drifted apart from the rest, up hill.

"Who is that?" Dynamon demanded.

"Keltry," came the answer. "I am just going up hill a little distance. When you exploded that last bomb I thought I saw something that looked like the edge of a volcanic crater."

"You can't see anything in this darkness," said Dynamon. "Wait till it gets light again before you do any exploring."

"Oh, I won't go far," said Keltry. "Really, I won't."

"Well, be sure that you don't," Dynamon smiled into his transmitter. Then he said, "Thamon, where are you?"

"Right here," and a figure moved over beside the centurion.

Dynamon's question was casual.

"Did you see anything that looked like a volcanic crater?"

"Come to think of it," the scientist replied, "I think I did. It's just up here a few yards."

"Shall we go along and have a look at it too, then?" said Dynamon, getting up on his feet. Just then, he stood rooted with horror as a piercing scream rang in his ear phone.

"Dynamon! Dynamon, I'm falling!"

"Keltry!" the centurion exclaimed. "What's the matter? Has something happened to your helmet?"

"Yes!" Keltry's voice was fainter. "I've lost it! It was unfastened, and when I stumbled, it rolled off!" Fainter and fainter grew the voice. "I'm falling down a black hole a mile a minute!" With a muttered sob, Dynamon scrambled up the slope. A moment later, his foot stepped out on empty space. He started to fall into nothingness.

"Keltry!" he cried into his transmitter. "Where are you? Answer me!"

Straining his ears Dynamon heard a tiny voice far away saying, "I'm still falling."

"I'm coming after you, Keltry!" the centurion yelled, and reaching up to the knob on his helmet, twisted frantically. By doing that, he multiplied the gravitational pull of the planet and was now falling much more swiftly than Keltry. How deep this black pit was, Dynamon had no idea, but he prayed it would be deep enough so that he could catch up with Keltry before she hit the bottom. It was a desperate chance but Dynamon was willing to take it.

"Keltry!" he shouted into the transmitter. "Can you hear me? I'm coming for you."

"Yes, I hear you, Dynamon," came the answer, and Dynamon's heart leapt as it seemed to him that the voice sounded a little stronger.

"Keep your courage up, Keltry," he said, trying to sound calm. "I'm falling faster than you are. There doesn't seem to be any bottom to this pit so I'm bound to catch up with you."

"Oh, Dynamon! You shouldn't have jumped after me. There's—there's only—one chance in a million that we don't crash."

KELTRY was bravely trying to hide the dispair and terror in her voice, but most important of all to Dynamon was the fact that she sounded—stil nearer! He resolutely put out of his mind the frightful probability that at any second, first Keltry and then he, would be dashed to pieces at the bottom of the pit. It seemed to him that he had been falling for miles, and he thought that there was beginning to be more air resistance now. He bent his head and peered downward, trying to pierce the inky blackness with his eyes, but he could see nothing. It was a fantastic sensation or, better still, a lack of all sensation. He seemed to be resting immobile in a black nothingness, with only the rushing air tearing at his cloak to indicate that he was falling.

"Keep talking, Keltry," he cried.

"Oh, you sound so much nearer!" There

was a note of incredulous hope in Keltry's voice.

"I told you I'd catch up with you!" Dynamon exulted.

Suddenly, his heart gave a great bound. He was still peering downward and it seemed to him that far away he could see a tiny pin point of light.

"Keltry!" he cried, "am I seeing things? Or is there something that looks like a star; way down there?"

"Oh, I think I see it!" Keltry answered breathlessly. "Dynamon, what could that mean?"

"I don't know," said Dynamon, "but it seems to be growing larger, and I'm getting much nearer to you."

Under his fascinated eyes, the star grew bigger and brighter by the second. In a few moments Dynamon, hardly daring to believe his eyes, thought he could make out the outlines of a flying figure between him and the light.

"Keltry!" he shouted. "I've almost caught up with you! Hold your hands up over your head."

"Oh Dynamon! I think I can see you."

The point of light which Dynamon thought was a star, was growing into a larger, brighter disk. Keltry's body was sharply outlined against it now, and she seemed to be scarcely ten feet away. Dynamon bent himself into a jack-knife dive and kicked his feet up behind him. The air pressure was tremendous now, and Dynamon began to realize that it was no star, or sun, or planet down below but the bottom of the pit. Rays of light spread upward, illuminating the smooth, shiny sides of the shaft. A few more agonizing seconds went past and Dynamon's hands grazed the tips of Keltry's upraised fingers. Dynamon dared not estimate how far above the bottom of the pit they were, but concentrated on gaining the few inches he needed to get a grip on one of Keltry's wrists.

"We've—almost—made it!" he panted. "Here—grab my right arm and hang on for dear life!"

An involuntary shout of relief came from Dynamon's lips as he felt Keltry's strong fingers close over his arm.

"Hang on!" he shouted, and his left hand flew up to his helmet and carefully turned the counter-gravitation knob. At the same time, he twisted his back around and fought his feet downward. A moment later, he gripped Keltry's torso under the arms with his knees. Frantically, he tried to estimate how far above the bottom of the pit they were. They might be five thousand feet—or five hundred feet. Slowly he turned the dial on his helmet, resisting the almost insuperable impulse to twist the knob too fast. If he tried to stop their fall too quickly it would tear their bodies apart.

Slowly, ever slowly, the air-rush diminished. By now, they were well down into the area illuminated from the bottom of the pit. And they could see that they were falling through a round shaft perhaps one hundred feet in diameter. Dynamon judged that they were less than one hundred feet off the bottom.

"Look out, Keltry," he said. "I've got to put on the brakes hard."

He gritted his teeth, and flicked the knob on his helmet. He stifled a groan as invisible ropes attached to his feet and hands seemed to be trying to pull him apart. But gradually the terrific pressure released. He moved the knob a shade, and released the grip of his knees on Keltry.

"There!" he grunted as they both landed lightly on solid ground. "There wasn't two seconds to spare."

KELTRY drew a shuddering sigh and put a hand on Dynamon's arm for support.

"Oh, Dynamon!" she whispered, "if I weren't such a well brought-up girl I would break down and cry from sheer relief."

"I don't blame you," said Dynamon in a voice that shook a little. "That was quite an experience, but we came out of it all right. Now, where do you suppose we are? How do you suppose this pit was ever formed?"

The two Earth-people stared around them curiously. They were bathed in a bright light, and yet there was no apparent source of illumination. It began to dawn on them that the rocks which formed the side walls at the base of the shaft, were themselves luminous, glowing with a curious greenish light. Dynamon tilted his head back and stared up into the darkening shaft. Suddenly, he uttered an exclamation and, seizing Keltry by the wrist dragged her to one side. A few seconds later, a round object dropped out of the shaft and bounced on the ground. It was Keltry's counter-gravity helmet.

Dynamon reached down and picked it up. "It's a good thing that these things are well built," he remarked with a smile, "or this would be smashed to bits. The knob is still set for plus ten pounds, and that was quite a fall. I wonder whether it still works."

He twisted the knob experimentally and the helmet started to sail upward.

"Say!" Dynamon cried. "It works, all right! Here, put it on Keltry."

Keltry accepted the helmet with a laugh, put it on her head and was buckling it under her chin when her blood suddenly congealed in her veins. A loud shout rang echoingly through the shaft. Dynamon whirled around and beheld a curious figure standing in front of a rock not sixty feet away. It stood upright on two legs, and cradled a sort of club in its arms. Its head was covered with long, yellow hair that fell down on to its shoulders, and the lower half of its face was covered with coarse, yellow hair. Blue eyes glinted from under shaggy brows in a menacing glare at the two Earth-people.

"It looks quite human, doesn't it?" whispered Keltry.

Dynamon nodded and slid his ear phone off his right ear as he saw the stranger's hairy mouth opening and closing. Keltry followed his example in time to hear the stranger's rumbling voice.

"Whoo-yoo?"

Dynamon touched Keltry's hand. "That sounded like 'who are you' didn't it?" he said wonderingly.

"It certainly did," Keltry answered. "I think that's some kind of human."

"If it's a human," Dynamon said, "then there must be some sort of breathable atmosphere down here. You notice he's not wearing any oxygen mask."

"Whoo-yoo?" the stranger repeated, "an whey cum fum?"

"He's speaking a kind of English!" said Keltry excitedly. "He said, 'who are you' and 'where do you come from!"

"By Jupiter!" cried Dynamon. "I think you're right. If he can breathe without a mask, so can we. I'll have a little talk with him."

A moment later the centurion stood bareheaded, helmet and oxygen mask in hand.

"We're humans from Earth," he told the stranger, pronouncing each word carefully. "Who are you?"

The stranger's eyes and mouth flew open in astonishment and the rod sagged in his hands.

"Humes! Fum Earth!" he cried hoarsely, then turned his head, and gave an ear-splitting yell.

A MOMENT later, a dozen or more short, hairy-faced creatures closely resembling the first stranger came tumbling through a passageway behind him and stood rooted with astonishment at the sight of Dynamon and Keltry. Their bodies were completely covered, the torsoes, with loose, gray tunics, and the legs with ugly, baggy tubes. They advanced cautiously on the two people from Earth.

"Take off your helmet and mask," Dynamon directed Keltry, "the air is perfectly good. We'll try and find out the mystery of how these humans ever got here."

He turned and addressed the first stranger, again enunciating slowly and carefully. Immediately the whole crowd burst into excited jabbering. Here and there Dynamon thought he recognized a word. Finally, one man taller than the rest stepped forward.

"Yoo cum thus," he declared.

"Certainly," Dynamon nodded with a smile, and reached out a hand to Keltry. The crowd, with wondering eyes, opened up a line and the two young people from Earth followed their self-appointed guide through it. A short narrow passageway led off at a sharp angle through the rocky wall of the pit, and presently Dynamon and Keltry found themselves on what appeared to be a hill top. Both of them gave little gasps as a vast and magnificent panorama spread out before their astonished eyes. It was as if they had stepped into a new world.

A gently undulating plain stretched away in three directions as far as their eyes could see. It was predominantly gray in color, but here and there, were scattered long, narrow strips of green. These green strips all had shimmering, silvery borders, and Dynamon couldn't help recalling to mind some arid spots back on the Earth that were criss-crossed with irrigation ditches. There were no trees on this vast plain, but strewn around in a haphazard way, were a quantity of great boulders. And these rocks, like the rocks at the base of the pit, glowed luminously. However, the landscape was clearly illuminated by some other source than those scattered rocks. Dynamon lifted his eyes upward and saw that above them, and stretching as far as the eye could reach, there was a softly luminous ceiling. There was no way of telling how high up this ceiling was. It might be twenty feet or twenty miles. The effect was like that of certain days on the Earth, when wide-spread clouds blanket the sky and diffuse the sun's rays.

The plain was by no means deserted. Here and there along the green strips four-legged creatures moved slowly, creatures that, on Earth Dynamon would have said were cows. Nearer at hand, a flock of small white creatures milled around aimlessly, and Dynamon could have sworn he heard the cackle of hens. Dynamon glanced over his shoulder and saw that the little hairy-faced men were filing out of the passageway to the pit. The guide tugged at his sleeve.

"This oo-ay," he said and pointed to his right.

Still holding Keltry's hand, Dynamon turned and followed the man, and the others fell in behind them. Their way eventually led toward a tall set of cliffs at the base of which a score or so of cave-like openings could be seen.

"These *are* humans, aren't they, Dynamon?" Keltry whispered.

"They certainly look like it," Dynamon answered, "although obviously they're very primitive."

"Then how and when did they come to Saturn?" Keltry persisted.

"I haven't the faintest idea," Dynamon shrugged. "Perhaps we'll find out.

Other strange humans came running up the hill and joined the crowd behind them. Apparently they were not all men, for some of them had no hair on their faces and wore long robes over their bodies. The guide led them straight to one of the openings in the cliff, then halted and faced the two adventurers impressively.

"The koo-een!" he announced in a loud tone.

Dynamon and Keltry looked wonderingly at each other and then back to the guide. At that moment a woman appeared at the mouth of the cave. She was small and delicately formed and strikingly beautiful. She had the bluest of eyes and golden hair that fell away on either side of a marble brow. A long-sleeved white garment gathered at the waist covered her from neck to toe, but its shapeless folds could scarcely conceal the delicious curves of her little body.

"Humes!" the guide shouted proudly, "fum Earth!"

THE woman's blue eyes widened as she stared solemnly at Dynamon and Keltry.

"Are you from Earth?" she said in slow musical tones. "So strange! So wonderful! How did you come?"

Dynamon grinned. "We came in a Cosmos Carrier," he said easily. "And to us, it seems even more strange and more wonderful that we find humans already on Saturn."

A shy answering smile came over the woman's beautiful face.

"We have been here hundreds of years," she replied in the same slow accents. "But come inside the Palace and we will talk."

She turned with an inviting look and the two adventurers from Earth followed her through a passageway lined with the, by now, familiar luminous rocks. They came out in a fairly large, high-ceilinged room, in the center of which was a sort of table made out of a long, trimmed slab of rock. At one end of this table was a high-back chair made of woven reeds. The woman walked over to the chair and sitting down in it, indicated stools on either side of her.

"Sit down," she said, "and tell me more about yourselves."

"Thank you," Dynamon answered, and turning to his companion said, "It's warm in here, I think we might take off these cloaks."

Keltry nodded, and putting her hand to the throat fastening, zipped it downward. Dynamon did likewise and the two stepped out of their cloaks. There was a sudden scream from the beautiful little woman, and her hands flew up in front of her eyes.

"What are you doing?" she squealed. "Why you're—you're practically naked! You're positively immodest!"

Keltry threw a startled glance at Dynamon's long, brown legs.

"Why, not at all," she said quietly. "We are dressed like everyone else on Earth at the present time. Modesty with us, nowadays, is something much more important than lengths of cloth.

The little woman kept her hands before her eyes and shook her head vigorously. "It's immodest," she insisted, "and you must put on your clothes at once. Don't you realize that I'm the queen?"

Reluctantly, Keltry and Dynamon stepped back into their heavy cloaks and zipped them up the front.

"Well! that's better," said the little queen primly. "My goodness," she said with a slight glance, "is everybody on Earth as big and brown as you two?"

"We're about average, I should say," Keltry answered with a smile. "And seriously, we didn't mean to offend you in the matter of clothes."

"Well we, on Saturn," said the little queen, "don't believe in indecent exposure. Now, you say you came in some kind of a carrier?"

"Yes," said Dynamon. "It's up on the surface. We were exploring in the darkness and fell down the long shaft."

"Why weren't you killed?" said the queen, blue eyes wide. Dynamon explained the counter-gravity helmets. It took considerable explanation, because the queen was inclined to disbelieve the whole story. She finaly accepted it, however, and then launched into a long series of questions about the Cosmos Carrier and about the state of the Earth. Eventually Dynamon

found an opening and started asking questions on his part.

"We're anxious to know about you and your people on Saturn," he suggested. "Have you a name or are you addressed only as Queen?"

"I am Queen Diana," the little woman stated. "The last of my line. I am a Bolton, and the Boltons have been rulers of Saturn ever since we came here."

"Bolton!" Dynamon shouted. "Are you a descendant of Leonard Bolton?"

"Yes!" replied the queen, with a delighted smile. "Do they still remember Leonard Bolton on Earth?"

"We know that he designed a contrivance called a 'space ship', but that's all. Did he actually build such a ship, and is that how you come to be here so many thousands of miles from Earth?"

"Yes," said Queen Diana, proudly. "It's all down in some books which I will show you. Leonard Bolton built a space ship which was big enough to hold ten families and their belongings. There was a terrible war going on and he thought the only place to find safety was another planet. So the 'space ship' left the Earth by means of a thing called a 'rocket,' whatever that is. And they wandered around for years in space till they finally came into Saturn's orbit, and the tremendous gravity pulled the ship right through the light outer crust into this Nether World. I don't know how many years ago that was, but we have been here ever since."

"Well that is an amazing story," said Dynamon. "And I would like to see those books you mentioned. How incredibly fortunate that the 'space ship' broke through into this Nether World, where there is an asmosphere that will support life. And it is pretty miraculous too, that the 'space ship' didn't break up from the force of hitting the outer crust."

"Well, the books say that it was broken up somewhat," the queen answered, "but nobody was hurt. And after they unloaded the ship, they took it apart so that they could use the metal in it for other things."

She was eying him admiringly.

"And the colony has survived over a thousand years," Dynamon mused. He could not help thinking how, in comparison with the people on Earth, the survivors of Bolton's expedition were a rather poor lot. They had made no progress at all in the thousand years, mentally or culturally; from all evidences they had, on the contrary, retrogressed at least to a degree. Then across his mind flitted a picture of the hardships these brave souls had to endure in establishing themselves on the new planet. At no time could they have even hoped to return to Earth.

With their limited equipment they had set out to make the most of their new world. The great caves offered natural shelter so it was small wonder that they made their homes in them.

Dynamon, although a soldier to his finger tips, had none of the haughtiness and cruelty which are so often found in the warriors of today. Quickly his pity for the colonists turned into admiration, and he turned gently to face Queen Diana again.

"Tell me," he asked, "Are we the first strangers you have seen? You haven't, by any chance, been visited by Martians, have you?"

"Martians," said the queen. "What are they?"

"At present, they are just about the worst enemies of human beings," Dynamon replied tersely.

"No," said the queen, "our only enemies here are the *land-krakens*. We have been fighting them for hundreds of years and we have never been able to exterminate them, because they're so hard to kill."

"Land-krakens," said Dynamon. "What sort of creature are they?"

"They are great, crawling monsters," the queen told him. "They have a dozen long, flexible arms that curl around their victims and strangle them. They lie in wait for our cows and kill them easily, and now and then, they catch a human being. They're terribly hard to kill even with bullets—they seem to be made of gristle and jelly."

Just as the queen spoke, there was a chorus of shouts outside the cave, followed by three or four sharp reports, in rapid succession. The queen stood up quickly, as one of her subjects rushed into the cave.

"Land-kraken!" he shouted. "Ter'ble biggun!"

WITHOUT a word, the queen picked up her long skirts and ran to the entrance of the cave, Dynamon and Keltry following close behind. An extraordinary sight met their eyes.

At the foot of the little hill, fifty or sixty shouting men were ringed around a horrible mass of thrashing, gray tentacles. Several of the men were pointing their black rods at the beast.

"Oh, it *is* a big one," the queen cried. "Our guns will be useless against that thick hide—the bullets will just skim off."

There were several more reports and smoke curled from the ends of the rods. Several long, grey tentacles rose up above the mass, and the crowd surged backward in all directions. Suddenly one of the slimy arms streaked downward and outward, and a moment later a struggling, screaming human was lifted high in the air. A thrill of horror went through Dynamon, and Keltry clutched his arm.

"Their ancient fire-arms are useless," she said in a tense whisper. "Perhaps a voltage bomb——"

But Dynamon was already running down the slope, fumbling at the black box at his hip. The concerted groan of dispair from the crowd suddenly changed to a shout as the unfortunate human somehow tore loose from the encircling tentacle and dropped to the ground. Just as the land-kraken was reaching for the doomed man with another long arm, Dynamon hurled a voltage bomb over the heads of the crowd. The little glass ball landed squarely in the middle of the writhing gray mass. There was a blinding flash and a loud report. A convulsive shudder rippled over the gray monster and its twelve tentacles suddenly went limp. The crowd looked at it in stunned silence for a second, and then raised a yell of triumph. A noisy mob of little bearded men escorted Dynamon back up the hill to where the beautiful little queen stood, waiting, her blue eyes shining.

"How marvelous! How heroic!" she breathed, as Dynamon came up to her. "You killed the kraken with one blow. How did you do it?"

"Well, you see, Queen Diana," Dynamon replied, patting the black box, "these little voltage bombs have long ago entirely replaced fire-arms on Earth. Their range is shorter but they are far more deadly."

"Oh! So wonderful!" the queen gasped. "I am so glad you came. You shall marry me and I'll make you King of Saturn."

"I am most honored and flattered by your proposal, Queen Diana," Dynamon smiled, "but I am afraid that isn't possible. Keltry and I must go back up the shaft and rejoin our expedition."

"Oh, but you can't!" said the queen suddenly. "Send the girl away if you want"— she waved a careless hand at Keltry—"but you must stay here with me forever."

DYNAMON saw Keltry's startled eyes on him and he felt an acute embarrassment. It was an impossible situation. He could not repress a little glow within him from the frank approval of the beautiful, imperious little queen. But at the same time, he knew that he must soon devise some means of making a graceful exit from her presence. His thoughts were interrupted by a sudden cry from the edge of the surrounding crowd. He turned his head and looked along the base of the cliff. A column of cloaked figures, helmeted and masked, were streaming out of the passageway to the pit.

"It's a search party coming after us!" cried Keltry.

They were twenty or so of the soldiers from Earth, and they covered the distance toward Dynamon and Keltry in a short time and forced their way through the crowd of bearded Saturnians. The one in the lead unfastened his oxygen mask and revealed the spectacled face of Thamon.

"Thank goodness, you're alive!" said the scientist fervently. "We never expected to find you. What a fantastic place this is!"

"You are in the kingdom of the Boltons," said Dynamon, "and this is Queen Diana."

The man behind Thamon unmasked, revealing the lean, dark features of Mortoch.

"Congratulations, Dynamon," said the Chief Decurion, dryly, as he in turn was presented to the wide-eyed little queen. "You certainly picked a sort of paradise to fall into. A paradise, I might add, presided over by an angel."

A coy smile crept over the queen's face, then died away at Mortoch's next words.

"I bring you grave news, Dynamon," the Chief Decurion said. "There are two Martian Carriers in the vicinity. We haven't seen them yet, but we intercepted a long-wave conversation between them. What do you intend to do about it?"

"Why, I think we should go right back to the surface," Dynamon replied. "Could you tell from their conversation whether they knew that we were on Saturn?"

"Apparently they knew we were somewhere around," said Mortoch, "but hadn't located us yet."

"Well, we'd better hurry right on up then," said Dynamon, "so that we can get back to our Carrier before they find it."

"Oh, but you can't go!" said the little queen in a shrill voice, "I forbid it."

"I wish we could stay, Queen Diana," Dynamon answered, "but there's dangerous work to be done up on the surface."

"But why go to the surface at all?" the queen demanded. "Why not stay down here and keep away from the danger?"

"No, Queen Diana," Dynamon said, keenly conscious of Mortoch's lurking smile. "Duty calls and we must go. Perhaps when we have finished our work we will pay you another visit. All right, men, here we go."

THE centurion, Keltry by his side, led the way back to the entrance to the pit, while the Saturnians, grouped around their little queen, gaped after them. As the little force stood in the bottom of the pit adjusting their helmets and oxygen masks preparatory to ascending to the surface, Mortoch leaned over to Dynamon.

"That wasn't such a bad idea of the beautiful Diana's," he murmured. "Personally, I wouldn't mind spending a few safe years down there with her. It would be better than facing those deadly Photo-Atomic Rays of the Martians."

"If it's safety you're interested in, Mortoch," said Dynamon, dryly, "we'll try and get you, as soon as possible, to the safety of the Carrier. Anyway, perhaps the Martians are just exploring and didn't come equipped with the Ray."

But as the centurion turned the knob in

his helmet and shot up through the great shaft, he felt in his heart no great hope that such, indeed, would be the case. If the Martian Carrier were in the vicinity of Saturn it was altogether likely that they had come prepared to destroy the Earth Carrier, and would be equipped with their best weapon. Dynamon hoped against hope that he and the little force would reach the surface in time to get to their own Carrier, whose thick walls the Martians' Ray could not penetrate. After that, it would be a case of maneuvering the Carrier in such a way as to try to disable the Martians' ships.

The humans, their gravity repellors turned up full strength, whizzed up the black shaft at a tremendous rate of speed. Even so, it seemed hours before a small gray disc above him warned Dynamon that they were nearing the top. He spoke some words of command into his radio phone and cut down his upward speed. In a few moments he stepped over the rim of the shaft into the gray light of the Saturnian midday. He glanced down into the valley in the direction of the Carrier and felt a shock of dismay go through him.

THE gray Earth Carrier was in the same place, but a half a mile on either side of it were two flaming red Martian Carriers. And out on the gray sand far from any of the ships a furious battle was going on. Some twenty tall, human figures were ringed around by a swarm of tiny, globular Martians. A continuous series of white flashes showed that the humans were desperately hurling their voltage bombs, but the encircling Martians were keeping well out of range and a dozen still forms on the ground showed that the invisible Photo-Atomic Ray was doing its deadly work.

All too clearly, Dynamon saw what had happened. In the absence of a commanding officer, himself or Mortoch, Borion had unwarily sent a force of soldiers out scouting. The Martians had swooped down, landed swiftly, and cut off the force from the Carrier. The humans were desperately trying to cut through to safety, but their situation looked hopeless.

Quickly, Dynamon turned and faced the men behind him and held up his hands in a gesture signifying that no one should use his radio phone. He had determined to try and help his beleaguered soldiers down in the valley, and the only way that could successfully be done was to surprise-attack swiftly on the rear of the Martians. He motioned Keltry and Thamon back into the pit and then, sweeping his arm forward in a wide arc, he plunged down the hillside. But before he had covered half the distance to the combat in the valley, Dynamon realized that his attack was coming too late. The Photo-Atomic Ray was cutting down the little force of humans like an invisible scythe. There were only nine of them left now and one by one these were falling. A thousand thoughts raced through Dynamon's head. Should he go ahead with the attack, counting on getting within bombing distance of the Martians unnoticed, before they could swing their Photo-Atomic Ray around? Or, should he change direction, skirting the enemy, and make a run for the Carrier? Suddenly, his blood froze in his veins as a voice sounded in his ear phones.

"This is suicide, Dynamon!" It was Mortoch's voice.

"It's suicide now!" said Dynamon through clenched teeth. "You fool! You have given us away!"

There was an instant reaction from the swarming Martians in the valley. A large group of them broke away from the combat and rolled over the gray sand toward Dynamon's detachment. The centurion halted his men abruptly. It was sure annihilation to try and stand in the face of the oncoming men of Mars.

"Back to the pit!" Dynamon commanded. "It's our only chance. Once we get down there we'll decide what to do later."

The little force just barely made it to the mouth of the shaft. The Martians were coming up rapidly behind them, and Dynamon could see the big, black cones which produced the invisible Ray.

THE descent down the shaft was rapid, Dynamon being the last to land on the shiny floor. Immediately, he marched his men through the passageway into the Nether World and detailed two men to remain and guard the entrance to the pit.

"I don't believe the Martians will follow us down," he said. "If they do, we can easily defend the passageway."

Then he turned and singled out the Chief Decurion.

"Mortoch," he announced, "you are under arrest. You disobeyed my orders in regard to using the radio phone, and by doing so you betrayed our presence to the enemy. I will dispose of your case later."

Mortoch stepped forward, a sardonic gleam in his dark eyes.

"And suppose I refuse to be arrested?" he said. "If I had not disobeyed the order, you would have led us into certain death." Mortoch swept the crowd of soldiers with a burning look. "Men, I proclaim that Dynamon is incompetent to command you. Henceforth, you will take your orders from me—and you, Dynamon, are the one who is under arrest."

"Mortoch!" Dynamon cried. "You are out of your mind!"

"Not at all," Mortoch returned. "I am merely assuming the command which should have been mine to begin with. Put your hands up in the air, Dynamon, and backward march till I tell you to stop. And let nobody else make a move"—Mortoch's rasping voice rose to a shout—"I have in each hand a voltage bomb which I shall not hesitate to throw if anybody attempts to cross my will."

"This is madness!" Dynamon cried hoarsely. "You can't hope to get away with this!" He strode forward angrily.

"Back!" roared Mortoch, and raised his right hand threateningly.

Dynamon staggered back in bewilderment from the soldiers who stood in silence, too shocked to make a move. Helpless against the voltage bombs in Mortoch's hands, the centurion stepped slowly backward, arms upraised. It was an impossible situation, and for the moment, Dynamon felt powerless to do anything about it. He reproached himself bitterly for not being more wary of Mortoch. Up till now he had been conscious of the Chief Ducurion's enmity, but he had never thought that the man would erupt into open mutiny.

Dynamon threw a swift glance over his shoulder and saw that he was only two paces away from one of those curious, luminous rocks. It was approximately cylindrical in shape, six feet wide and perhaps twenty feet tall. Dynamon took another step backward and turned his head to face Mortoch. His back was almost touching the rock now, and a desperate plan formed in his head. That was to make a sudden leap around the rock. Once behind it and protected by its mass, he would have time to pull out one of his own voltage bombs and await Mortoch's next move.

BUT Dynamon had not truly measured the state of Mortoch's mind. There was a sudden scream from Keltry as Mortoch, with a lightning movement, drew back his right arm and flung the voltage bomb straight at Dynamon's chest. The little glass ball sped unerringly across the intervening twenty feet. There was no time to dodge. Dynamon pressed his back against the rock and closed his eyes. It was the end.

Dynamon felt the little bomb bump his chest. But—wonder of wonders! There was no blinding flash—no explosion. There was just a silvery tinkle as the glass ball shattered at his feet. Dynamon opened his eyes and found that he was still alive. An incredulous shout went up from the horrified crowd and Thamon started running toward him.

"Tridium!" shouted the scientist. "You have discovered tridium!"

As in a dream, Dynamon saw the soldiers overpowering Mortoch and heard himself say, "What do you mean? Where is the tridium?" He stared about in wonder.

"The rock!" cried Thamon excitedly. "You touched the rock and were instantly insulated against the electric charge. Great heavens! What a discovery! Every one of these luminous rocks must be made of tridium."

Dynamon turned around and placed a hand on the glowing rock. Instantly, he felt himself enveloped in an extraordinary transparent aura.

"You see!" cried Thamon, and struck at the rock with his metal rod. Evidently, it was almost as soft as chalk, for several pieces as big as a man's fist chipped off and fell to the ground. Thamon stooped down and picked one of the pieces up and immediately he, too, stood in a curious, gleaming aura.

"It's tridium, all right!" exclaimed the scientist. "There can be no doubt about it. We knew it was on Saturn and we knew what its properties were, but we didn't know what it looked like. Do you realize what this means, Dynamon? It means that we may finally have found the defense against the Photo-Atomic Ray!"

Dynamon felt a little dizzy. Not only had he been snatched from what appeared to be certain death but he had inadvertently made a discovery that might save the people of the world from conquest at the hands of the Martians.

"Thamon, are you quite sure?" he said. "Are you quite sure that this will work against the Ray?"

"No," replied Thamon promptly. "I won't be *quite* sure until we've tested it out. From a theoretical standpoint, this glowing cloud, this aura that surrounds us as we touch a piece of tridium should insulate us against the Ray. But to be absolutely certain, somebody will have to expose himself to the Ray. Someone among us must go up to the surface holding a piece of tridium in his hand and face the Martians. If he is killed, then I'm wrong. But if he is not killed, then the Martians are at our mercy. We can walk up to them untouched and crush their egg-shell skulls with our bare fists."

"I see," said Dynamon gravely. "Then, one of us must be a heroic experimental guinea pig?"

"Exactly," said Thamon.

Dynamon looked over the silent group of soldiers, at Mortoch, shoulders hunched in the grip of two stalwarts. Then he bowed his head in thought for a moment.

"Men," he said, finally, "this is not a case of calling for volunteers. I think any one of us is brave enough to offer his life for the good of the rest of the human beings, but I think we should decide who is to do this dirty work by drawing lots."

"No!"

It was Mortoch. In his eyes was a wild, hunted look, and his voice was hoarse, but there was deep sincerity in his tones.

"Dynamon," said the Chief Decurion,

"I went off my head with jealousy a minute ago. The madness is gone now, and I would give anything if I could undo what I did. You must give me the chance to redeem myself. If I am killed, so much the better for me. And if I am not, so much the better for all the human beings in the world."

Dynamon looked long and searchingly at the Decurion. Finally he said, "Mortoch, I cannot deny your appeal. Take this piece of tridium and go up the shaft. We will be close behind you to observe the experiment."

Just then, there was a shout from the two soldiers who were guarding the passageway to the pit.

"Martians!" they cried. "They are coming down on us! The shaft is full of them!"

Dynamon walked straight toward Mortoch and placed the piece of tridium in his hand.

"Your ordeal is at hand," he said cimply, as, in a flash, the bright aura transferred itself to the person of Mortoch.

THE two soldiers guarding the entrance to the pit were backing away to either side and throwing voltage bombs into the passageway as Mortoch ran toward them.

"Stop!" he shouted, never slackening his pace. "This is my job! Get out of range!"

He halted six feet away from the mouth of the passage and raised his arms up in a gesture of defiance. An admiring gasp went up from the crowd of watching humans at the tall, lean figure bathed in its luminous glow. Then a deathly silence shut down abruptly as four little figures erupted through the passageway. Martians!

They were scarcely two feet tall, with spindly little bodies and legs, but their heads were more than twice the size of human heads and looked doubly grotesque in their combination helmet-masks. One of them was holding a big, black cone—the Photo-Atomic generator. Quickly the little creature leveled it at Mortoch and pulled a lever on the side. An ominous high-pitched hum filled the air and everyone knew that the death Ray was being poured in all its deadly violence on Mortoch.

Thamon was the first to raise his voice in a shout as Mortoch, unharmed, strode forward and felled the Martian with one blow of his fist. The air rang with human cheers as Mortoch seized two more scurrying Martians by the legs and dashed their brains out on the ground.

"It works!" Thamon yelled, hysterically. "It's tridium! We're saved!"

The scientist was hacking crazily at the rock with his metal staff and jubilant soldiers swarmed around him, picking up pieces of tridium. In a few moments the whole force, every man surrounded by the luminous aura, was bolting through the passageway into the bottom of the pit.

For a short time the Martians tried to put up a battle. But with their chief weapon nullified, they were slaughtered by the dozen, and the survivors began flitting up the shaft. In the midst of the turmoil, Dynamon kept his wits about him. He knew that in order to realize the full value of the tridium discovery, the Martians on the surface must be kept from learning about it. He raised his voice in a mighty shout over the clamor.

"Masks on! Up the shaft at full speed! We must not allow a single Martian to reach the surface!"

Swiftly the Earth-soldiers fastened their masks and took off straight upward. Each one of them clung to their precious lumps of tridium, and in a short time the dark shaft presented an extraordinary spectacle. Each of the twenty-odd humans was bathed in his own ghostly envelope of light, and the fleeing Martians, looking downward, must have felt as if they were being pursued by a squadron of giant fireflies.

The survivors of the massacre below had a head start of their pursuers, but being so much lighter in weight, their gravity-repellors could not push them up through the atmosphere as fast as the humans could go. Gradually they were overtaken and destroyed by Dynamon's force —the last Martian being caught just at the upper mouth of the pit.

DYNAMON quickly gathered his men about him while he took stock of the situation in the valley. The three Carriers were in the same position as they were before, but there were no Earth-soldiers left standing. A little circle of fallen bodies offered mute testimony to the hopeless battle put up by the force of three decuria which had made that ill-fated sortie from the Carrier. Now, the Martians from both of the red ships—excluding, of course, the group that had been cut to pieces in the pit—were gathered in a body near the Earth Carrier. Dynamon guessed that they were waiting to see what the Earth people were going to do next. They would soon find out, the centurion thought grimly. Even though there were probably close to two hundred of the evil little creatures down there, they would be no match for the brawny humans insulated against the Photo-Atomic Ray.

Swiftly, Dynamon formulated a plan of action. His first consideration was to try and seize both Martian Carriers. If possible, they must be prevented from leaving the ground and carrying back to Mars the warning that, at last, the humans had found a defense against the Ray. With that in mind, the centurion divided his little force in two. One decuria with its decurion he put under Mortoch, and the other, he commanded himself. Each group was to strike boldly at one of the Martian ships, Mortoch the nearer one; himself, the farther one.

Dynamon issued his commands by signs, hoping to remain unnoticed by the enemy if he refrained from using the radio-phone. But as he led his group off along the hillside, a sudden activity among the Martians in the valley told him that he had been sighted. They came streaming across the valley floor toward the heights on a shallow crescent, each wing spreading to perform an enveloping movement.

What an unpleasant surprise the nasty little devils are going to get! thought Dynamon, and he switched on his radio-phone.

"Follow me, now, on the dead run!"

He dug his toes into the yielding gray sand and ran along the hillside, bending low into the wind. It was heavy going, but the humans were able to make faster progress than their enemies because of their greater weight. Dynamon saw that he and his group were outrunning the Martians and would probably reach their objective sooner. Two thoughts arose in his mind to worry him. One was, that the Martians inside the red ships might lock their doors and take off before he and Mortoch, respectively, could reach them. The other was the fear that Borion, inside the Earth-Carrier, not knowing of the new defense against the Ray, would sally out in a desperate attempt to save—as he might think —the two isolated detachments of humans.

However, Dynamon reflected, those were eventualities over which he had no control. All he could do under the circumstances was pray for good luck.

A GLANCE down into the valley told him that he and his little force were abreast of the Earth-Carrier by now, with a half a mile still to go to reach the Martian ship. The Martians, running parallel, were falling behind a little. Rapping out a command into his transmitter, Dynamon changed his direction slightly, and swung downhill on a direct line with the red ship. At the same time, he and his men readjusted their gravity-control so that their speed was almost doubled. Away to their left, the Martian horde was dropping behind. Dynamon gave an involuntary shout of triumph. He and his party was going to win the race.

As the little knot of speeding humans approached within a hundred yards of the Martian Carrier, another cheer broke from Dynamon's lips. The door at the side of the Carrier swung open and a score of little creatures carrying the once-dreaded black cones tumbled out. The Martians inside the ship, far from running away, were coming out to fight—mistakingly confident that the twelve humans were at their mercy!

Quickly, Dynamon issued orders that two of his men should immediately penetrate the inside of the Carrier and seize the control-room, while the rest stayed outside and engaged the Martian warriors. Then, panting for breath, but none the less confident, the decuria closed in on the Martians.

They were within twenty-five yards of the dwarf-like little creatures before the Martians discovered that something was amiss with the Photo-Atomic Ray. The

ugly little men hesitated in momentary dismay, and then started to make a dash for the inside of the Carrier. But by that time, it was too late.

The twelve humans, clothed in their life-preserving auras, swept down on the Martians like avenging angels. All the pent-up hatred against this diabolically cruel enemy now found release. At last, the Martian superiority in weapons was broken. Dynamon and his men waded implacably into the terrified little ogres and slew them without mercy. The whole business was over in less than two minutes.

Without the loss of a man, Dynamon had annihilated the defenders of the Carrier, and two of his soldiers were inside in possession of the control-room. There remained now the job of handling the hundred or so Martians who were moving over the gray sand toward his victorious decuria.

But this force of the enemy had realized that something was radically wrong. They were no longer running, but, in fact, were slowing up to a halt about fifty yards away. Dynamon swung an arm and began to walk toward them. The black cones came up, pointing, all along the long line of Martians. Dynamon's men fanned out on either side of him, walking forward slowly, inexorably.

The line of Martians wavered uncertainly, and then began to fall back in terrified confusion, as the humans remained unharmed by the Ray. Dynamon's voice crackled in nine sets of ear-phones, and the decuria lunged forward. In a moment, they were in the midst of a panic-stricken mass of scurrying Martians. Again, the soldiers from Earth slew pitilessly, until in a short while, fifty-odd of the harried little creatures lay dead. The rest were scattered in headlong flight over the valley.

THE business was accomplished none too soon. The thing which Dynamon had feared might happen earlier, happened now. A force of humans, unprotected by tridium, emerged from the big gray Carrier and hastened toward Dynamon. A few minutes earlier and these men would have been mowed down by the Ray. The centurion sighed with relief and ordered the newcomers back to the Cosmos Carrier.

The danger was over.

Twenty minutes later, Dynamon had joined forces again with Mortoch's detachment and was marching back to the mouth of the pit, where Keltry and Thamon were waiting. The past hour had seen a complete and sweeping triumph for the humans. Mortoch's attack on the other Martian ship had been as successful as Dynamon's. Now, both of the Martian Carriers were captured, and their crews and warriors cut to pieces. And, all this had been accomplished with the loss of but one man. One of Mortoch's soldiers had fallen and dropped his lump of tridium. The man had instantly died under the Photo-Atomic Ray.

There remained only one more piece of business to conclude successfully the expedition to Saturn, and Dynamon set about it promptly. Once again he led the way down the pit to the Nether World.

There was great excitement at the bottom of the shaft. The Saturnians were disposing of the bodies of the Martians who had fallen in the first onslaught when Mortoch had proven the efficacy of tridium. And, as Dynamon landed among them, closely followed by Thamon, Keltry and the soldiers, the Saturnians crowded around in an condition bordering on hysteria. They had never before seen Martians, or even dreamed of their existence, so it was not to be wondered at that the primitive humans of the Nether World were excited when the sudden, fierce combat broke out almost in their midst. With the greatest difficulty, Dynamon quieted them down enough so that they heard and complied with his request to be taken to their Queen.

"Queen Diana," he said directly, "in your kingdom, you have any quantity—thousands of tons—of this luminous rock which we have identified as tridium. This substance is the one thing which can save the people of the Earth from the death-ray of the Martians. Will you give me your permission to carry away some of these rocks back to Earth, so that our armies can defend themselves against our enemies?"

The little Queen gave Dynamon a long languorous look.

"If you stay here and be my King," she answered, at length, "I will permit your people to carry away as many of the rocks as they want."

Dynamon's heart sank. He had hoped that Queen Diana had got over that idea. What was he going to do?

"Well, Queen Diana," he said, slowly, trying frantically to think of some way out, "I can't tell you how flattered I am at your proposal, but I don't see how I can accept it."

"Why not?" the queen demanded, imperiously.

DYNAMON shook his head helplessly. He was trying to think of some tactful way of telling this spoiled little woman that his heart already belonged to Keltry.

"Well, perhaps you have noticed," he began, "that someone else on this expedition has a—a claim—er—"

"Who do you mean?" the Queen interrupted, "The tall, dark man? The one called Mortoch?"

"Mortoch?" said Dynamon wonderingly.

"Yes, isn't that what you're trying to tell me? Mortoch! That's very interesting," said the Queen dreamily, "Come to think of it, I *had* noticed that he looked at me very intensely."

A great light dawned on Dynamon. The Queen was jumping to a quite different set of conclusions. He had tried to tell her that he was in love with Keltry, and she thought he was telling her that Mortoch was in love with her, the Queen!

"I think that is very generous of you, Dynamon," said the Queen with a brilliant smile. "You are standing aside in favor of Mortoch because in your eyes, his bravery in facing the Martians gives him a greater claim on my hand."

Dynamon nodded wisely.

"He is a very handsome man," the Queen went on, looking off into space, "perhaps you're right."

"He is just outside," said Dynamon rising. "Let me bring him in to you."

Before the little Queen could say anything more, Dynamon walked briskly out to the mouth of the cave and hailed Mortoch.

"I remember hearing you say," he said, as the Chief Decurion came up to him, "that you wouldn't mind staying here with Queen Diana. Well, it seems that you are to have your wish. The Queen is determined to marry one of us, and right at this moment, she is inclining toward *you* as a husband. I think it's a fine idea."

Mortoch turned startled eyes on the centurion. Then he began to grin.

"Is that a command?" he asked.

"It is," Dynamon replied.

"I could do lots worse," said Mortoch, "although I'm liable to get homesick now and then."

"Don't forget," said Dynamon, "you'll be King of Saturn, or at least, of this part of Saturn. Go on inside, now, she's waiting for you."

Not long afterwards, Queen Diana, her eyes shining, appeared at the entrance to her cave. Her hand rested lightly on Mortoch's arm, and she announced to her people that at last she was taking a husband and giving the Nether World of Saturn, a King. As cheer after cheer went up from the bearded Saturnians, Dynamon bent over the Queen's hand and kissed it. He, then, received gracious permission to take away as much tridium as he needed.

KELTRY stood between Dynamon and Thamon and the three of them stared into the bow periscope screens in the control-room of the Carrier. Borion came over and joined them.

"Well, there she is," said the navigator, fondly. "There was a time back there on Saturn when I kind of doubted that any of us would ever see her again."

The chief image in the screens was a glowing sphere about the size of a man's head. It was Earth. Already, the watchers in the control-room could make out the outlines of the continents.

"But at that, I guess we got off lightly," continued Borion, "We lost thirty-nine men—including Mortoch—but just think what we're bringing back! We've got enough tridium in these three Carriers to divide up among ten thousand men. I was afraid we might have trouble with so much of the stuff—afraid it might affect the magnets."

"No, it's a curiously inert substance," said Thamon, "I suppose that's why it can absorb the terrific shock of the Photo-Atomic Ray so easily. What's the news from Headquarters, Dynamon?"

"It's pretty sketchy," said the centurion, "Argallum was afraid to say too much for fear the Martians might be able to decode the message. But it looks as if we are going to be just about in the nick of time. The Martian invasion began ten months ago, just about the time we were leaving Saturn. Even though they came without warning in thousands of ships, our people managed to beat them off for quite a while. Some cities were destroyed, but Copia wasn't touched—too well guarded. But then, even though our people maintained, and still do maintain, superiority in the air, those Martian devils found some remote desert spot unguarded and landed thousands of their men. They were all equipped with the Ray, of course, and our land forces simply couldn't stand up against them. They've been driving steadily ever since, and right now, they're within seventy miles of Copia."

"Whew!" gasped Borion.

"I should say we *are* in the nick of time," said Keltry.

"Heavens!" exclaimed Thamon, "I shudder to think what would happen to the World right now, Keltry, if you hadn't fallen down that pit!"

"That's right," laughed Dynamon.

Just then, a communications man walked into the control-room and handed Dynamon a message.

He read it avidly.

"That's good news," the centurion remarked, looking up from the piece of paper, "Argallum is sending a heavy convoy to meet us. How soon will we be landing, Borion?"

"Well, we should hit the top of the stratosphere in less than an hour," the navigator replied. "From there on down—at reduced speed—will probably take another two hours."

"In that case," said Dynamon, "I think we'd better shut down on all conversation. Even Argallum doesn't know what we're bringing back—I'm taking no chances on having our secret get out to the enemy.

He only knows that we are returning with two captured Martian Carriers. So, make your dispositions, Borion, because in five minutes I'm going to order everyone on all three ships to landing stations."

THE next three hours were tense ones for the returning expedition. Even though a convoy had been promised, Dynamon was apprehensive about possible attacks by the Martians, who, he was sure, must know something of what was going on. But as it worked out, a perfect cloud of gray Cosmos Carriers came out to meet the voyagers from Saturn, and Dynamon was able to set his ships down at Vanadium Field without mishap.

A heavy guard was thrown around the precious cargoes, and the young centurion was whisked away to Government City.

"What did you find?" The Commander-in-Chief's face was haggard.

"We found tridium," said Dynamon, "tons of it. We had an opportunity to test it, and it proved to be a complete defense against the Ray."

"How difficult is it to get at?"

"Not difficult at all," said Dynamon, "we brought back enough to equip nearly ten thousand men."

"Heaven be praised!" said Argallum fervently, "We might pull out of this situation yet. Those devils have been sweeping everything before them. We cut off their communications with our air power but that didn't stop them. They've been living off the land, and they're so powerful that they've been able to overrun territory at will."

Dynamon glanced at his watch. "It is almost noon," he said, "It will take just one counter-attack to break through their line and roll it up in both directions. If you throw attack-units forward as fast as they can be equipped with tridium, you will have the Martians in a rout before sundown."

And it was so.

Dynamon stood beside Argallum two hours later, on a little knoll sixty miles out of Copia. A wide plain stretched before their eyes and across its width, a beaten, discouraged army of humans gave ground slowly before hordes of tiny, malevolent creatures from another planet. As the two men watched, a fresh column of Earth-soldiers issued forth from a woods in the center of the plain. There was a curious greenish shimmer surrounding this new column — a will-o'-the-wisp, mirage-like quality — and it advanced without hesitation straight into the serried ranks of the terrible Martians.

"Great Heavens!" cried Argullum, "They're walking right up to them! And not a man is down! Look! The Martians are reeling back! Our voltage bombs are killing them like flies!

Dynamon turned away from the scene of carnage with a curious smile. He knew that Argallum in his gratitude would probably want to throw every conceivable honor and promotion at him. For bringing three Carrier loads of tridium back from Saturn, he, Dynamon, would very likely become a World-wide hero. And yet, he reflected, it was a feat which could never have been accomplished if it hadn't been for a series of unrelated incidents. If Keltry hadn't stowed away, she couldn't have fallen down the pit, thus leading to the discovery of Queen Diana's Nether World. If Mortoch had not rebelled and tried to kill him with a voltage bomb—. If he hadn't happened to touch the rock with his back—.

Dynamon turned and looked out on to the battle field where the victorious Earth-soldiers in their tridium-auras were vengefully slaughtering the hideous Martians. And he thought of the incident which had to precede all the other incidents so that he could bring back the tridium. That was the incident which had occurred hundreds of years before, when a man named Leonard Bolton had built a "space ship" and had traveled to Saturn in it, breaking through the burnt-out crust into the Nether World, boring the long hole with his clumsy medieval Carrier. That was the hole that Keltry had fallen into.

Dynamon shook his head. Leonard Bolton had built his "space ship" in the year 1956, the last year but one of the long series of frightful wars, in which the divided peoples of the World tried to destroy one another—and very nearly succeeded.

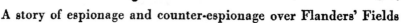

Printed in the United States
129561LV00003B/44/A